Unopened Letters from Dead Men

D1501455

Unopened Letters from Dead Men

Jeff Regan

Creators Publishing
Hermosa Beach, CA

Cover art by Peter Kaminski

CREATORS PUBLISHING
737 3rd St
Hermosa Beach, CA 90254
310-337-7003

Library of Congress Control Number: 2018930173
ISBN (e-book): 978-1-945630-82-8
ISBN (print): 978-1-945630-83-5

First Edition
Printed in the United States of America
1 3 5 7 9 10 8 6 4 2

Acknowledgments

In the 17 years since the first draft of my novel, many different emotions have occurred for me — so many highs and lows — providing a perspective of respect for every attempt people have ever made to convey what matters to them to the reader. My story had gone through all the phases, yielding hope and anxiety, until I was finally resigned to the fact that I had done the best I could and would have to find peace of mind in the knowledge that I hadn't given up. Yet I had.

Then a nephew I admire very much asked for a copy of my book for Christmas in 2015. I was afraid he would think it was awful. Knowing him as I do, I thought he would simply say the novel was great while his body language would say the book was below average and my disappointment would find new affirmation. But instead, he showed excitement and said, "It's very good. I don't know why nobody will publish your book."

I finally submitted my novel to Creators Publishing, and my editor, David Yontz, was a major force in giving my novel what it really needed: a new beginning. David's attention to detail was extremely thorough, and the effort and improvements he made have my greatest respect.

My appreciation for my previous editor, Jen Howard, is also extremely high. She went through many drafts, providing encouragement along the way with much-needed criticism, and I always felt she was as much a mentor as she was an editor.

I also want to thank Ross Browne and The Editorial Department. I needed your services desperately, and you provided the best editorial fit for someone in need of so much guidance.

And many thanks to family members who were supportive through the years. I appreciate you all more than I have ever shown.

This novel is dedicated to the memory of my father,
Dan Regan Jr.

Contents

Chapter 1

Billy waited for Karen to look at him one more time — just once — as she danced with the other cheerleaders, but they'd already turned toward the student section, waving their pompoms in the air with uniform perfection. Jesus, why couldn't he ever catch her? How did she always know when he was trying? Maybe she'd let her guard down. At least he hoped. So he waited. But when they turned back around, her dreary gaze went past him, and he felt as lifeless as the basketball in his hands. Lonny Green came over, snapped his fingers near Billy's ear and laughed when Billy jumped. Then Lonny pointed across the floor at the Rawlings players doing layup drills.

"Man, those snakes got something up their sleeves."

"Why?" Billy said.

"You're getting mugged tonight," Lonny said.

Billy shot the ball and turned toward Karen. It was no use. He joined the team huddle, wishing he could be somewhere else. Then his father's head turned toward him, and Billy stood upright. Coach Randle, a tall, wide man with a western twang, told them to be quiet and then whistled the team quiet.

"All right, guys," he said. "Rawlings is the worst-shooting team in the conference. You know they're a bunch of runts. But remember, they're as stingy as it gets, and nothing's coming easy."

Billy's father leaned forward, ignoring Simeon Bledsoe, a guy who flailed his arms around when he spoke, and Billy waited for him to stand up and clap his hands with everyone else. But he didn't. The buzzer sounded. Billy walked out to the center of the court, and the referee tossed up the ball for the tipoff. Lonnie, though a couple of inches taller than his guy, was out-jumped, but the Rawlings player tapped the ball to Billy. Billy ran toward the basket and went up for a layup, but the two Rawlings guards waylaid him from both sides and knocked him to the floor. As he was lying on his back, stars lit up his vision, and the crowd booed. Lonny reached over and pulled him to his feet.

"I told you they were up to something," Lonny said.

And he was right. Every time Billy touched the ball, they clobbered him. But Lonnie got hot, and his teammates kept feeding him the ball. Lonny had hardly ever scored in double figures, but he was tearing them up enough to keep the game close. At halftime, Richland trailed Rawlings by a basket, and in the second half, they were either up or down by 2 points the whole way. Finally, at the end of the fourth quarter, Billy ran to the side of his defender, leading him away from the ball. He went to the perimeter and stood with his hand in the air. The ball came at the same time two defenders collapsed on him from the post. Their weight against him, he swiveled around on his pivot foot, looking for a referee to call a timeout. But Lonny was standing alone underneath the basket. Billy whipped the ball to him so hard it made a smacking sound when it hit his hands. Lonny nearly bobbled the ball out of bounds before controlling it and flipping it in the air.

The ball glanced off the glass and fell through the net. Lonny pumped his fist and slapped Billy on the back as they ran down the court. But Billy's man, a stick-thin farm boy with a redneck tan, hurried ahead. The ball came to him, and he sank a 15-footer. Up in the bleachers, Billy's father stood up with his rolled-up program clenched in his fist. So with a few seconds to go, Billy ignored the aches of his battered, scraped-up legs and called for the inbounds pass. Lonny lobbed the ball toward him, but not directly, and Billy had to out-jump his defender to get it. He pulled away from the double-team and shot the ball, releasing it a moment before three defenders slapped at his arms, pulling him backward. The ball bounced around on the rim before it fell off and rolled out of bounds.

The roaring fans began stamping their feet on the bleachers, making it impossible to hear the officials' whistles as they pointed at the Rawlings player who'd fouled him hardest. Billy pumped his fist, rolled onto his stomach and looked up to the seat where his father always sat, first with Billy's mother and then by himself after she'd died. But his mom's seat had been empty for almost a year now, like a cavity on an otherwise perfect set of teeth.

He could imagine her cheering him on, her hair done up in a beehive, a hairstyle he had made fun of. A lump caught in his throat. Lonny's massive torso eclipsed his vision before Lonny bent over and pulled him to his feet. "Hit them both, man," he said, laughing. "Let's send these jokers on their way."

Billy walked to the free-throw line — the crowd now silent, the rednecks hopeful he'd miss at least one. He took several deep breaths and bounced the ball three times. Sweat trickled into his eye as he took his shot, making his motion a little less smooth. The ball bounced around the rim and then fell through the net. He wiped his face on his jersey and then bounced the ball three times and shot again. This time, the ball sailed at a perfect arc, and Billy turned his back, the crowd's cheers confirming what he already knew. The kids in the student section, jumping up and down, their red and black Felix the Cat sweaters swaying in an uncoordinated wave, stamped their feet and made so much noise the Rawlings players had to motion to one another to signal the play. Finally, the mousy kid with the deep voice took the inbounds pass, dribbled down the court and took a midcourt shot that went over the backboard and bounced off the wall. The buzzer sounded, and Billy's teammates ran toward the locker room, jumping up and down. He walked several feet behind them, waiting for his father to come down the bleacher steps, but his father wasn't anywhere around.

In the hallway, Coach Randle motioned for Billy to hurry up. Billy picked up his pace and jogged past him and into the room, shivering almost at once; the concrete walls were as cold as an igloo's, and the radiator heater was so worn down kids shivered even when they were sitting on top of it. Lonny and Chad flanked him, their breaths coming out as cold fog when they laughed.

"Sorry about the pick," Chad said.

Pick, singular? Chad had blown more than one. But Billy shrugged. "Doesn't matter. We won anyway."

Lonny clutched his hand and pumped it. "Twenty points! I'll bet you never saw that one coming."

Sharp pain shot through Billy's arm. "C'mon, man. You break my arm and you'll have to do that every night."

Lonny tipped his head back and laughed so loudly it echoed. Billy walked past them to the rear of the room, where a row of wooden folding chairs sat against the wall. Once seated, he rested his head in his twitching hands. The coach stood at the lectern and cleared his throat. "Guys, that's the worst offensive execution I've ever seen. If it wasn't for our defense…"

Billy was puzzled. His father had never left before the end of a game. What kind of reception awaited him at home? Maybe it wasn't too hard to imagine. After all, he had seen him sulking before, sitting in the darkness of his study, the ice in his drink clanging against the glass as he twirled it around. Billy's mother had always been the perfect buffer in times such as this, seeing things his father never did and pointing them out whenever he'd start in. It often seemed as if she knew more about basketball than either one of them — or at least she paid more attention. But she couldn't help him now. She had died on her way to pick up Al Jr. — no big surprise — because he had missed the bus, again, and hit a patch of ice that sent the car into the path of an oncoming semi. Her voice, sometimes the only reasonable one in the house, was gone.

Billy licked the sweat off his lips. Coach Randle paused before speaking in a sleepy monotone. "What'd I say, Billy?"

"You said our offense stunk but our defense was pretty good."

"Yeah, five minutes ago," he said. "Believe me, guys. We'll go over everything on Monday. Have a good weekend, and stay out of trouble."

Billy slipped behind the sophomore starter, Cody Garner, trying to get to the door Lonny had already exited. Coach Randle veered through everyone until he stood behind Garner and blocked the doorway. "Are you OK, Billy?"

Billy smiled. It was so uncomfortable the muscles in his face ached. "Sure, Coach. I'm just a little tired; that's all."

A somber frown crossed Coach Randle's face. "I'll see you Monday."

Out in the hallway, Lonny paced back and forth, his stringy hair flipping around each time he turned. He was reaming two sophomore benchwarmers, Phil Firth and Mark Mueller, about their lack of intensity.

"Hell, Lonny," Phil said. "How fired up can you be in 20 seconds?"

"That's 20 seconds more than I got," Mark said. He was a lanky redhead whose long mop was too thick to fall below his shoulders; instead, it meshed thickly around his head like a helmet around his red, splotchy face.

Billy let the locker room door shut behind him, and his three teammates turned around. Lonny danced an awkward jig, not helped by his 6-foot-5-inch body and a head so large everyone called him "The Melon" behind his back. "I'm going to buy 20 Tribunes to send out to all the coaches who said I wasn't good enough to play for them."

"Are you sure 20 will cover it?" Billy said.

Phil and Mark laughed until a quick glance from Lonny shut them up. Billy understood. Lonny had always been the class clown, his pranks often resulting in a trip to the principal's office. The only time he was ever halfway serious was when it came to basketball. They had been teammates since the fourth grade, when they were on the B-Team Warriors at Daniel Boone Elementary School. One time, during a pep rally in the fifth grade, their coach, Mr. Molsen, called them out one by one. Lonny was the first one called — and was even referred to as the main hatchet man — but he went out on the floor wearing a pained smile, knowing it only meant he was always the last benchwarmer to come in at the end of the game. He was always the last one to make the team until a 6-inch growth spurt in the ninth grade moved him to the middle of the bench. Now, in their senior year, Lonny had started every game for the first time ever.

But the ride was almost over. Lonny's future, more than likely, would be not on the hardwood floors of a college campus but in the rice paddies of Vietnam. When they were younger, it didn't seem possible the war would still be going on by the time they graduated. Even President Johnson talked as if the Americans were going to crush the Viet Cong soon. But the notices still came in the mail, and the hallways at school were thinned out by all the boys who'd said the hell with it and run away. Who could blame them? The death toll of Richland's alumni had already gone into the dozens, and the kids started taking sides. Some began calling themselves flower children and wearing peace buttons. They encouraged the drop-out-and-run campaign at school and spouted off about knowing where the kids had run off to yet would only laugh if anyone asked them where.

Vietnam seemed to be the last thing on Lonny's mind as he waved his hands in dismissal at Phil and Mark. "I'll be at the Y tomorrow if either one of you benchwarmers wants to rebound for me."

"We'd be chasing your bricks all over the gym," Mark said. Billy and Phil laughed, and Lonny's face turned red before he, too, began to laugh, mockingly.

"Did you score 20 points tonight?" Lonny said. Mark and Phil walked off down the hallway. When they were gone, Lonny asked, "Your dad's not here?"

"No, he already left," Billy said. "He must not be feeling good. Think you can give me a lift?"

"Yeah, let's go," Lonny said. "I can't wait to tell my dad about this one. It sucks he couldn't come."

Billy sighed. "I don't know. I wish my dad would stay at work sometimes."

They walked through the thinned-out gym, Lonny babbling on about the game, his stride getting longer and longer until Billy thought he was trying to outrun him. But once they went out into the frigid, swirling wind, Lonny slowed down a bit and snapped his coat all the way up. Billy had time to think. He'd scored only 6 points, 16 below his average, and his father never accepted anything like that. Even 21 points wouldn't do. All of his other coaches had gone along with his father's wishes, letting Billy take as many shots as he wanted. Coach Randle was different. Even though Billy had become the first freshman in school history to make the varsity team and had soon become a starter who led the team in scoring, Coach Randle expected him to follow his game plan, whether it revolved around him or not. Not one shot could be taken out of the flow of the offense. It had taken only two games of riding the pine for Billy to get his message. And even on nights like tonight, when Billy's shots simply weren't falling, his father would sulk and call him into his study, fix a drink and then nitpick his mistakes for a half-hour, eventually losing his temper.

For example, last year, after they'd nearly lost to Grass Creek, his father said, "The guy was 3 inches shorter than you. You could've backed him up to the rim every time."

"But Chad was a lot quicker than his guy."

"Don't interrupt me," his father had said. "If you keep playing like that, you won't get a decent scholarship offer."

"I want to play for Evansville," Billy said. "Coach McLowery reminds me of Coach Randle."

"Coach Randle's a bum," his father said, his voice rising. "You could go to IU if you hadn't—"

Billy stood up and went to the door, his father close behind, and nearly bumped into his mother. Once past her, he saw Al Jr. sitting in a chair in the front room, smiling, probably hoping they'd go at it even more. Billy thought they might, until his mother went inside the study and closed the door. He then put his ear up to it to listen. Though their voices were muffled, he still heard what they said.

"Settle down, Al," she said. "You don't need to get on him every time he doesn't score 50 points."

"He's not — he could go to—"

"Evansville's a fine school," she said. And the subject stayed closed until after she had died.

They got into Lonny's beat-up dark blue Chevy and headed home. Civil servants stood at the intersection in orange vests, waving cupped flashlights, as if people wouldn't be able to find their way without them. Billy's nerves almost caused him to retch, which forced Lonny to stop bragging and look over at him. He started all over again once Billy had caught his breath.

Lonny headed down Broadway and then turned on 20th Street. At the end of the block, where the street ended and turned into an alley, Lonny pulled up in front of Billy's green-slated two-story house and parked. Billy looked up at the darkness of the house. The curtains on every window were pulled shut. The only light was the dim glow of a kitchen lamp, which was always on, even during the day. Maybe his father hadn't been angry about the game at all. Maybe he had just been tired and gone to bed. Yet when Billy looked over at Lonny, whose frown lines almost made him look middle-aged, Billy couldn't move, almost couldn't breathe.

"Something wrong?"

Billy smiled and shook his head. "No. Maybe I'll see you at the Y tomorrow."

"Yeah, we could play two-on-two if Phil and Mark show up," he said. "We'd smoke those jokers."

"I guess we would."

Billy opened the door, got out and waited for Lonny to drive off to the end of the block and turn before climbing the concrete steps. He bent over and took the key from underneath the welcome mat and opened the door, making as little noise as possible, and stepped inside the dark foyer. He listened for movement for several seconds before finally shutting the door and climbing the steps. His footsteps were light until a loud creak came from a weak spot halfway up the stairs.

In the kitchen, a chair slid back and toppled over. Purposeful footsteps came toward him, and the foyer light came on, making his eyes squint until they focused on his father at the bottom of the stairs.

Billy tried to move further upstairs, away from his father's presence. His father was in his 50s — with a receding hairline, not helped by his vain comb-over — but he was built as solidly now as ever.

"One for 6!" he said. "I've got to watch you stink up—"

"We won!" Billy said, his voice so loud it made his father recoil. "But you'd know that if you'd have stayed."

His father was up the stairs in a flash, grabbing Billy's letterman jacket and pulling him forward. The stench of liquor filled the air, and he flipped Billy backward, causing him to hit the floor. His vision blackened momentarily.

Billy sat up and scooted away, waiting until his father's left foot was about to land on the step, and kicked at it right before it did, tripping him up. His father fell hard, his forehead bouncing off the floor when he landed next to him. Billy jumped to his feet and ran to the door, afraid to turn around; he didn't even shut the door behind him. Halfway down the block, he heard his father's voice cutting through the whistling wind.

"Don't come back, you ungrateful punk!"

Running aimlessly, Billy touched his head where he had landed. There was no bump, but his sweat-soaked hair was starting to freeze. He cussed and yelled. Everything about the night sucked, and now, with no one to turn to and nowhere to go, he slowed down to a trot.

After his mother's death, loads of people — teachers, teammates and other students — had said they'd be there for him. But they were liars. The refrigerator had started stinking, and he threw away the cause, a tuna casserole his mother had made the night before she died — the last meal they had all eaten together. When he went to school the next day — unkempt and wearing clothes from the day before — all of his classmates, including Karen, had kept their distance and brushed him off with nervous laughs.

The embarrassment hardened him and made him start avoiding everyone — especially Karen, who acted relieved. Soon he was spending his lunchtime in the library, where a pretty, sympathetic senior, Cherri Sands, worked as a student helper. She was always nearby, putting books or magazines away or sorting through things when she had nothing else to do.

One day, she sat down across from him and said she'd never seen anyone as unhappy as he was. Her words worked his nerves for a second, until he realized she wasn't making fun of him. Before he knew what he was doing, he told her that when he was alone in the house, he could almost hear his mother's voice or the light swishing of her feet walking across the carpet. When he had finished, his clenched hands were trembling on the tabletop, and she cupped his hands with hers and held them there until they steadied. Her hands were much smaller than Karen's, and her long nails were painted yellow, matching her dress. He was powerless; she had found out more about him than Karen ever cared to know, and soon after that — he really didn't think he meant for it to happen — she gave him a ride home in her Volkswagen Beetle. Once they were inside, he kissed her.

The phone downstairs rang several times as they made love upstairs. He hadn't thought it could have been Karen until the next day, when she came up to him tearfully and as pissed off as he had ever seen her.

"Why was that tramp's car parked in front of your house?" she asked, her voice low and harsh.

He looked down, ashamed, and said nothing. She ran off down the hallway, but Billy felt confident it would only be a matter of time before she would forgive him — so confident, in fact, he told Cherri he couldn't see her any more. She laughed and asked him how many times a day he gawked at himself in the mirror. It stung, but he couldn't be without Karen. Months had passed since then, and maybe Karen had finally forgiven him, but he doubted it.

Then it dawned on him; his face became hot, and his breaths came out in labored gasps as he picked up his pace. Al Jr. had come back from Vietnam a couple of months ago. He'd jetted before their mother's funeral, leaving Billy all alone to fend for himself. At the time, Billy understood why. But what he couldn't forget or forgive was that Al Jr. had high-hatted him 10 days before Christmas. Earlier that month, Dom Henry, a kid from the neighborhood, had come up to him while he was shooting baskets out back and said he had seen Al Jr. when he was at the veterans hospital in Indianapolis visiting his cousin. Al Jr. had been lying in a bed, covered all the way up to his neck, sleeping.

"How'd you know it was him then?"

Dom had frowned at Billy as if Billy were nuts before laughing and patting his shoulder. "I've known Al all my life. Besides, there was a nameplate outside his door."

The next week, Billy told his father a lie; he asked to borrow the car to go play a three-on-three tournament down at Broad Ripple. He expected his dad to say no, but his dad shrugged his shoulders and said to give him a ride to work and drop off the car at the bar when he came back. Billy went home and got a couple of small gifts, filled up the Impala's huge gas tank and went on his way, happy he'd finally get to see his brother.

But the old hospital looked as if it should have been torn down years before. The inside was just as dreary; the men there weren't what he thought soldiers and Marines would look like. They had long hair and full beards; their eyes were vacant. At the end of the hallway was an office enclosed in glass with two sliding windows in the center. Inside the room was a very pretty girl wearing her hair in a plain bun and no makeup. She seemed to be hiding from something, probably the weirdos walking around in the hallway. He tapped on the glass, and she looked up at him.

"Can I help you?" she said, smiling.

For a second, Billy wasn't able to say anything. When he was, he stammered. "I'm here to see Al Hennessy."

She flipped through her registry a couple of times before finding his name. Then she pushed a button on her intercom. "Pvt. Hennessy, you've got a visitor."

"Who?"

She released the button and gazed up at him. Billy smiled at her. "I'm his brother, Billy."

"Your brother—"

"I don't care," Al Jr. said. "I don't want to see anyone."

The girl fidgeted, and Billy felt like an idiot standing there holding his gifts. His first thought was to hand them to the nearest soldier on his way down the hallway, and he probably would've if he could've moved. But he kept staring down at the intercom, the girl's finger still on the button, hoping that if he stood there long enough, Al Jr. would break down and ask to see him. He stood there for what must have been a whole minute before the uncomfortable look on the young woman's face made him uneasy. He handed her the gifts — a card, a box of chocolates and a GE transistor radio. "Will you see he gets these, please?" He then hurried off down the hallway.

Then, only a couple of weeks ago, while cruising around with Lonny, he'd seen Al Jr. walking into a rundown apartment building and rolled down the window. "Hey, Al!" Al Jr. had stood up straight, like a stalked beast, and scampered inside without a backward glance.

Well, Al Jr. would have to deal with Billy now, and by God, Billy was going to let him have it, and have it good. Billy changed directions, running toward the south side of town. A screaming woman yelled at someone in the distance as he crossed the Third Street Bridge. Finally, when he was on West Montgomery, Al's neighborhood, his aching lungs forced him to slow down. He coughed and caught his breath. The stench of musty, rotting wood hung in the air. Houses were missing windows, and roof tiles littered their lawns.

Billy found the house Al Jr. had gone into. Shadows on the porch moved; two men sat in the corner, drinking wine. He hurried past them and through the screen door and then checked the mailboxes situated underneath a low-wattage light. There it was: "A Hen. 1B." The hallway was so dark Billy didn't see how anyone could possibly be living there, and he worried that Al Jr., who'd been one step ahead of him lately, had already moved on. But there was the sound of movement inside the apartment, and he pounded on the door.

"Who's there?" Al Jr. said, his voice cracking.

"Billy!"

The long silence was unbearable, but then shuffling footsteps came toward him, and three deadbolt locks were unlatched. The door opened up, spilling light out in the hallway. Billy backed up to the wall as his brother's handless left arm emerged from the shadows.

"Jesus, Al," he said. "What happened?"

Al Jr. came into the light, but the person standing there didn't look like the person Billy remembered. He wore an army jacket, a pair of tattered bell-bottoms and unpolished combat boots, and his once fleshy face was now gaunt. His gaze slowly lowered to his arm before he looked back up.

"I was running toward a hill, when everything went black. I woke up on a chopper with one hell of a headache and this."

"I'm sorry."

"Why? You didn't shoot me," he said, stepping back and waving for Billy to enter with his handless arm. Billy went past him and into the cluttered and cramped living room. Empty liquor bottles and food wrappers were strewn all over the floor. Rust-colored wallpaper peeled down from the ceiling, revealing a yellow wall that must've originally been off-white. The ceiling was blackened with dust. A broken-down bright green couch and chair — probably picked from the same person's trash — flanked an ancient television set sitting on two concrete blocks. An island-style bar separated the living room and kitchen, and on the stove was a cast-iron skillet so reddened with rust he doubted it had ever been used. On the counter were several more bottles of different kinds of booze with varying amounts in them. The bedroom door — thank goodness — remained shut. Billy turned toward Al Jr., whose face twitched uncontrollably as he tried to smile. "I haven't got around to hiring a maid yet."

•••

Chapter 2

"At least you know you're a slob," Billy said. His damn smirk, something Al Jr. had seen so many times growing up, made everything too real. Al Jr. looked away from him, rubbing his face. He'd been sitting on the couch, half-awake, thinking the noises outside had to be a dream or, if they were real, the two winos, Hamlin and Dill, stumbling in from the porch, their bottles finally as empty as their wallets. His stomach ached. What was Billy doing here?

He was probably going to let him have it, just like the time when he'd shown up at the hospital bearing gifts to soften him up so he could hammer him and then gloat about it. Billy was a great gloater. But the chocolates had been the expensive kind, and the radio had been so nice he'd been able to pick up Richland's radio station all the way down in Indy. And the Christmas card had simply said, "I'm glad you're OK. — Billy." Now he wasn't sure why Billy was there or whether he should feel guilty or suspicious. Drinking too much made everything mushy.

"Are you OK?" Billy said, his voice tense. Billy hadn't been smirking; the expression on his face was more like a sickened grimace. And for some reason, his hair was wet. The R on his letterman's jacket was torn, and so was the tongue on one of his sneakers.

"What happened?" Al Jr. said. "You been in a fight?"

"Dad threw me down the stairs," Billy said, frowning as he noticed the tear on his jacket.

"Jesus," Al Jr. said. "Have you called Karen?"

Billy sat down on the couch, massaging his temple with his index finger and thumb. "She doesn't know," he said. "We're finished."

"Finished?" Karen, as much as it had always pained Al Jr., had become a bigger part of the family than he was, and though he had often made fun of Billy for being whipped, he'd always envied him. The girls Al Jr. always dated weren't popular, let alone cheerleaders, and even then he wasn't able to keep them interested for very long. Billy's only problem was that girls liked him too much. To think that Mr. All-American, Mr. Charming, could blow something was mind-boggling. He sat down and frowned at Billy. "What happened?"

"I just screwed up," he said, his jaw clenched. "I don't really want to talk about it."

"Maybe she'll take you back."

Billy laughed, slapped his knees and then stood up, running his fingers through his hair. "I doubt it, man. If anything, she'd get the laugh of her life watching me beg to sleep on this damned filthy couch of yours."

"Beg? You haven't even asked. Jesus, Billy, you come pounding on my door — I wasn't even sure if you were real."

"Can I?"

Al Jr.'s stomach churned, forcing liquor fumes up his throat. His hand began to shake as he wiped his mouth. If Billy noticed anything, he kept a straight face, and Al Jr. turned away from him and toward a whiskey bottle sitting on the table. He unscrewed the lid and guzzled from it. "Doesn't that hurt?" Billy asked.

"No," Al Jr. said, shaking his head and wiping his mouth with his sleeve.

"You're not going to let me stay?"

Al Jr. paused. "You can stay here — for a while, anyhow."

Billy slumped back on the couch. "Do you have any food?"

Food? Al Jr. almost laughed. He picked up a discarded bag of chips and crumpled it up. He shrugged and shook his head.

"Have any money?" Billy said.

"I've only got 20 bucks, and it has to last until Wednesday."

"C'mon, Al," he said. "I've got money at home."

"Well, then you should've brought it with you."

"Oh, yeah," he said. "It's in my room. If I could've only got past Dad."

Billy's stare forced him to turn away; this was Mommy and Daddy's fault. They had coddled him for as long as Al Jr. could remember. Billy — just as he was ready to do now — would pout over things, things Al Jr. never even thought of, until given in to. Hell, according to their mother, the first words Billy ever said were "I want." She'd always laughed about it, saying that when she would ask him what he wanted, he would say, "I just want." Damn, nothing ever changed.

"When's the last time you ate?" Billy said.

Al Jr. was so lightheaded he thought he might get sick. He gagged and coughed again and tried to remember. Maybe it had been the chips on the floor or at the church down the street, the Methodist one, when Reverend Lesaux had spotted him walking down the sidewalk with a sack full of booze and invited him in for their weekly supper. But that had been Wednesday or maybe even Tuesday.

"You can't remember, can you?"

"I think Tuesday."

"Three days ago," Billy said, and then he laughed. "You look like a damn scarecrow, Al. You always had 20 pounds on me, but look at you."

"So what?"

"So you don't think a Garry's pizza sounds good?"

The guys at Garry's hand-tossed their dough and stacked their pizzas with pepperoni and sausages and every kind of vegetable. Al Jr. and Billy could get there by 11 if they hurried, and Billy was already heading toward the door, looking over his shoulder with that smug smile of his. Al Jr. put on his parka and ran to catch up. Hamlin and Dill jumped back in the shadows as he sprang off the porch.

Al Jr. caught up with Billy, and they crossed the Third Street Bridge as a train rumbled across the overpass. Once it passed, he heard music coming from a downtown bar. Conflicting signs hung in almost every storefront window — "support our troops," "impeach Johnson" — and none of them made any sense. In December, everyone in the hospital, on the news, everywhere, had praised Johnson. The news had run pictures of him shaking hands with troops in Vietnam, and Gen. Westmoreland had said they'd wiped out close to 100,000 of the National Liberation Front. Hell, hadn't the president even been named Time's man of the year? Al Jr. wanted to throw a rock through one of the windows.

They were close enough to Garry's to smell pizza lingering in the air, and a song, "Mr. Pitiful," played faintly and mixed with the mingled voices of people in the bar next door. Cars flew in and out of the parking lot as they crossed Market Street. Billy hurried to the door of the shack, where a squat, greasy middle-aged man stood behind a picture window and tossed pizza dough into the air. Billy waved for Al Jr. to hurry up. The man put the dough on a large-handled pizza pan and grabbed a pad of paper. He looked from Billy to him and smiled. "What can I get you boys?"

Al Jr. pulled his $20 bill from his coat pocket. "A large combination pizza."

"A combination of what, buddy?"

"Everything but anchovies."

The man's nostrils flared, and he winked. "Need something to sop up the booze, huh?"

Al Jr. handed him the money without answering, and as the man took it, his eyes stopped and widened on Al's left arm. The smartass smirk disappeared, and he broke the twenty and handed the change back. Al Jr. headed to a small table in the back, where Billy sat with his back against the wall. Billy leaned forward and nodded his head toward the man. "What's up with him?"

"I don't know," he said, putting his change away, "but maybe you should go get the pizza when it's done."

They sat in silence until the man tapped his bell and set the pizza on the counter. He waited until Billy had brought it to the table before saying that he would be closing in 10 minutes and that they had better hurry up. Al Jr. took two of the square-cut pieces in his hand and crammed one in his mouth as he spoke. "I don't think you've got anything to worry about."

"Jesus, pal," the man said. "Slow down. You guys sure are a lot different than we were coming back from Korea."

Al Jr. crammed the other in his mouth and picked up two more. Billy picked up two pieces and tried to keep up with him. Within a couple of minutes, there was only one piece left, and both of them stood up. Billy reached out for the piece of pizza, paused and looked over at Al Jr. "Are you going to eat this, pig-man?"

Al Jr. shook his head and grabbed his stomach, which had cramped. He rushed outside and doubled over, steadying himself against the building. He took several deep breaths. At least the alcoholic fog in his head had gone away. Once the cramp was gone, he stood up and saw Billy and the man laughing inside.

"You could've got the pizza and brought it back." Al Jr. said when Billy came out.

"Who in the hell wants to eat cold pizza?"

Al Jr. took a deep breath. "Man, that guy was a real wiseass."

The quiet walk home seemed to take an eternity. Once they were inside, Al Jr. went to the living room closet, grabbed a pillow and blanket, and handed them to Billy, who frowned and smelled them.

"Christ, Billy," Al Jr. said. "They're new."

Billy stretched out on the couch and pulled the blanket up around his neck. By the time Al Jr. came out of the bathroom, Billy was already snoring.

ooo

Billy sat up, his heart racing from a terrible dream. The room swallowed him up; the walls pounded with a pulse of their own. After several seconds of silence, his heart stopped racing, and he sprawled out on the couch.

Boom! Boom! Boom! The noise came again, this time from his brother's room, and he ran toward the light switch and flipped it on. The noise sounded once more, followed by an awful high-pitched cry. Someone was in Al's room beating him to death; he was sure of it. He searched the room for a weapon, grabbing an old Louisville Slugger propped against a wall. But when he went to open Al's door, the handle wouldn't budge. He put his ear against the door. Awful thrashing sounds and moans came from inside, so he rammed his body into the door. He crashed through, his momentum carrying him to the middle of the darkened room.

But the only one there was Al Jr., who was sitting up in bed. Billy turned on the light. Al Jr.'s eyes were fixed on him, but he wasn't really seeing him; they were cold and deadened and seemed to linger somewhere just above his head. Al Jr.'s mouth began to twitch, and he stood up, moving slowly with an awkward gait that almost forced him to fall backward. The mumbles from his twitching mouth began to make sense.

"You think you can torture me, too?" he said, stumbling toward Billy and wrapping his cupped hand around Billy's neck. He tightened his grip.

"Al!" Billy said. "Wake up!"

The grip slackened as life returned to Al Jr.'s face. His eyelids fluttered, and he frowned at his hand before pulling it back. "What happened?"

Billy felt wetness on his neck. When he touched it, his hand came away with a smear of blood on his palm. And there was something else strange. The wall above the bed's headboard was splattered with knuckle-shaped bloodstains. Around the room, there were other such spots on the wall. There were so many with identical patterns, in fact, he wondered how they could have accumulated in the little amount of time Al Jr. had been there. "Jesus, Al, I didn't know you were a sleepwalker."

"What're you talking about?"

"You remember me coming in here? Trying to choke me?"

Al Jr. waved his arms at him and scanned the room until his eyes stopped on a coffee cup lying on the floor. He picked up the cup and filled it with rye from a bottle on his nightstand. As he drank from the cup, he grimaced. "Why'd you break in my door?"

"Because I thought you were being murdered in here."

"I wasn't."

"Man, what's wrong with you?"

"What?"

"You need to see a doctor."

"Sure, Billy," he said. "They'd dope me up and send me to that damned hospital again."

"You should come to Evansville with me."

"Just imagine the hippies getting a load of me," he said. "They'd spit in my face and call me a murderer."

Stories like that had circulated around school. Many were openly hostile toward not only the government but also the service members coming home. Some kids assumed he agreed with their twisted way of seeing things just because of his college deferment. They asked him all the time whether he would come to their student rallies. One time, he did.

They were marching across the street from the Marion County Courthouse. The signs kids carried called for troop withdrawal and impeachment, and on a couple of them were messages advocating an overthrow of the government. They walked in large circles, pumping their fists in the air while waving their signs, and tried to pull him in, but he couldn't bring himself to march with them. Instead, he looked up at the courthouse steps, where officers stood smacking their batons onto their open palms. He pulled all the way back to the sidewalk across the street, where he could stand safely.

Their leader, Andy Cross, came after him, pointing his finger as his sign dragged on the ground beside him. "You can't stay on the outside of this! Come on, Billy!"

Billy began to walk toward him, when a young man in a tattered army coat walked by on the other side of the street. A couple of the kids zeroed in on him, went over and called him names, said he should be dead. Billy waited for the guy to slug them, but he moved past them as if they weren't there and kept on going down the sidewalk. Billy thought of Al, by then gone for about four months, and walked to the bus stop, where he bought a ticket and rode a Greyhound home, a more preferable option than catching a ride from Andy.

Al Jr. looked at him now, nodding his head and smiling as if he was studying him, before filling his cup again. Billy started to walk out of the room, when Al Jr. said something in a low voice. He turned around. "What, Al?"

"I was warned about the so-called peace lovers," Al Jr. said. He paused. "But I never gave them any thought until they came around spouting out their shit. I'd give anything to see them in the jungle, see how tough they'd be with Charlie on their asses. They'd curl up in a ball and beg for their lives."

He put his cup down and buried his face in his hand, cupping his chin while he used his stump for support. Billy leaned forward. "What is it?"

"I was feeling sorry for myself in the hospital, you know, thinking about facing people with this," he said, raising his arm in the air. "And then they brought us Mike." He paused again, a bittersweet smile coming across his face as he took another drink. "The guy had so many visitors that first day I was jealous of him. He kept asking, 'Is Angie coming?' And his dad kept telling him she would. But it didn't seem like she would. Everyone left, and it was close to curfew, when I heard a clip-clop coming from the other end of the hallway. It was dark when she passed my room, but I could tell she was afraid."

"Of what?"

"Him," he said. "She went into his room, and he sounded happy. But she started screaming and ran out of there, all the way down the hallway. I went to his room and pushed the door open all the way. He was crying and asking her to come back, and I saw why she ran: His face was gone."

"Damn, Al."

"Everybody on our floor rallied around him, the guys up there," he said. "All of us were messed up, but nothing like him. After a while, he lightened up. He even started joking around."

Billy smiled at him. "So he was OK."

"Yeah, until they came with their goddamn signs, raising hell," he said. "Mike's window was open, and he started begging for them to quit, but they only got louder and started chanting 'baby-killing faceless freak' over and over again."

Al's voice wavered, and he covered his face with his hand. Billy waited for him to finish.

"What happened?" Billy said.

Al Jr. took a deep breath. "He jumped out the window. I went over to it and looked down. Jesus, those bastards were spitting on him."

Billy wanted to say something so the room wouldn't be so quiet, but Al Jr. looked up at him, the scowl on his face more feeble than tough.

"If I went to Evansville and those bastards spit in my face, I'd kill them."

•••

Chapter 3

Big Al climbed the stairs and knocked on Billy's door. There was no answer, so he opened the door and stepped inside. The room was dark and still. When he turned on the light, he saw Billy's room for the first time since Janet died. Clothes lined his floor, covering the carpet, and his basketball (something he rarely left home without) sat on top of a mound at least 2 feet high, next to his poster of Jerry West. So he couldn't have gone to the Y, where he'd often complained the balls were too bald to hold on to, unless he went with Lonny. Maybe they'd left early and he'd just been so skunked out he hadn't heard the door close.

He went to his study, found his Rolodex and flipped through it until he found the number for the Greens' house. But Lonny said he hadn't seen Billy since dropping him off the previous night. Big Al sat on the couch and trembled. Now everything came back, and he remembered Billy lying at the bottom of the steps. The fearful way Billy had looked at him was a reminder that at the age of 52, Big Al didn't know himself as well as he'd thought and that past demons still haunted him. The emptiness of the house made it so he could hear everything. He fled without showering.

At work, it was the same way. Even though they'd been open for hours, there wasn't even one car in the parking lot. Eric Rolston always walked to work, despite having a car; the empty parking lot was probably why no one ever seemed to show up until after Big Al did. Everyone probably thought they were closed. Why not? Several bars had gone under in the past year. Inside, he heard Eric moving around but couldn't see him, and he shut the door so that the bells jingled loudly.

"I'll be with you in a second," Eric said, hurrying to put the last of the mugs away.

"Take your time."

Eric wiped his hands off on a towel. He was slight in build with shoulder-length blond hair he had kept short until the past few months. He wiped away spots on the last mug, looking from it to Big Al before his face reddened and he put the mug down. "What happened to you?"

"Nothing. I just tripped at home," Big Al said. "Any customers yet?"

"No."

Big Al headed toward his office. "Come and get me if you get swamped."

Eric let out a short, nervous laugh as Big Al closed the door. The oblong office was dimly lit. He turned the light up and turned toward the shrine — Billy's trophies, which had been accumulating there since he was big enough to hit a basket on a 10-foot rim. He had Billy's fifth-grade free-throw title and mental attitude award; his city and AAU championship ribbons; his three consecutive Danny Ferron awards, given every year for the best high school player in the county. All of them represented not only his son's greatness as a basketball player but also his greatness as a father. At least they had.

He sat down behind his desk. Lowering his head onto his folded arms, he slipped back to a different time, a different place, when he'd lived just outside a small town near Gary named Leesburg. The face he imagined didn't belong to the grizzled man he would eventually become; it belonged to a small, asthmatic 6-year-old boy huddled underneath a moth-ridden blanket on a hot summer night waiting in fear. The darkness had always terrified him. He was afraid of what could come out of the shadows.

The trouble had always started the same way at about the same time. At least once a week, his mother would pace around downstairs complaining about the late hour, the absence of his father and the fact that Al was still up when she'd told him to go to bed already. He'd walk upstairs slowly, listening for anything but silence, hoping to fall asleep without hearing what he was really afraid of. Then it would come, faint at first and then louder: horses whinnying in the distance, coming closer to the house so the maniac whipping them could unleash his rage on the one he really wanted to hurt — Al, the boy he'd never been able to forgive himself for fathering.

One night, Al had done something he'd never done before. He prayed to see patience and love on his parents' faces. But that night, the horses were moving faster than they ever had before. Whatever ailed his father would soon ail him, and he pulled the cover over his head and put his pillow around his stomach. The horses came to within 50 yards, and a husky, unfamiliar voice called out.

"Whoa, whoa!" the man said. But the horses were going so fast they didn't stop until they were up to the porch. Al got out of bed and went to the window, where the full moon cast light on the backs of two brawny men dragging something heavy and limp before dropping their load in the middle of the yard. Then they ran to the buggy and jumped up in the cab, and the bigger of the two whipped the horses with one quick motion. Then they were gone, and the only thing remaining was a cloud of dust floating in the air and the lump they had left behind.

As the dust settled, his mother took ginger steps toward it. He heard her sobbing, until she let out a shriek so shrill it made him jump and run down the stairs and out on the porch, where he could at last see what it was they had left behind. His father. Limp as a rag doll. His mother kneeled over him, cradling his head and rocking back and forth, whispering. Then, as though she felt Al's presence, she turned her head toward him. The outline of her face was pitch-black.

"Go get Dr. Stevens," she said, almost panting. "You hear me? Hurry up!"

Al jumped off the porch and ran down the road. He didn't even realize he was barefoot until his foot came down on a pointed rock. He yelped in pain but kept running until he became winded. He slowed to a trot until he was close to Dr. Stevens' large farmhouse.

Then he picked up his pace and ran down the doctor's long tree-lined lane to the front porch, yelling, "Dr. Stevens! Dr. Stevens!"

The front door opened, and Dr. Stevens came out holding a kerosene lantern, waving it around so much the light highlighted every one of his wrinkles. Confusion came across his face as he leaned over, put the lamp down on the porch and grabbed hold of Al with a surprisingly firm grip. A mosquito landed on the old man's cheek, and he slapped at his face, the sharp sound making Al recoil backward.

"What's wrong, boy?" he said. "You nearly scared Anna to death."

"My daddy's been hurt!"

The doctor let go of him, hurried inside and came back out holding his black bag and pointing toward his Ford Model T. "Don't just stand there, boy. Let's go."

Al turned and jumped off the porch. He ran with the doctor's hand at his back, and the doctor opened the passenger-side door, lifted him up by his pajama top onto the running board and tossed him inside. Then he cranked the engine and tore off up the road, kicking up a cloud of dust that made it almost impossible to see. On the road, the rows of corn were nothing but blurs, and the doctor kept driving at that speed until they made it back to his parents' ramshackle house. He pulled off onto the grass, his head swiveling around. "Where's your pa?"

"By the porch."

The doctor drove around to the other side of the house, a dismayed frown on his face as he stared through the windshield. Al couldn't see over the dashboard, so he grabbed at it with his hands and pulled himself up. His mouth opened; his head went light. His mother was facing him, her white nightgown and cheeks drenched with blood. The doctor reached over and pulled him down in his seat.

"You'd better stay here."

Then the doctor grabbed his bag and got out. Within seconds, the doctor's steady voice began conflicting with his mother's frantic cries.

"No!" she said. "Do something!"

"I'm sorry, Mildred. Do you have something to cover him up with?"

"No," she said, whimpering, "he's going to be OK. I swear he just said my name a few seconds ago."

"That's impossible."

Al fumbled with the door handle and climbed down off the running board. He went around to the front of the car and then backed away from the lump in front of him. His father's body was lying in an unnatural position, his limp arms sprawled out to his sides and his legs spread out like those of a child about to make a snow angel. Yet it was his head that was in the strangest position; it twisted against the free-flowing motion of his limbs, almost as if he were trying really hard to see something — or him. The headlights cast enough brightness for Al to see that his father's eyes maintained the same cold gaze in death they had held in life.

He heard movement coming at him from behind and turned toward the sound. His mother stepped into the light, her hands trembling and head tilted down.

"I'll bet you didn't even kick up any dust," she said, whispering. "You worthless little…"

Her voice trailed off until it was nothing more than an incoherent whimper, and she buried her face in her hands. Red-streaked tears came through the cracks of her fingers. She frightened Al so much he turned away. And when he did, her hand came swinging down, the back of it sending him backward to the ground. Stars lit up his vision, and then everything was completely dark. Above him, the doctor argued with her, and when Al's vision cleared, the old man was holding her back. She reached out at Al as if she wanted to slap him again, but getting slapped by her was nothing compared with his father's hard blows. He wouldn't have felt her slap at all had she not hit him directly in the face. So he just stayed there as the doctor held her waist until the fight was gone from her and she slumped in his arms. Only then did he finally let go, and she dropped to her knees. Al thought she was finished, until she made another feeble lunge toward him, but she was spent. For a second, he felt sorry for her, and he almost went over to comfort her.

"That's enough, Mildred," Dr. Stevens said, pointing down at him. "This boy didn't stab Gilbert. And I couldn't have saved him even if I'd have been there when it happened."

"I'm sending you to the county home," she said to Al.

"That'd be in his best interest," Dr. Stevens said. "I'll be glad to take him away from here."

She glared up at the doctor and then stood up in the light. There was weariness on her otherwise youthful face as she turned away and walked toward the house. For a moment, Al thought she might tell him to come inside, but she remained silent.

"Mommy!"

She stood straight up, stiff as a board, and hurried up the steps, turning only slightly. "Go away, Al. Dr. Fancy Pants here will take you to your new home." Then she went inside.

Al went toward the house, waiting for her to come back. After several seconds, he ran up to the porch to open the door, but it was locked. He ran around to the side of the house and looked up at her room, but the curtain was drawn shut. His legs went out from underneath him, and he fell to the ground crying. Dr. Stevens' brisk footsteps approached from behind. The doctor leaned forward and helped Al to his feet.

"It's all right, boy," he said, and then he smiled. "You can stay with us tonight."

Al turned to run away but stopped. Out of the corner of his eye, he could see the doctor's face — his many lines, downcast eyes and sad, almost apologetic, expression, which offered neither comfort nor restraint. Al knew that he could run as fast and far away as his short legs would go and that when he got tired of running, the doctor would probably still be standing there, waiting for him to return. So he froze, until the doctor put his hand on his shoulder, gently guiding him back to the car. Once they were close, Dr. Stevens shielded Al from his father's body and helped him inside. While the doctor cranked the engine, Al stood up in his seat and turned toward the house.

The door opened, and his mother came outside holding a small suitcase. She walked over to the doctor and handed it to him. She turned away, and the doctor opened the door and tossed the suitcase in the back seat. He motioned for Al to sit down, and then he got in and drove off the grass to the dirt road. As the car sped by the endless wave of fields, Al wondered what it would be like sleeping in the doctor's house, but the doctor didn't turn onto his lane. He kept driving all the way to Leesburg, where the county home and the sheriff's office were both on Main Street across from each other. Al stared up at the big white house and began to cry again; the doctor meant to get rid of him right then and there, he thought. And sure enough, the doctor pulled up in front of the house, smiled down at him and patted his arm. "C'mon, boy. You're going to be all right."

"Will they beat me up here?"

Dr. Stevens frowned, and his fingers tightened around the steering wheel. "I don't know."

Al wiped away his tears and looked up at the house again. The large windows all had white curtains, and because there were more windows downstairs than up, the house looked like a grinning face. The front yard was filled with so much shrubbery there wasn't even a path to the door. He waited for the doctor to tell him to get out of the car and was surprised when instead he told him to wait. The doctor got out and went across the street to the sheriff's office. Left alone, Al noticed the shrubbery moving and swaying, almost waving at him, and he opened the door, hoping the doctor wouldn't be too angry with him for not doing as he was told. Right away, he heard the deep voice of the sheriff as he laughed in an unpleasant way. The sheriff was holding a kerosene lantern and standing next to his car, which had a star painted on the door. Their voices were muffled as they spoke, and Al moved to the rear of the car, where he could hear them better.

"So, Gilbert finally went and got himself killed," the big sheriff said. "Did Mildred recognize them?"

"I don't know," Dr. Stevens said. "She didn't say."

"Well, I'd better get out there," he said, turning toward his car. Then he stopped abruptly as Al's shadow moved with the lamp's flickering flame. "Who's there?"

Al stepped out of the shadows. The sheriff knew Al well; he had been out to their house several times, always asking his father to step outside as he pulled on his walrus mustache. Sometimes Al would go to the window to spy on them. He couldn't help himself. Those visits were the only times he ever got to see his father scared.

Twice, the sheriff made him go to jail. Those nights had been peaceful, but the following days, after his father returned, had been the worst, the beatings more painful. Now the sheriff seemed confused as he waved the lantern in Al's direction.

"What's he doing here?"

Dr. Stevens told the sheriff of Al's situation. Shaking his head, the sheriff pointed at the county home. "I wouldn't wake Mrs. Orville up at this hour. The jail's empty. He can sleep in there."

"No," Dr. Stevens said. "He can stay with me. Besides, Anna might not believe me if I show up empty-handed."

"Well, I'd better get out there," he said. "Guess I'd better bring Fisher along."

He crossed the street to a small house with a sign hanging from an awning over the front, knocked on the door and waited as the lantern inside turned up and a skinny man came outside. They left together in a horse-drawn buggy. "Where're they going?" Al asked.

"To fetch your pa."

Then they left, passing the slowly moving carriage on their way back down the dirt road. Al nodded off and didn't wake up until the doctor shook him. "C'mon, boy. You can't sleep out here."

Al stumbled out of the car and followed him to the house, where the door flung open and a woman much bigger than the doctor stepped out on the porch wearing a nightgown.

"Don't you ever light out of here like that again," she said. "Where've you been?"

"The Hennessy house," he said as his wife's gaze lowered toward Al. "I can explain."

"I certainly hope so."

Dr. Stevens' reaction was one Al often thought of when he, too, had become an older, married man. The old doctor — the most patient man Al had ever known — rubbed his palms on his tweed trousers, shifted in place and then flung his hands in the air.

"Can we get this boy inside?" he said. "His father died tonight, and — we'll discuss it inside."

Mrs. Stevens gave Al a stern look, and he followed her in. The living room was as big as the whole downstairs of his parents' house. A large fireplace sat across the room beside a large winding mahogany staircase. Mrs. Stevens led him upstairs to a large bathroom — a claw-foot tub sitting in the middle of the room.

"Undress, young man," she said as she ran the bathwater.

"Yes, ma'am," Al said. Then she left the room and went down the stairs. Within seconds, Al heard the old couple arguing in the living room below him and froze. Violence usually followed arguing. So he began to tremble when the doctor's wife came upstairs and frowned when she entered the bathroom. Then he remembered she had told him to undress.

"I'm sorry," he said, undressing as fast as he could. Her folded arms went limp and her serious expression softened into one of horrified pity. She fled the room. At the top of the stairs, she called out to her husband.

Al wondered what was wrong with her. Looking down, he saw what had always been — a body more black-and-blue than white. But the doctor came into the room and knelt down next to him. His face held that sad, apologetic frown. "How're you feeling, boy?"

"I'm all right, sir."

Mrs. Stevens knelt down beside her husband. "Was he in an accident?"

"No," Dr. Stevens said, "though I'm sure that's what his mother would say."

"Who could do such a thing to a child?"

"His father."

Al never made it to the county home. That night was the beginning of the second half of his childhood. When he went to school in the fall, he didn't go as the mangy son of a failed farmer and thief. He went as the charge of the only doctor within 20 miles. The doctor took him out on house calls, where he saw babies born, broken bones mended and many people taking their last breath.

But he never forgot the first half of his childhood — what it was like to be afraid of those who should've loved him. And as the clock chimed next to the shrine, he wondered whether Billy now felt the same kind of fear.

•••

Chapter 4

Billy heard Al Jr. call out in the night. "Who's over there?"

Billy leaped up from the couch and went over to the light switch. When he flipped it on, Al Jr. was standing just inside his room, squinting against the light, his face a splotchy mess of red dots and his puffy eyes encircled by black rings. At first, Billy backed away from him, worried he was sleepwalking again. But Al Jr.'s eyes followed him.

"Jesus," Billy said. "I've been here for two days."

Al Jr. slumped against the doorframe. "I thought you might've gone home by now."

"You said the same thing yesterday."

"I did?" Al Jr. said, coming out of his room and sitting on the edge of the couch, rubbing his forehead with his fingers. "This place is too small for two people."

"Yeah," Billy said, sighing, "you said that, too."

Al Jr. opened his mouth to say something but stopped. He went to the kitchen, poured a shot and drank it. When he came back into the living room, both the bottle and cup dangled from his fingertips, and he sat down at the table before pouring another. It was only 7 in the morning, and Billy couldn't imagine anyone drinking so early, especially Al Jr. At the few parties they had been to together, Al Jr. was always an embarrassment. He could never drink more than a few beers before stumbling around and slurring his words. Yet he always had the Hennessy love for hard liquor. One time, when Al Jr. was 14, his friend Freddy had smuggled a bottle of 100-proof bourbon, and the two of them had sat in the garage loft drinking. Billy hadn't known they were out there until he went out to play basketball. He heard movement from the loft and ran toward the house, but Al Jr. caught up with him, his cigarette swinging wildly in the air, and tackled him from behind. Billy jumped right up, but Al Jr. had just lain there laughing, his smashed cherry burning a hole in his sleeve. He was hung over for the next few days, and Billy never saw him drink like that again.

Until now. He was guzzling more booze than Billy had ever seen anyone drink before, and it hardly had any effect on him. Billy almost got sick watching him. "Damn, Al. How can you drink this early?"

Al Jr. downed another shot before nodding at his stump. "It helps numb the pain."

Billy went to the bathroom with his clean clothes. A pile of moldy clothes sat on the floor next to several magazines with President Johnson on their covers. The orange towel on the floor smelled like a dirty mongrel. He opened the door and stuck his head out. "Do you have a clean towel?"

Al Jr. mumbled something under his breath as he stood up and went to a closet. He came into the hallway holding out a hole-ridden towel set and handed the towels to him. Billy sniffed them and hung them up.

"Where'd these come from?" Billy said.

"With the place," Al Jr. said. "What's it matter if you're just going to throw the same clothes on?"

"I went home and grabbed some clothes — my money, too," Billy said. "Don't you remember anything?"

Al Jr. shrugged and walked back down the hallway. Billy went into the shower and groaned; the only soap there was a bottle of dish soap with so little left he had to pour water in the bottle just to get enough to lather up his rag. He had to wait for the low-pressure water to heat up. Once it did, he took only a few seconds to wash, dry off, dress and hurry from the bathroom before the many stenches gagged him.

Out in the living room, Al Jr. sat on his chair pooch-lipped and pouting. His whole face was red — the dots had disappeared—and his eyes held a dull glint. With a rolling motion, he stood up and went back to his room. Billy put his coat on and called out to Al Jr., "I'll be back around 5:30 or 6."

Al Jr. came back out grimacing. "I'm sure Dad's forgotten all about the other night."

"I'm not."

Al Jr. disappeared inside his room. The door closed behind him, and Billy felt the emptiness of the room all around him. He could hear a dump truck rolling through the alley out back. He remembered his first day of kindergarten, when he'd thought he could get out of going to school by hiding underneath the dining room table.

His father, a little leaner and with a lot more hair, had stood over the table, waiting for him. Al Jr. was smirking behind his father one second and the other telling Billy to hurry up. Then his mother came out from the kitchen, dropped down on her knees, lifted up the tablecloth and smiled at him.

Billy grabbed hold of the oak support beam. "I'm not going," he said.

"You're going to make lots of friends."

"But I want to stay home with you, Mommy."

His father and brother joined together in telling him he was acting like a baby. But he didn't care; he wasn't ready to quit being the baby yet. His mother turned toward his father and brother and told them to shut up. Then she reached out for him and waited for him to take her hands. Something about the way she smiled made him reach out to her. He clung to her as she pulled him out.

"Do you know what they do in kindergarten?" she said.

"No."

"They paint pictures and take naps," she said. "Don't you like to paint?"

"Yes."

"Know what else they do?"

"Huh-uh."

"They go outside and play at recess."

"What's recess?"

"That's when you get to go play on slides, monkey bars, and there's so many swings little boys like you don't have to fidget around waiting their turn," she said, her smile widening. "It's like the park except bigger."

Billy imagined a place where little kids ran around without any grown-ups telling them what to do, and he couldn't wait to get there. He pulled away from her and went toward his brother and father. Al Jr., in a white T-shirt and rolled-up jeans, held his Lone Ranger lunchbox close to him. He liked to say they only let big boys bring their lunches to school because the little squirts like Billy needed their mommies to spoon-feed them their lunches. Once Billy showed he was going to school willingly, Al Jr. seemed to lose interest in the whole scene and walked out the door ahead of their father. Billy hurried to catch up with them but paused at the door to say goodbye to his mother. She wiped away a tear and forced a smile, coming over to him and giving him a hug. Then she pulled away, still holding him by his arms. The clock on the wall ticked; otherwise, there was silence.

Al Jr.'s cheap dime store clock ticked away, too. It was getting late, and he only had a little time left to get breakfast at the small diner at the bottom of Jefferson Hill. Buttoning up his coat, Billy went out in the hallway, where a cold draft came in from the many cracks in the front door. The temperature had to have dipped down into the teens already, and his fingers stung even when he put them in his pockets. As he crossed the bridge, his lungs ached from the swirling wind blowing up from the river, and his legs cramped up. By the time he reached the cafe, he was so cold he didn't even care whether he made it to school.

He sat at the counter, waiting while a young waitress went around the room pouring coffee. After she filled his cup, he ordered eggs over easy, bacon and toast. The coffee warmed him, and he thought about Eric Rolston. Surely, Eric knew what was going on. It was probable that Eric had already said something to calm Billy's dad and everything was all right. Billy probably could go home whenever he wanted. But did he really want to? Even if all was forgotten, he couldn't stand to think things would go back to the way they were before, the two of them barely speaking to each other and staying away from the house as long as possible. And what about Al

Jr.? Sitting around all day getting plastered. It was amazing he hadn't already fallen through that dirty picture window of his. He was so whacked out he was constantly getting skunked, raising hell and walking around in his sleep punching the damn walls.

Now Eric could tell their father about Al Jr., and by the end of the day, they'd find a way to help him; there wasn't any reason to think otherwise. Billy's food came, and he had everything down before the waitress brought her carafe around to fill his cup. He tried to remember what his father always left for a tip, but when he couldn't, he handed the waitress $2 and told her to keep the change.

When a jalopy pulled over on his way to school, he didn't think twice about taking a ride, no matter who was driving. So he said thanks to the zit-faced kid surrounded by a cloud of marijuana smoke and wearing an all-leather outfit with a red bandana around his neck. The kid rolled his head to Hendrix, singing along — or at least trying. Billy slumped down in his seat, hoping no one would recognize him. After the kid parked in the lot, Billy got out and hurried toward the entrance.

Once inside, he cut through the mass of kids blocking the freshman hallway and went upstairs. All the seniors stood around, waiting for the first bell to ring, and he had to scan the hallway for several seconds before he saw Lonny slouching over, his back turned, on the other end. He cut through the crowd, waving off everyone who tried to talk to him along the way, until he was close enough to see that Lonny had cornered Tonya Stalling — a perfectly stacked bottle-blond cheerleader. Every time she tried to move, Lonny would block her path and put his hands on the wall.

"Why don't we go to Hop's after the game?" he said to her.

"I don't think Scott would like that at all," Tonya said.

"Isn't he in Bloomington?" Lonny said, leaning close. She tried to back away.

"You know he is," she said. "So why ask?"

"Is he coming home this weekend?"

"No."

"And I suppose you think he's going to spend all weekend alone studying, huh?"

"What's that supposed to mean?" she said. "Why wouldn't he be?"

Billy flicked Lonny's ear before he could answer her, and Lonny's head shot to the side as he turned around. Tonya slunk away from him and down the hallway. "Damn it, Billy," Lonny said. "I had her right where I wanted her."

"Right, creep," Billy said, laughing. "You've been following her around since the third grade."

"She was going to say yes, and you—"

"Oh, now I've ruined it for you."

"Yeah, you're good at that."

"At least you smeared Scott," he said. "I didn't ruin that for you, did I?"

The sad look disappeared, and a wide grin replaced it. He tilted his head back and laughed so loudly some of the nearby kids jumped and turned toward them. "She'll be freaking out all day."

Billy leaned forward. "I need you to do me a favor."

"What?"

"I want you to call my dad's bar and ask for Eric."

Lonny's forehead wrinkled up as he frowned. "Your dad called me Saturday and asked where you were. Where were you?"

"My brother's place."

"Why?"

Billy told him what had happened, and Lonny's eyes widened as he whistled. "He could've broken your arm or something. We would've been screwed."

"Thanks."

"Why was he so mad?"

"Because I couldn't score."

"You were getting mugged out there."

"Doesn't matter," he said. "Dad thinks I'm better than Jerry West."

"Nobody's better than him."

"So you'll do it, right?"

Lonny looked down and away. "He'll know it's me."

"You can hang up if he answers."

"Why don't you call him?" Lonny said encouragingly. "He said he wanted you to."

Billy slumped. "That's easy for you to say. You weren't the one chucked down the stairs like a bag of trash."

Billy walked away. The bell was about to ring. The breakfast he had eaten made his stomach feel sour, but maybe it was more than that. Why did people only want friendship when they could get something back? Not one person he knew cared about anything besides himself or herself. He thought about ditching, going back to the apartment and lying down on the couch until the disappointment went away, but then he ran into Rich and Ralph Blynner. They stared at him with the serpent eyes on their matching faces, identical hairdos swooping out like rams. Everything about them was the same — their builds, especially — except for the way they dressed. Rich wore loud, bright sweaters, slacks and black leather boots, whereas Ralph preferred tie-dyed shirts, bell-bottoms and Chuck Taylors. They were both as good at getting in trouble as they were at playing basketball, which was why they weren't his teammates anymore. A stupid prank in middle school — they'd stolen their crosstown opponent's mascot, a 6-foot stuffed bear, and been caught hanging it from the flagpole — had ended their playing days for good. Blacklisted from there on out, they sank to the bottom of the social circle as everyone from their middle school team shunned them except for Billy.

"What's up?" Rich said.

"I need a favor."

Ralph looked at Rich before smiling at Billy. "You need some grass?"

"No, man," Billy said, waving his hand at him. "I just need someone to make a phone call for me."

Even their heads tilted the same way as they smiled. Rich shrugged. "It depends."

"On what?"

"We want to go to Duke's party this weekend." Rich said, his smile disappearing as he cocked his thumb, using it to point at himself and his brother. "Every time he sees us, he tells us to leave."

"How come?"

Ralph shrugged. "He thinks we stole his tap."

"Did you?"

"What the hell would we do with a tap?" Rich said, shaking his head. "He's the only one around here who even gets kegs."

"Well, why—"

"Because we get blamed every time something gets lifted when we're around," Ralph said.

This was the first time Billy had given Duke's party any thought. Lonny wouldn't go; he was always preaching about how bad it looked for the starters when the benchwarmers saw them sloshed, and as a result, it was unlikely that anyone on the team except for Garner and a few other underclassmen would go. And there was no way Billy would take a chance at being mocked by Garner for showing up with Mueller or Firth. Showing up with the Blynners wouldn't be much better, but at least they were seniors. They stared at him with intense desperation. Billy couldn't care less what the other kids thought. "We'll have a blast."

ooo

Al Jr.'s feet ached. Pacing from one end of the apartment to the other made him feel confined — even more so than when he was in a foxhole waiting for the rounds to quit coming — and he checked the door locks again. Maybe Billy would go away if he couldn't get inside. Of course, he would pound on the door, bitching and howling the whole time. But he'd get the hint. After all, Billy was the one with promise, and if their father had to get a little rough with him, then that's just the way it was.

Maybe it had been raining or storming on the day Al Jr. first understood about Billy; the memory was so old he could barely remember it. It could've been snowing outside. Maybe that's why they'd been playing basketball in Billy's room with the small wire rim that hung lazily from the closet door. Their father always played against them, scooting around on his knees so they'd at least have a chance. But still, their father rarely lost, except when they'd hit the impossible shots from across the room. He said they'd always have to play that way — someone bigger than they would always be close to the rim — but they tried to take the ball inside, where their hurried shots rarely had a chance. Their father would block the foam ball, sometimes fouling them so they'd have to take free throws from the makeshift foul line at the end of Billy's bed.

They were about the same height at the time, probably no more than 8 and 7 years old. But Billy's arms were long, and his motion was already athletically fluid, whereas Al Jr. was wide and clumsy, his arms stubby. The only way he could score was to barrel in, but Billy could twist and turn in the air, making hard shots look easy, the ball bouncing around the rim before dropping through the net, always followed by their father's praise.

It was after one of those difficult shots when their father threw the ball at Al Jr., with his face drawn into an intimidating scowl. Al Jr. froze with the ball clenched in his hands before lowering his head and barreling forward. The ball sailed through the air and was dropping toward the rim, when his father reached up and smacked it back down. It bounced off Al Jr.'s face.

"The ball was coming down," Al Jr. said. "That's goaltending."

"Sorry, Al," he said, smiling. "Not even close."

"I didn't know you were a cheater."

Something dark came over his father's face he had never seen before, and his father raised his hand. Al Jr. closed his eyes and waited for the slap. But it never came. When he opened his eyes, he was stunned to see his father looking at his hand in tears. He wiped them away and went to the door.

Of course, Billy glared at Al Jr. and followed their dad out of the room. Al Jr. wished he could go, too, so he could apologize. Yet he couldn't; his father had been wrong. So he left the room, taking small steps down the stairs to the den below Billy's room. Soon he heard his father's door open and his plodding footsteps, followed by Billy's lighter ones, going back to Billy's room, where they played without him.

"What's wrong, Al?" his mother asked from the kitchen archway.

He lowered his head. "Nothing."

She came over to him and lifted his head with her fingers. It seemed as if she already knew what had happened, so he told her everything, his voice getting smaller as her smile went away.

"Oh, Al. You need to tell him you're sorry."

"Why?" he said. "He was cheating."

The noise coming from Billy's room became louder and was soon followed by the sound of their laughter. It was the first time they left him out but not the last. From then on, he played with them less and less, until he quit trying to fit in with them at all. It was better to fade into the background than listen to how he wasn't as good as his little brother.

His mother would try to get him to play with them, but he'd go outside, where there was no possible way he'd hear them. Leaving them alone was what they had wanted, and he had always respected that. Why couldn't Billy leave him alone now?

●●●

Chapter 5

Rich and Ralph should've been waiting for Billy after practice, but they were 20 minutes late. What a day, full of letdowns. Nobody could be counted on to do anything he said he'd do. And Rich and Ralph might as well forget about the damn party on Friday. Hell, he didn't even care about going. The cold wind swirled around, blowing fresh snowflakes in his face, and he began walking toward Al Jr.'s apartment. In the distance, a muffler-less car was coming closer, and he turned toward the circular road going around the high school as it came within sight. A cloud of blue smoke hovered over the hood as the car pulled up to the curb and stopped. Soon the fumes reached him, and he coughed.

Through the mist, Rich and Ralph were smiling as he opened the passenger-side door of the burgundy Edsel and climbed in the back seat. The heater's air finally warmed him, and he blew into his cupped hands. "Man, what took you guys so long?"

Fumbling with the gearshift, Rich said, "It takes a while to start this thing up when it's cold like this."

"Great," Billy said. "Aren't you guys worried about getting gassed in this deathtrap?"

"You get used to it," Ralph said, turning around in his seat until he faced Billy. "Where're we going?"

"The side street by 300 and Montgomery," he said. "There's a phone booth there, and Al lives a block and a half away."

The brothers exchanged smart-alecky smiles. "I guess we're slumming it, Ralph."

Billy leaned forward in his seat. "He's on disability and can't afford anything better."

Rich blushed. "Sorry," he said. "I was just joking."

Though the Blynners didn't know anything, none of it was funny. Not at all. If he had kept on running the night his dad threw him down the stairs instead of going to Al Jr.'s place, he would've been all the way to Indy by now, and he wouldn't have stopped. He would have gone as far as his thumb would've taken him, maybe all the way to Florida. Running had crossed his mind many times in the past year. But Al Jr. had changed everything. He was such a weakling and always had been; sometimes Billy felt as if he were the elder brother. Even their mother had told Billy it was his job to watch out for Al Jr. But it was ridiculous to think he could keep Al Jr. from doing dumb things. Hell, Al Jr. would do something just to show off for kids who thought he was nothing but a square, like the time the creep down the street had him roll down the hill at the end of the alley in a trash barrel and the milkman nearly ran him over.

And the girls he liked — oh, Lord, like Peggy Morris. She was one of those bra-burning girls who didn't even want anything to do with boys, yet Al Jr. asked her out right after he got his license. He'd actually believed their father would let him take the Mustang out— with a girl who'd accused them of being pigs for watching a basketball game just because there were cheerleaders dancing on the floor, even though her boobs bounced around freely in her T-shirt. Oh, how their father had looked at her when she'd said that. No wonder his date with Peggy never happened.

Yet Al Jr. managed to get hold of the car keys and take the Mustang for a joyride one night right before Thanksgiving after their father had fallen asleep on the couch. Everything would've been all right if Al Jr. hadn't scratched the door pulling through the narrow opening of the garage. It wasn't a deep scratch or a large one, but their father noticed it right away. Man, was it the strangest holiday ever — their mother preparing everything in silence, wearing her orange harvest sweatshirt and bright green pants. Everything about her was cheerful except her face.

After supper, Al Jr. stood up and turned to go to his room. It was then that their father confronted him about the car. Al Jr. said nothing; he only looked down and clenched his jaw. Their father went to slap him, but he ran around the table.

"Stop it, Al," their mother said, standing up.

"I'm tired of him going against everything I say," their father said.

"I'm sorry," Al Jr. said.

"You're always sorry."

Al Jr. looked down and said nothing; their mother went over and stood in between them. "Go upstairs."

Al Jr. had done as she said, taking ginger steps around their father and hurrying once he was past him. He had gone to his room and stayed there the rest of the night, maybe even the rest of the weekend.

Rich said something to Billy and waited for an answer. "What?" Billy asked.

"Are you sure there's a phone booth around here?"

"Yeah," Billy said, "it's on Tammany Street — the other side street."

Stanley Street ran along the opposite side of West Montgomery. All the houses there were small, and half of them had been abandoned long ago. Stanley led into the empty businesses of Tammany Street, a string of mom and pop stores where the owners had died off years ago and were never replaced, where outdated signs announced chuck roast on sale for 52 cents a pound and beans at 6 cents a can. There was even a newspaper hanging up with a picture of Harry Truman holding up a newspaper announcing he'd been beaten by Thomas Dewey. When the car pulled over, Billy got out, and Ralph came over and whistled. "This place could be one of those Hollywood ghost towns."

Billy motioned for Rich to get out of the car. Rich left the engine idling and got out, glaring over at Ralph, still facing the store's window, and then came over to the open door of the booth. "Why don't you just make the call? You can hang up if your dad answers."

"I've got to talk to Eric. If I hang up, Dad will think he's being pranked and he'll answer every time."

Billy handed him the receiver, put his coin in the slot and dialed the number. On the other end, he heard the phone ring four or five times before Eric answered. "Al's."

Billy took the phone from Rich and tried to close the sliding glass door. It jammed and then shut as Rich got out of the way. Alone, Billy put the receiver up to his mouth and spoke.

"Hey," he said. "It's Billy."

"Hi, Billy," Eric said. "You want to talk to your dad?"

"Don't say my name. He didn't hear you, did he?"

"Huh?" Eric said. "I don't—"

"Just listen to me," Billy said. "I'm not staying with Dad. I'm staying with Al Jr. He lives on West Montgomery — 334, I think. It's easy to spot. The place is practically falling in."

"What do you want me to do? I'll go get your—"

"No, don't! We got in a fight!" Billy said, turning toward Rich and Ralph. Both of them had the same look of dumb confusion. He turned away from them, speaking in a low voice. "Al's a wreck, and Dad needs to know. Will you tell him?"

There was a long silence. Billy thought the faint line had finally gone dead. But then he heard Eric breathing. He clutched at the handset and crooked it under his chin. "Are you still there?"

"Yeah, I'm still here," he said. Billy heard his father asking who was on the phone. After saying his wife, Eric spoke a little louder. "But I think it'd sound better coming from you."

"We need your help," Billy said. He turned around to make sure the Blynners weren't nearby, but Rich paced like a damn duck in a shooting gallery, and Ralph had his face smashed against another storefront window, his hands cupping the glass.

On the other end, Eric whispered. "If it was just me, I'd talk to him, but I can't afford to make him mad and get fired."

Billy put the phone down to his chest and sighed. Rich stopped his pacing and glanced at him. Billy wiped his face on his jacket sleeve before putting the phone back up to his mouth. "Kiss my ass, Eric."

Then he hung up before Eric had a chance to speak and left the phone booth. He headed down the sidewalk. The Blynners got in their car, and Rich rolled down the street toward him, catching up before he was even halfway down the block. Rich rolled down the window and gave him a worried look, probably afraid he wouldn't go to the party with them now.

"C'mon," Rich said. "I'll give you a ride."

"It's just a little ways," Billy said. The anticipation of the phone call had made him run way too hard at practice, and his feet were sore. So he shrugged, got to the car and collapsed down in the back seat. He gave them directions to Al Jr.'s place, and then blocked them out as they babbled, almost drowning each other out. Then Rich said his name and stared at him through the rearview mirror.

"What?"

"We're taking a road trip at spring break," he said. "Where would you go, California or Canada?"

"You wouldn't even make it out of the county in this heap," Billy said. "That's stupid."

Ralph turned around in his seat, nodding and smiling. "We'll hitchhike the rest of the way. Maybe we'll get picked up by a hippie sitting on a bunch of weed."

"You're going to do all that in a week? You guys will never make it back in time."

Ralph turned back around. "Wouldn't that be a shame?"

"This is it," Billy said as they reached Al Jr.'s place. The car came to a stop. "You guys are coming in, aren't you?" Billy asked.

They looked at each other. Billy could only see the back of Ralph's head, but he saw Rich's eyes widen for a second before he noticed Billy staring at him. Then both of the twins gazed forward, thinking — Billy just knew it — of an excuse not to come in. But they couldn't. They got out slowly, first Rich and then Ralph, and Billy was already on the porch waiting for them before they stepped onto the walkway. He motioned for them to hurry before going through the screen door and down the hall to Al Jr.'s door. When he went to open it, the handle wouldn't budge, and he pounded on the door. "C'mon, Al! It's me! Open up!"

Shuffled footsteps came toward the door and stopped. All three locks were unlatched, and the door opened, releasing the stench of hard liquor. Al Jr., wearing a smiley-face shirt and baggy trousers, leaned out the doorway while his stump rested against the doorframe. A scowl came across his face. "Why'd you bring them here?"

"They gave me a ride," he said. "You remember Rich and Ralph, don't you?"

"Yeah," Al Jr. said. "You used to hang out with them before you got a fat head."

Billy turned around to give the Blynners an apologetic smile, but they were fixed on Al Jr.'s stump. They kept backing up to the front door until they were close enough to go out. Billy followed after them, but Al Jr. stepped back and opened the door all the way.

"Wait," he said. "You don't have to go."

Billy turned around and headed into the apartment. Al Jr. looked like a clown trying to balance himself on a beach ball. His eyes were thin red slits. The Blynners filed in the doorway sideways and jumped when Al Jr. shut the door a little too hard. Rich smiled at him. "What've you been up to, Al?"

"What do you think?" Al Jr. said. "Tying one on, man."

None of them spoke. The silence in the room lasted so long the Blynners began moving toward the door again. Finally, Billy said, "These guys are going to Canada or California."

Al Jr. smiled unpleasantly. He picked up his prosthetic hand and waved it in the air at them. "Canada, huh? Are you trying to run away from this? You'd be damn smart to."

"C'mon," Billy said. "They didn't come here to talk about Vietnam."

Al Jr. fumbled to put his hand back on. When he couldn't, he threw it on the floor. "Oh, I forgot. Life's one big party?"

"Not around here."

"Get on with yours," he said, pointing to the door. "Go to Canada or California or fucking Timbuktu for all I care."

Rich had already opened the door and motioned for Ralph to follow. Al Jr.'s stare seemed to go beyond Billy to a bottle of whiskey on the table; he walked toward it. Halfway there, he tripped and fell forward. Sprawled out on his stomach, he began speaking in a garbled way that sounded like a foreign language. Then — as if he'd said something funny — he began to cackle wildly, before his laughter trailed off to guttural snoring.

Rich came back in the room — Ralph had already gone outside — and stood over Al Jr. He smiled at Billy before going out the door. "I'll see you later."

"Hey!" Billy called out to him. "Can you give me a lift tomorrow?"

Before the screen door thwacked shut, he heard Rich's fading voice. "Sure, Billy."

• • •

Chapter 6

Big Al filled his coffee mug and paced from room to room, wondering just where Billy was staying. Maybe Billy had run away with one of those free-loving communes and was halfway across the country on a spray-painted bus. Or maybe the people he was with weren't so friendly, one of those cults in which God and destruction went together. Maybe Billy was one of their sacrifices and needed his dad to come and save him. Or maybe he had just kept running and was still running now. Big Al drank his coffee. Nothing made sense. Unless Billy had forsaken him; the thought made him sick to his stomach, and the coffee threatened to come back up. But what else could it be? Coach Randle — as worthless as he was — would be ringing the town bell in alarm if anything had happened to his meal ticket.

Janet had always joked (at least he'd thought she was joking) he would be left in the dark if it hadn't been for her. He had to admit she was probably right. He never knew what was going on in Billy's mind unless Billy had a ball in his hands. Even then, he was sometimes left in the dark — for example, when Billy was a freshman and his interest in basketball was waning. At first, Big Al had thought Billy had come under the influence of the new breed of kids who wore loud clothes and let their hair grow down to their asses while they wore sunglasses to hide their red eyes. But Billy's

clothes never had the scent of burning leaves Big Al's patrons
complained about on their kids' clothes.

Once, he had a scare when he came home at noon to fix a
sandwich. Movement came from above him, and the smell they
talked about was faintly in the air. Taking light steps, he went
upstairs and opened Billy's door. But the room was empty, and he
turned toward Al Jr.'s room. He opened the door and saw Al Jr.
lying on his bed pretending to be asleep, while the scent lingered in
the air. On the other side of the bed, the no-good loafer Freddy
Brown was hiding on the floor. He had tried to crawl underneath the
bed but was too big to fit. They had skipped school and smoked a
couple of joints was what Al Jr. told Janet and him. Pressed further,
he said Billy had nothing to do with it, and Big Al relaxed, thinking
that whatever it was, at least Billy wasn't turning into a hippie. But
Billy's aloofness still bothered him. Finally, several days later, he
couldn't take it any longer and said something to Janet. She laughed.

"What's so funny?" he said.

"You're really a — what is it they say?" she said. "Oh, yeah, a
square."

"A square?" he said.

"Somebody who doesn't get anything."

"Huh?"

"I know you'd like to keep Billy on the court all night long."
She paused. "But he's got a girlfriend now."

He remembered feeling naive and relieved at the same time. He
wasn't pleased, but at least he knew what was going on.

But he didn't have Janet's guidance to help him now; he didn't
have anything but a phone book and a telephone. Before leaving for
work, he called the high school. The secretary put him on hold
before telling him Billy was indeed there — and had been all week.
So whom could he be staying with?

He planned on giving plenty of thought to this question in the
dark solitude of his office, away from everything that could muddle
his mind. But once he came in view of the bar, he saw the cars of his
least prosperous customers lined up in the first row of the parking
lot. All three of them were eyesores from an another era. Mort
Simpkins drove a rust-colored pickup truck from the '40s that had no
tailgate and sloped downward at an awkward angle. Lester Brigg's

station wagon had dents from the many collisions Lester had had when he was too drunk to walk, let alone drive. Davy Lee and Howard Meeks always showed up together in Howard's '58 Bel Air, which had been the group's pride and joy until Howard parked it on a hill one day and the car slid down and slammed into a couple of trees and crumpled in the passenger-side door. The two of them now had to get in on the driver's side. None of them spent any more money at Al's than they did on their cars.

But what were they doing here on a Thursday? Their regular day was Tuesday, the day of dime beers and quarter shots, and even then, they never came before noon. He went inside and found them sitting at the center table, wearing tattered black coats and staring somberly in their beers. Mort was smoking a filterless cigarette, his hair oiled back in a strange way. Lester, a chubby man with a friendly face and his hair combed across his scalp, turned around and nodded. "Good morning, Al."

"Good morning, guys," Big Al said, going toward their table before stopping abruptly. "How's it going?"

All of them lowered their heads except for Mort. He kept on staring, and Big Al was about to ask him what was wrong when he spoke first. "What's the long face for, Al? You worried about Rionsburg?"

"Those bums," Big Al said. "Billy can handle them all by himself."

"Fired up, is he?" Lester said.

"You'd better believe it," Big Al said. "He'll break the scoring record yet."

Eric came out from behind the counter and frowned. "How's Billy been?"

"Fine," Big Al said, smiling at him before looking away. "What brings you guys here so early? Surely not to talk about Rionsburg."

Mort's face tensed up, and the rest of them acted surprised by what he had said. Big Al took a step closer to their table. "C'mon, guys. What is it?"

"They're burying Stan today," Mort said quietly.

For a moment, Big Al couldn't catch his breath. He suddenly noticed how stale the air was from every cheap cigar ever smoked in there, and it made him nauseated. When he finally caught his breath, he asked, "What happened? When did he die?"

Mort regarded him suspiciously. "You never heard he had cancer? All the people who know him never told you that?"

"No," Big Al said. "No one ever told me."

"Yeah, he died on Monday," Mort said, his head tilted. "I can't believe you didn't know."

"How could I?" he said. "He quit coming in here after he stiffed me on his tab."

Mort shook his head slowly. "That's Stan for you. You should've seen him Saturday, coming in and out of it and asking if his daughters were there yet. Of course, they never showed up."

That had to be nonsense. He had known the girls, Cynthia and Doris, since they were little more than babies. They had always run up to Stan, both of them hugging and tugging at his legs. Even years later, long after their mother had left him because of his drinking and inability to hold a job, Stan had made it sound as if the girls still wrote him regularly and their bond was so strong nothing could ever come between them. Maybe he had made it all up or was seeing things the way he wanted to. Either way, he was convincing, often making a big show of the gifts they had sent him.

But no. All of it was nothing but a smokescreen for a lonely old man to make himself feel good. Big Al wondered why none of the guys had said anything sooner than today, when there was nothing left to do except bury him. He asked them why they'd kept quiet.

Each one of them slumped. Mort folded his arms and sat back in his seat. "Because none of us thought you'd care."

"What?" Big Al said, running the fingers of both of his hands across his head. "I carried him when no one else would even let him in the door," he said. "Besides, I never said he couldn't come back."

"No," Mort said, "but you treated him like dirt."

"Things have been tight around here," Big Al said. "Nobody spends much more than a handful of nickels anymore. Hell, we barely make enough to keep the lights on."

"A handful of nickels are better than nothing," Howard said.

"I guess you're right," Big Al said. He told Eric, "Don't charge them for their next round. Put it on Stan's tab."

They all mumbled their thanks. They didn't sound grateful, but he didn't care. They could have whooped and hollered, and he'd still have had the same sick feeling. "When's the funeral?"

"Eleven o'clock," Mort said, "at Mount Hope."

Big Al hurried into his office and closed the door. He sat down so hard the chair made a cracking sound, and then he buried his head in his folded arms. Poor old Stan, always coming in there with his pockets empty and filling the air with vows of the rounds he would buy once his ship finally came in. And the nonsense about how he could have made his fortune 10 times over if he would have just gotten the loan to buy the land where they were going to build the mall. He never admitted to any kind of failure. Only once did he ever seem beaten.

About two months after Janet died, Stan came in empty-handed. It hadn't been the first time but might as well have been. Everything was a struggle for Big Al; people doing things they normally did got on his nerves. Stan approached the bar after no one had bought him a drink. His once red hair was nothing more than a few tattered wisps of stringy white going in every direction, and his clothes were so baggy he had to walk holding his pants up. He looked closer to 80 than 62. He sat at the bar waiting for his usual drink, a martini with two shots of gin and hardly any vermouth. Eric went to make the drink, but Big Al wouldn't let him. With his back turned, Big Al could feel Stan staring at him, begging for a drink he couldn't afford.

Big Al picked up the gin and vermouth, but when he turned around to make Stan's drink, he was already gone. And though Big Al meant to apologize — maybe tell him how everything, including friendship, seemed meaningless and insignificant since Janet died— he never got the chance.

They'd been friends so long he couldn't even remember when they'd met. But the past started coming back to him, little by little, until he felt old and stupid for not remembering sooner. In 1942, wandering around in East Chicago, he heard about how Joel Lydon, the owner of a prosperous nightclub bearing his name, was in desperate need of bouncers. Most of the men were off to war; the ones remaining were tearing up his place. So Big Al moved to Richland with little more than the clothes he wore. The place was filled with women. But that didn't give a man like him the upper hand. Far from it. He was regarded the same way as any other man not serving overseas — as an idle loafer with no worth. He could have told them he had gone to every recruiter from all the services. None of them would have him because of all the broken bones he had suffered in childhood. But the shame of not being good enough made the subject something he always avoided. So he went about his business as a bouncer as if there weren't anything he couldn't handle. Soon he found himself fighting more than he had ever done in his life, often seeking confrontations when there wasn't any need to, the chip on his shoulder getting bigger each time. He didn't care; he wasn't good enough for the people he wanted to be around and despised the ones he was.

It was then, around March, when he first noticed Janet dancing the Charleston by the jukebox. She was tall and slender with an easy smile he only saw when she didn't know he was staring at her. It didn't surprise him she looked down on him just as everyone else did, and he wished he'd noticed her sooner, when he would've had a better chance of making a good impression. Still, he found the courage to approach her. But then he froze. She was prettier up close; her cheeks dimpled up when she smiled, and her brown eyes had a soft, comforting quality in them — at least they had until she saw him approaching with two beers. He tried to hand her one, but she wouldn't take it. Instead, she sized him up, frowning the whole time, before she turned and walked away. He thought that he had just been too bold and that in time, she would soften up and give him a chance. But she didn't. The drinks he kept sending her way went untouched. Finally, he asked her to dance, but she said no. Then he slunk off to the other end of the bar. He began to think she was just out of his league, but he cornered her one more time as she was coming off the dance floor.

"Why won't you have dinner with me?" he said.

Janet folded her long arms and tried to walk around him, but he shifted so she couldn't. So she simply turned around to go back out on the dance floor. Reaching out, he put his hand on her shoulder, and she jerked away from him and turned back with her hand high in the air. Then she lowered her hand and pointed right in his face.

"Why would I want to spend time with someone who drinks every day," she said, "and fights all the time like a little kid?"

"I can't help it if I have a reputation."

"Were you born with it?" she said. "What's your mother think? You do have one, don't you?"

Her unwavering reproach made him dizzy; approaching her felt like a big mistake. He tried to speak, but his voice caught. He cleared his throat. When he spoke again, his voice was barely above a whisper. "I haven't seen my mother in over 20 years. She could be dead for all I know."

For a moment — which he would have missed had he not been looking right at her — her expression softened. "You're just bumming your way through life, Al. For me to…" She paused. "I'd have to see some change."

He smiled. "I can change."

"It's not that simple," she said, crinkling her nose. "How often do you bathe?"

"I took one yesterday."

"Uh-huh," she said. "When's the last time you held a job?"

"I worked all weekend."

"For what, booze money?"

He lowered his head and watched her hand coming off her hip. She put it under his chin and lifted his head until their eyes met. "You've got too much time on your hands."

Then she let go and walked off, disappearing on the crowded dance floor without so much as a backward glance.

The following Monday, he went to Beta Die — a dirty, smoldering hellhole — and filled out an application. When he returned it to the secretary, she asked him to wait. Then she picked up the phone and smiled. "I've got a live one."

After several uh-huhs, she hung up and led him down to a room at the end of the hallway, where she told him to wait. Though it wasn't quite spring yet, he began sweating, and the walls were so thin he could hear men's voices blending with the humming sound of machinery and, about every five seconds, a slamming sound. He started to take off his jacket, when the door on the other end of the room opened and a tall stocky man with an unlit half-smoked cigar came in and called back to someone inside the plant. "The kid's gone if he smashes that die, Abel."

Shuffling through a stack of yellowed papers, the man acted as if he were the only one in the room, and Big Al squirmed in his seat. The man must've been about 60, but he was as solid as any man he'd ever seen. The white button-up shirt he wore was nearly gray with metal shavings, and the rolled-up sleeves revealed scrapes and burns on his forearm. When he finally found Al's application, he looked it over for only a few seconds before flinging it on the table.

"OK, kid," he said, his cigar bouncing in his mouth as he extended his right hand, which was missing a pinkie and half its ring finger. Big Al shook his hand, and the man smiled slightly. "Name's Dick Henkin, Al. Normally, we hire men with experience. Now we're just hiring men. When can you start?"

Big Al pulled his hand away, careful not to let his gaze linger too long on Dick's missing fingers. "I can start today, Mr. Henkin."

Dick went through his desk drawers and pulled out a box of matches. He struck one on a piece of sandpaper and lit his cigar. "Just be here at 7 in the morning."

The next morning came fast. He rarely got up before 10, and when his alarm clock rang at 6, he was so groggy he nearly fell down getting out of bed. Things didn't get any better at work. He was handed a pair of holey gloves and a thick set of goggles before being led out to the plant, where it must've been at least 90 degrees. His foreman, Abel Herman, put him with Stan Evans, a man with the reddest hair he'd ever seen, and pointed up to a machine situated next to a cauldron of molten metal. Up there was hotter than everywhere else in the plant; sweat rolled down his forehead and seeped through the goggle's seals. Abel stood next to him for hours and didn't say much of anything except for what to do. Finally, around 10, he tapped Big Al on the shoulder. "Just remember to pour and hit the button as fast as you can. Spray the die after every few dips so the metal doesn't stick. Remember, if it does, we're screwed. Those things are worth more than both of us put together."

Stan stood at the bottom of the steps mimicking Abel's nervous, overly animated movement, and then Abel turned around and headed down the steps toward him. Walking away, Abel patted Stan on the shoulder and went over to another miserable-looking metal dipper. Stan climbed the steps and smiled a gaping, wide smile.

"Don't let him scare you," he said. "They can't keep anyone around here. Hell, you could run Dick over with a forklift, and they'd just move him and tell you to get back to work."

Big Al laughed and held out his hand. Stan took it and pumped it. "I'm Stan Evans," he said. "I think I've seen you at Joel Lydon's Lounge. You're a bouncer?"

"Not anymore," he said. "Name's Al Hennessy, and I had to find something a little more respectable."

Stan frowned but still seemed to be smiling. "I don't know if I'd call this place respectable."

By the end of the week, Big Al understood what Stan had meant. Though the machines broke down constantly, Abel still demanded he put out more parts. And Dick — the rude bastard— would throw his cigar butts and empty paper coffee cups in the cauldron, sometimes causing the metal to pop and burn Big Al's arm. Every now and then, Big Al would see Dick and Abel standing off to the side scowling. But those were minor irritants compared with the way the heat parched his lips and dehydrated him so much his tongue thickened like leather, making him crave a beer long before noon. And though Stan was probably the most likable guy he had ever met, he was also one of the most annoying. An incurable prankster, Stan would wait until Big Al was deep in thought— always about the day Janet would be his — and then throw scraps of trash at him. Big Al would turn to yell at him, but Stan would time his throws so he was never caught in the act. Then he'd smile that damned toothy grin of his.

There was a knock on Big Al's office door, and he nearly tipped his chair over standing up. "What?"

"Smitty's here," Eric said.

Big Al reached into his pocket for the key to the cooler. When he opened the door, Eric regarded him so strangely Big Al asked what was wrong.

"I'm sorry I knocked so hard," he said, taking the key, "but I've been out here for five minutes saying your name."

"Oh, I'm sorry," Big Al said. It didn't seem possible for Eric to have been out there for so long, though it didn't matter; Smitty always had a couple of beers before unloading the truck. Then it struck him: Eric thought there was something wrong with him.

"I just…"

"It's all right," Big Al said, slapping him on the shoulder on his way around him. Smitty sat at the bar in his baggy suit and his ridiculous milkman hat, which still wasn't big enough to cover his ears. He lifted his beer in the air. "Here's to Stan."

Big Al poured himself a beer. Then he lifted his mug and clanked it off Smitty's mug. "To Stan."

Both of them took a couple of sips. Big Al wondered whether Smitty felt as strange as he did toasting someone who'd bummed more beer than he'd ever paid for and never put much money in either of their pockets. Yet it felt right. In better times, before Janet died, before there was any real friction with his boys, Stan had been as much a fixture there as the stools and bar. Smitty always gave him a six-pack of beer, and Stan — who never had anything — would hand them out to whoever was there at the time, keeping only one for himself. Smitty always sat alongside him and never unloaded his truck until their beers were gone.

"I heard he had cancer," Smitty said, pushing his hat back on his head. "Guess that explains it."

"Explains what?"

"Why I haven't seen him here in a while."

Big Al started coughing; a lump in his throat nearly made it impossible to breathe. Out of the corner of his eye, he could see, or imagined, an odd look on Eric's face. His own face felt hot and red. He downed the rest of his beer before putting his jacket on. "I've got to go now. You want to come to Stan's funeral with me, Smitty?"

"Can't," he said as he drank the rest of his beer. "Got to be in Kokomo by noon."

"Well," Big Al said. "I'll see you next week then."

Eric pointed up at the clock. "It's only quarter after 10."

"I don't want to go straggling in there like a bum."

ooo

Big Al drove under the archway at Mount Hope Cemetery. A wreath blew across the road. Just beyond the gate was a 30-foot

World War I monument, a soldier standing with his rifle at his side overlooking the sun-bleached markers so worn down by time the names on them were no longer legible. The narrow road widened in the newer section, and he headed toward a line of mausoleums on top of a hill. Down in a pasture below was a canopy where several men in tattered coats passed bottles hidden in paper sacks. A tall minister stood solemnly in front of the tent and kept checking the time on his watch.

A beer can sat on top of Stan's casket; Big Al planned on saying something after he parked the car, but then the minister removed it, and a bony hand reached out of the flap in the canopy and took the can from his hand. Big Al drove past a string of jalopies lined up nearly to the end of the road and parked. He got out of the car and loosened his tie. He recognized some of the men gathered there. Dan Riggle, Bart Tenner and Shelley Brian, in particular, stared at him sullenly. All three had been banned from his bar for picking fights with some of his more respectable patrons after their panhandling efforts failed. No doubt they would use Stan's death as an excuse to get back in his bar, where, he was sure of it, they would pick up where they'd left off, and he'd have to go through the trouble of banning them all over again.

He almost got back in his car, especially because Stan's own daughters hadn't bothered showing up. But Stan deserved to have someone there who wouldn't use his death as an excuse to weasel free beer.

"I don't believe it," a squeaky voice called out from behind him. "Al!"

Big Al turned around and smiled. Nick Dooley, the town's biggest little man, came forward with his arms open and hugged him. He lifted him off his feet and repeated his name over and over.

"Come on, you big lug," Nick said, laughing. "Don't break my back!"

Big Al put him down but continued to hold on to his arms and smile at him. "How've you been keeping yourself?"

"Busy," Nick said, his smile now gone. "I had to come and pay my respects to Stan, though. I didn't even know he was sick."

Big Al's jaw felt as if it were clamped shut. Nick took a few steps toward the tent before stopping and gazing around as if he were counting headstones. "Poor Stan. God knows he didn't catch any breaks. Maybe he's found his rainbow now."

"Yeah," Big Al said, "and hopefully there's a waterfall full of free booze at the end of it."

"That's awful, Al."

Big Al felt his face redden; he hadn't meant to bad-mouth Stan. But he didn't like Nick's reaction. Nick was a bachelor with no kids and no responsibilities, and it had probably been a long time since he had to worry about money. Still, he smiled at Nick as if he'd just been joking. "Well, how much did he owe you?"

"He quit coming to my place a long time ago," Nick said. "It's a little too rowdy for the old-timers, I guess."

"Never found that quiet little place you were always looking for, huh?"

"I quit trying after you said no."

From underneath the canopy, a scratchy song began to play on an old gramophone; the Irish tenor sang "Danny Boy." Stan had often stood at the jukebox listening to the song, rocking back and forth and singing along. Hell, Stan was the only person who ever even played it. Everyone else preferred to listen to the lively music of the big bands, including Big Al. But the song made him think of Stan when they were both much younger and not so broken down by time, laughing it up at Joel Lydon's Lounge and acting as if they would live forever. Nick fidgeted and nodded toward the tent. "Are you ready to go in?"

"Yeah," Big Al said. They walked side by side into the tent and sat in the last row. The smell of cheap cologne and even cheaper wine filled the air, making it hard to breathe. Mort, Davy, Lester and Howard sat in the front row, talking to one another. Shelley Brian sat behind them and kept looking back over his shoulder and then whispering into Bart Tenner's ear. Then the two of them laughed before the minister came inside and gave them a withering glance that shut them both up.

Soon the minister, Reverend Forgey, began his eulogy, speaking in a voice that occasionally cracked as he talked about imperfections, infidelities, living in sin, just about every shortcoming Stan had ever had. He spoke of Stan's daughters as if they were right there in the tent with them. By the time Reverend Forgey finished,

Big Al was so ashamed he stood up and hurried past everyone else. He was almost to his car, when Nick called out for him to wait. He turned around and tried to smile. "I'm sorry, Nick," he said, "but this place gives me the heebie-jeebies."

Nick hugged him and lifted Big Al up off his feet. After he let go, he stood back and smiled. Big Al slapped him on the arm. "You're like an ant. They say they can lift eight times their body weight."

Nick waved at him and walked away. "Don't be a stranger, Al. Stop by sometime."

"Bye, Nick," he said. Turning around, he caught a glimpse of the sun's bright glow reflecting off Janet's headstone.

ooo

Big Al stood near the window of the bar as an old pickup truck pulled onto the parking lot, a cloud of black smoke rolling out of its tailpipe. When the truck parked, the three men sitting inside didn't get out but instead passed around a bottle, content to wait for reinforcements. Big Al turned, pointed at the cash register and told Eric, "They're starting to show up. Make sure you keep the drawer closed. One of those rumdums wouldn't think twice about sticking their grubby paws in there and cleaning us out."

As soon as he said it, several car doors, at least 20, opened and shut. Peeking out the window, he saw that the parking lot had filled with jalopies, and their owners stood in a huddle, conniving and plotting, before turning toward the bar and approaching. It unnerved him; even if he gave them a round on the house, it would only make them want more. Eric came over to the window and whistled.

"We should flip the sign over," he said. "Maybe they'd go away."

A good idea — at least it would've been 20 minutes prior— but by the time he said it, more of them had shown up, including Shelley Brian, Bart Tenner and Dan Riggle, who got out of a car driven by Charlie Reeser — the self-proclaimed king of the drunks. All of them — including the first wave of guys, who were already near the door — paused and waited for him to get out. Reeser beamed at their numbers before coming toward the building, the rest of them filing in behind him. Soon they filled the room, and Big Al and Eric went back behind the bar. They were all talking at once until Charlie motioned for silence. Then he took off his hat, a ridiculous fishing cap with hooks sticking out of it, and held it out in front of him. When he spoke, his voice was low and humble.

"Out of respect for poor old Stan," he said, "I think it only fitting for you to provide his friends with enough booze to soak our sorrows and reflect on his greatness."

Big Al nodded his head. "And I think it only fitting I should send my light bill to you when it comes in the mail."

A collective groan broke out; terms such as tightwad, penny pincher and squeaky were bandied about until Big Al finally raised his hands in the air. "OK, OK. Once Eric takes in 20 bucks from the lot of you, the rest is on the house."

Charlie threw his cap on the ground and pointed at him. "That's bullshit!"

Big Al shrugged, came out from behind the bar and went to his office. The noise level rose and then tapered off with each jingle of the door's bells.

"It's not right, Eric," Charlie said. "Stan deserved better than this."

Big Al slammed the door shut. He didn't even remember seeing Charlie at the funeral, but one thing he said was true, at least to Big Al. Stan deserved better than to have a bunch of drunks who'd never been there for him in life pretending their only purpose of the day was sending him off in style. Hell, even Mort and the guys were better than that. They'd never come in there begging for booze, making it sound as if he were stepping on Stan's grave by refusing them. What a joke.

Finally, after his nerves settled and all of them were long gone, he opened the door and went back out to the bar. Eric stood by the window, massaging his temples as if he were afraid they had only left to get reinforcements. "Thanks for leaving me all alone with those vultures."

"How much did they spend?"

Eric laughed and pointed at the cash register. "You can look for yourself. They got mad after I wouldn't let them have Tuesday prices."

Big Al went to the cash register and opened the drawer: two crinkled-up $1 bills, both of them so grimy he wondered whether they'd been pulled out of someone's sock. Panhandling money. "I feel sorry for the next bar they hit."

•••

Chapter 7

Billy's back ached, undoubtedly from the way Al Jr.'s couch bowed at the center, and Billy sat up and cradled his head. His usual game day breakfast — eggs, pancakes, toast and bacon — wouldn't happen today. It was probably for the better; after not eating well for so many days, the sight of so much food might make him sick. Besides, nothing tasted the same since his mother died. When his father cooked breakfast, the eggs were overdone, the pancakes doughy in the middle and the bacon flabby and soft. But it didn't matter. Al Jr. didn't have any food anyhow, and he didn't feel like going to the diner at the bottom of the hill.

He'd never gone this long without seeing his father. Even basketball camp never went a full week. Part of him felt guilty because he wasn't sure he even wanted to see his father. But there was no way his father would stay away from the game because of some silly argument. He wouldn't waste a chance to nitpick him about every wasted possession, every little mistake. It only took a glance up in the stands to read the old man's mood. If his arms were folded, then he'd better watch out; if he clapped in that strange way of his — with one hand coming up, the other down — then it was the ref or the coach screwing up. No matter what, his dad was never satisfied unless they were blowing the other team out and Billy had more points than everyone else.

The bedroom door opened, and he saw Al Jr.'s silhouette in the darkness. He stood there for several seconds before letting out a little laugh. "It's Billy day!"

Al Jr. went to the bathroom and re-emerged a short time later — going straight to his room and shutting the door without saying another word. Some things never changed. Al Jr. had always been moody on days when Billy had a game. It was something Billy learned in the fifth grade. He'd run up to Al Jr.'s room after having a great game and pound on his door.

"What?" Al Jr. would say, sounding as if he just woke up.

Billy remembered one particular night, when he had gone into the darkened room and turned on the light. Al Jr. was stretched out on his bed with headphones on, listening to that crappy doo-wop music nobody except him listened to anymore. He took them off and looked at him. "What?"

"I scored 20 points and had seven rebounds," Billy said. "And I had three steals."

Al Jr. put the headphones back on. "Well, I guess I don't care, I don't care and I don't care."

Billy had always understood why he felt that way. In those days, their father would nag at Al Jr. all day long, nitpicking everything he did, even though Al Jr. did the best he could to stay out of their father's way. The double standard always made Billy feel uncomfortable. His mother would wait until she thought the boys were out of earshot and then stick up for Al Jr., who was too much of a weakling to stick up for himself. At least that's what Billy had thought. Then a strange thing happened — something so weird it didn't seem possible.

And of course, everything started with their father and his damned jealousy. The previous year, Billy may have been the most popular athlete at school, but there was one kid dominating more than the cover of the Richland Tribune's sports section, a kid everyone except his father admitted was the best prospect in the whole area. It was a given Dirk Smith would play professional football one day. Scouts from all over the country — the Big Ten, the ACC, the SEC and Notre Dame — came to see him play. And the atmosphere in the Felix Bowl was so intense that every game felt as if Richland were playing for the state title. The stands weren't big enough to seat everybody, and cars lined the road next to the stadium. Though Dirk never touched the football unless it was fumbled to him, his value wasn't measured in personal statistics. At 6 feet 5 inches tall and weighing over 300 pounds, Dirk, an offensive tackle, could move the line even though he was always double-teamed. Richland's four-year total in yards gained was several thousand more than that of any other era. Big Al hated him. The mere mention of his name was enough to send Big Al to his study in a funk. The day after Dirk finally announced he was going to play for the Michigan Wolverines, the Richland Tribune devoted nearly the entire sports section to him. Big Al pretended not to have seen the paper, but he sulked all through supper.

"Jesus, Al," their mother said. "You're acting like a bear with a sore ass. What's wrong with you?"

He picked at his food with his fork. "Nothing," he mumbled. "I'm just tired."

After supper, he went to his study and closed the door. The next morning, Billy found the sports section crumpled up in the trash.

In the past, Billy's path had rarely crossed with Dirk's, but all of a sudden, there was Dirk, a few feet away every time he walked down a hallway. When he mentioned it to Lonny, Lonny pulled him aside and then told him what had happened in a low voice. Dirk's father had been to all the bars toasting his son, ending up at Al's place. The word was that Roger Smith had tried buying Big Al a drink and that when Roger had tried to hand the shot of whiskey to Big Al, Big Al had knocked it out of his hand. Later that night, Billy waited for his father to come home and followed him to his study. His father didn't deny what he'd done and actually tried to shrug it off.

"Why'd you do it, Dad?" he said. "Now I've got some gigantic nut ball following me around the hallways."

"Roger didn't have to come into my place bragging about Michigan."

Billy nodded. "I knew you were ashamed of Evansville."

"It's not that."

"Yeah, right. What else is it?"

"The only reason the slob's doing anything at all is because he's a damn moose."

Then he sat down at his desk and pretended to pore over a stack of papers. From there on out, Billy avoided Dirk as much as possible, going in the other direction even if it was out of his way. It was easier, and besides, he'd never had anything against Dirk. After a while, Dirk quit glaring at him in school and even said hello occasionally, acting so friendly Billy began to get suspicious. But after nothing happened, he quit worrying about Dirk and went about his business. But then one day, while he was shooting free throws in the gym, a nerdy, freckle-faced kid with a mop of curly orange-red hair came running through the entranceway toward him.

"Dirk's beating the hell out of your brother!"

Billy's hands were so rubbery the ball slid right out of them. His head felt woozy, and he ran out of the gym. Outside, he heard a commotion on the other end of the parking lot, where a huddled mass of kids gathered around, shouting in excitement, slapping one another on the arms. Then some of them began yelling for Dirk to stop, and all Billy could see was Dirk's tilted head sticking up above the crowd.

"Crawl," Dirk said, speaking in a calm, creepy voice, "like your dad does at closing time."

Some of the kids stepped far enough apart for there to be an opening, and through it, Billy saw Al Jr. lying facedown on the pavement and propping his head up with his hands. He started laughing — Billy couldn't believe it — and then tilted his head up as far as it would go. "You mean crawl the way your dad does whenever he's kissing some recruiter's ass?"

Laughter broke out among the crowd. Dirk's face reddened, and the glimmer went out of his eyes until they were as lifeless as a reptile's. He backed up several feet. For a moment, Billy thought he might just walk away, but as he got to the edge of the crowd, he turned around and ran toward Al Jr. as if he were about to kick a field goal. Billy cut through the crowd and ran at him. As they were about to collide, Dirk straight-armed him, but Billy dived, landing in Dirk's path, the wind leaving him as Dirk's foot nailed him in the midsection and turned him over onto his backside.

Dirk fell forward, twisting in the air. His head bounced off the pavement, and he landed on his back. He moaned. Their only hope was to get out of there before Dirk got up and killed them both. But as Billy hopped to his feet, Al Jr. sprang on top of Dirk, grappled his ears with his fingers and gouged him. Thrashing around, Dirk let out a loud yell as he swung Al Jr. from side to side, his large hands wrapping around Al Jr.'s wrists, squeezing them so tight Billy thought he might break them.

Some of the kids turned toward the school and made a wide path. Coach Thompson, the varsity football coach, came running toward them. "What's going on over there?"

Once he came inside the circle, he reached down and pulled Al Jr. up to his feet and tossed him aside. Dirk sat cross-legged, rubbing his eyes.

"What the hell are you thinking, Dirk?" he said. Then he turned toward Al Jr. "Did you start this?"

For the first time, Billy got a good look at his brother. His left eye was swollen, and the right one wasn't far behind. And his lips were right out of an abstract painting. Despite it all, there was such a look of smug satisfaction on Al Jr.'s face that Billy thought he may have had his bell rung a little too hard. Al Jr. smiled at Dirk. "He was running my dad down, so I punched him in that big mouth of his."

"You mean sucker punched me!" Dirk said, his voice cracking.

Coach Thompson cocked his thumb and waved his fist in the air, pointing away from them. "Get lost, Hennessy," he said, "and stay away from my player, or I'll have you run out of school."

Billy tried to follow Al Jr., but Coach Thompson grabbed his arm. "Oh, no, Billy boy. You, Dirk, Coach Randle and I are going to have a serious talk."

Billy followed Dirk and Coach Thompson to the Felix Bowl across the field. Inside, the locker room smelled musty, and they headed into the coach's office on the other end of the room. On his wall was an autographed picture of Ara Parseghian, alongside a picture of his players carrying him off the field after they'd won the state title in '66. Billy sat down in one of the lawn chairs, put his head down in his hands and waited for Coach Randle to arrive. Once he did, the two coaches took turns scolding them, saying how much they had to lose and how they'd disappointed everyone. After much berating, they finally let them leave.

"I'll have to call both your fathers," Coach Thompson said as Billy reached the door.

"Oh, Coach, c'mon," Dirk whined, but Billy had already shut the door behind him. He had no doubt Dirk had picked the fight and would've been kicked out of school if he'd been just another kid. Walking away with the warm air of an Indian summer day blowing around the scent of burning leaves, he passed several kids playing ball on the court at Daniel Boone Elementary School. They were playing 21, three of them mugging some short kid double-dribbling his way to the basket. Normally, he'd join them to take advantage of one of the last nice days of the year, playing until nightfall with kids whose names he could never remember — kids who only played for the fun of it, something he rarely got to do. None of them was very good — actually, they stunk pretty bad — but it was fun to play their reckless style of ball, in which there were no picks being set or coaches standing on the side criticizing everybody's damned fundamentals. But when they called out for him to play, he said, "Not today."

Their house sat off in the distance between two rows of stuccos. The sun reflecting off the window in the front room played tricks with the light, and he swore the curtain kept moving. Another unwanted bawling was coming. Just what the hell had Al Jr. been trying to prove? Anything Dirk could've said would've been nothing compared with the way their father acted.

Then, as the tree line slightly shaded the sun, he saw a glimmer shining off his father's wedding band as his hand let go of the curtain. Billy was going up the steps, when the front door opened and his father came out on the porch wearing his white beer-stained apron; his mother stood inside wringing her fingers and running them through her hair.

"Is Al here?" Billy said, backing away from his father's intense stare.

"Never mind him," he said, standing off to the side while holding the storm door open. "He got what he was asking for."

His mother straightened up to her full height and put her hands on her hips. "You mean he got what you were asking for."

"Janet," he said, "please."

She turned around and went upstairs. At the top, she turned around. "I'm going to find out what happened, and if I'm right, you owe Al an apology."

Big Al waited until she turned the corner, and then he tapped Billy on the chest and pointed toward the study. "Let's go."

Billy lowered his head and sat down in front of his desk. His father was in no big hurry to scold him and seemed content just to break him with silence and self-righteousness. After several moments, in a quiet voice, Big Al asked what had happened and sat back in his chair, listening as Billy told him everything, starting with the kid running into the gym.

Big Al cocked his head up to Al Jr.'s room above them. "There's no reason in the world you should risk everything for that bum up there."

Billy sat forward in his seat. "But he was about to get his head kicked in."

"So what?" he said. "Besides, Michigan won't be so hot for Dirk after pulling a stunt like that."

Billy stood up and headed to the door, sickened by his father's callous words.

"I'm not done yet."

Billy turned around and leaned against the doorframe. "Haven't I heard enough?"

A scowl came across his father's face. For a moment, Billy feared he would tell him to close the door and sit down until he was excused, but his father simply pointed upstairs. "Don't let him drag you down. That's all I ask."

He could hardly keep a straight face. Drag him down?! What a hypocrite. Why did the old man always have to act like an angel even when he was the one who'd screwed everything up in the first place? He wanted to ask him what it felt like being so perfect, to make others answer for what they did while staying above it all. But he said nothing, his only answer a slight nod as he left the study. About halfway up the stairs, he heard his mother and brother arguing, her pleading voice drowned out by his stubborn one. As he approached the door, they quit talking; his mother jumped when she saw him standing there. Then she came out and shut the door, tears rolling down her face.

"What is it, Mom?" he said. "Did he tell you what happened?"

"Yeah," she said, wiping away her tears. "I told him I'd make your father say he's sorry, but he doesn't want me to say anything."

"Dad's never apologized for anything."

"Maybe we could get him committed," she said. "I think it'd do him some good sitting in a padded room with a straitjacket on."

Billy smirked, but his mother didn't smile. He waited until she was downstairs before knocking on Al Jr.'s door. There was no answer, and he put his ear up to the door and listened, but all he could hear was the junky psychedelic crap Al Jr. was listening to these days. So he went in. The light was off, and he felt along the wall for the switch. The room filled with light. Their rooms were practically the same dimensions, their beds ordered from the same Sears catalog, but the similarities ended there. Billy had posters of Jerry West, Elgin Baylor, John Havlicek and Wilt Chamberlain, whereas Al Jr.'s walls were covered with wild-eyed rock stars with funky multicolored backdrops that were so lifelike Billy wouldn't have been surprised if they'd jumped out of the prints and gone crazy.

Al Jr.'s snores garbled into words as he mumbled, "Mom." Then he pulled the pillow off his face, leaving it covered with a rag full of ice.

"Mom went downstairs."

Al Jr. let out a moan and sat up slowly. The rag slipped from his fingers, leaving his face exposed. Now his whole face looked like some awful painting, but nobody would ever call it artwork; an enormous bruise engulfed his bloodshot eyes into one big black eye, and his lips actually seemed to pull away from each other. He tried to speak but immediately grimaced in pain. He put the rag back over his face and stretched back out on the bed. "That bastard didn't pull his punches."

"Are you OK?"

"I'm just great, Billy," he said, drawling out his name. "If you came up here to bitch, I don't really want to—"

"I almost got kicked off the team over your—"

"Oh, please," Al Jr. said. "If they'd have kicked anyone anywhere, it would've been me."

"What were you thinking?" Billy said. "Maybe I should've let Dirk…"

Al Jr. sat straight up and punched his bed. "Goddamn you! I didn't ask for your help, and I didn't want it! Now get the hell out of here, and shut the damned light off!"

Al Jr. hadn't raised his voice at him in a long time. Then Billy finally understood; he felt like an idiot for not getting it sooner: Al Jr. had only wanted to prove himself. And the beaten, wounded expression on his face accused Billy of screwing up the one chance he would ever be given.

ooo

"You're acting awful skittish, Al," Eric said. "What's wrong?"

Big Al made a sharp turn away from the sink and knocked over a mug with his arm. He reached for the mug but not in time, and it shattered on the ground. "Why'd you ask me a dumb question like that for?"

"Sorry, Al," Eric said, backing up. "You've been a nervous wreck all week."

Eric grabbed the broom and dustpan from the supply closet. Big Al took them from him and swept up the glass. "Billy's gone. He left last week. He's going to school, but I don't know who he's staying with."

Eric blushed and picked up a piece of glass Big Al missed. "I'm sorry, Al."

"You don't act too surprised."

"It's not like I just met you," Eric said. "I could tell something was wrong."

That much was true. After Janet died, Eric had seen him at his worst. At Janet's funeral, Big Al had been drinking for two straight days, and Eric and Stan had to practically carry him to his seat, each one of them propping him up on either side. Her death almost killed him. Only once before had he ever felt as helpless, and the day was supposed to be a once-in-a-lifetime experience, a chance to see the Cubs beat the mighty Yankees.

They had traveled to Chicago on the first day of October in 1932 for the third game of the World Series, the Cubs already down two games. Early in the morning, Dr. Stevens, who made the trip to Wrigley at least once a summer, surprised them by saying he had three tickets for the game and asked his wife to load up the picnic basket for the short ride. Anna was fine when she prepared ham and butter sandwiches, but during the ride there, she began to cough. The doctor didn't seem too worried until after Babe Ruth and Lou Gehrig blasted back-to-back home runs. Then he couldn't wait to go, saying he couldn't stand to watch anymore. He looked at Anna, who'd started to sweat and shiver, and then felt her head.

"She's burning up, Al."

On the drive home, she slept and coughed. As soon as the car was parked, the doctor told Al, "Help her to the room by the parlor. I'm going to town to get some ice."

"Yes, sir."

"I'm all right, Mark," she said, her voice faint. "It was just a long day."

Al helped her out of the car. At first, she walked mostly on her own, but as they climbed the steps on the front porch, she began to lean on him. By the time they made it to the room by the parlor, she was almost too weak to walk, and her footsteps became lighter as she slumped against him. It was hard to keep her up. At the foot of the bed, he let go of her, and he had to pull her all the way to the headboard. His back ached, and he went to the window and looked out for the doctor, but the dust in the air hadn't even settled yet. He wished the old man had stayed and sent him instead. Anna's breathing came out in a rattling sound. He had heard the moribund sound before, on house calls with the doctor. It didn't seem real; she'd couldn't have acted any healthier loading up the picnic basket earlier in the morning. Al had to do something, so he ran outside and filled up a bucket from the well.

In the distance, a car came down the dirt road, and he prayed it was the doctor, but the sound faded. Al went back inside, found a rag and went to the room to sponge off Anna's forehead. Her breathing was so faint that at first, he feared she'd already passed away. As he dabbed the sweat off her face, she began to cough slightly and whisper for her husband. But by the time the doctor came up the driveway, going as fast as he had the night Al summoned him for his father, she hadn't said anything for a while. The doctor packed ice all around her, but the fever never broke, and later that night, she quit breathing while the doctor cradled her head.

Many people came to the house for her wake. Most of them went to their church, but some were people the doctor had helped. Others were Anna's friends from the reading circles she had attended in town. All in all, close to 500 people filed in, stopping at the casket to comfort the doctor and say goodbye to Anna. Up until then, Al had always thought of how charmed his life had turned out; his early years were so long ago he hardly ever thought about them anymore. And he always imagined his life would revolve around the old couple. He'd spent years doing his chores and going on one house call after another, feeling pride at the relief on people's faces as the old man showed up with his black bag and calming smile. It had all been a wonderful dream he thought would never end. Maybe it took the old man's sitting by his wife's open casket to make Al see the falseness of his security. And the doctor's daughter, who'd come all the way from Philadelphia with her husband and daughter, regarded him as if he were leeching her father dry. She asked him questions about money and other things he had no knowledge of, making him feel like a conniving lowlife even though he'd never asked for anything.

Later that night, Al packed his clothes into a wool blanket. He planned on hitting the road while everyone slept. Early in the morning, he tiptoed downstairs. He was halfway toward the back door, when he saw the doctor's dark silhouette sitting at the dining room table.

"Going somewhere, boy?" the old man said.

Coming closer to him, Al could see things he hadn't noticed before. Dr. Stevens appeared more frail, as if the pounds had melted off him overnight, and the sad smile was gone; now he just looked plain sad.

"I thought I might go…" Al said, but then he stopped. The old man's face held so much disappointment he couldn't stand the thought of lying to him. So he took a deep breath. "I'm leaving, sir."

"Why?"

"You've been so kind to me," Al said, pausing because his voice cracked. "Your wife, too. I don't think I should take advantage—"

"Take advantage of me?" he said. "Did Millie say something to you?"

"No, sir, not really," he said, "but I don't think she—"

"Likes you?" Dr. Stevens said. "Well, Al, come to think of it, she's never really had much use for me, either."

"Why?"

The doctor scooted away from the table; up above them, someone moved, and he stared up at the ceiling for several seconds. "She's always said if I had any ambition, I'd have gone to the big city," he said, whispering. "But I'm a country boy, always have been, and she couldn't forgive me for it."

"But, sir," Al said, "isn't there plenty of country outside of Chicago?"

"I'm sure there is, and I'm sure I could've made a fortune, but poor people need doctors, too."

Then they didn't say anything, and the doctor went over to his pie safe and reached inside. He came out with a handful of bills, which he gave to Al. "You've always done what we've asked of you and never wanted anything in return. If you're leaving, I want you to have something to get you by."

Al counted the money; there was over $30. He handed it back to the doctor and smiled. He no longer wished to leave, deciding that if the doctor could take his daughter's contempt, then so could he. After Anna was buried, they were all alone again. Millie and her family took the first train back to Philadelphia.

One Saturday during the following spring, they went to a small farmhouse to check up on a farmer's pregnant wife after having breakfast at a small diner. The sun had just begun to show above the horizon; a warm breeze blew their jackets about as they walked toward the house. The doctor dropped his bag and reached down, clutching at his arm before falling facedown in the mud, his stethoscope twisting behind him.

"Are you OK, Al?" Eric said.

The dustpan was tilted at an angle, and the glass was close to falling onto the floor. Big Al emptied the broken glass into the trash can and told Eric what had happened with Billy. Eric didn't say anything.

"I was pretty loaded," Big Al said, "but that's no excuse."

He put the broom and dustpan away before sitting down on a barstool. "I've got to convince him it won't happen again."

○○○

Billy said something, but his words were so absurd Al Jr. asked him to repeat them.

"We're going to a party tonight, and I want you to come with us."

"What're you talking about?" Al Jr. said. "Who're us?"

"The Blynners and me."

Al Jr. felt his stomach rumble, and Billy stared at him as if he'd asked him nothing more than to pass the butter. Al Jr. went to the bathroom and retched into the toilet, but nothing came out. It was just what his old squad leader, Sgt. Tucker, used to call a case of the nerves. He splashed some cold water on his face and used his shirt to dry off. When the dull ache went away, he went back to the living room.

"You're such a square," Billy said. "We're going to have so much fun you won't—"

"No way, Billy," he said. "Besides, I doubt they'd want me around after the other day."

"What the hell was that about?"

"I don't know," Al Jr. said, rubbing his neck. "Everything's a blur."

"You jumped all over them. Man, you were acting like an ass."

Al Jr. sat down in his chair and sipped whiskey from his cup. "Whatever you say."

In their silence, Al Jr. could feel Billy's bad vibes. Out of the corner of his eye, he saw Billy staring at him self-righteously, his lips pooched out — the same damn way their father always had whenever he was ticked about something. Finally, Al Jr. couldn't take it any longer. "What?"

"I wish I hadn't brought them here."

"Oh, please," Al Jr. said, twisting around in the chair. "If you'd have left them out in the car, you wouldn't have had anyone to feel sorry for you."

"What're you talking about?"

"Poor Billy has to slum it," he said, his voice rising. "How long are you going to keep it up before you just go home?"

"I'm not ashamed of you."

"You're not?" Al Jr. said, turning back around and letting out a humorless laugh. "How many times did you ever say 'hi' to me in the hallway at school? Never. You always looked away or down your damn nose at me."

"What?"

"Hell, you wouldn't even be here now if you had somewhere else to go."

"Who's feeling sorry for themselves now?" Billy said. "And if I'm so ashamed of you, then why'd I invite you to a party?"

Al Jr. grabbed at a fifth of cognac, but his hand felt weak, and his fingers began to tremble so badly he nearly tipped it over. The intensity on Billy's face was as unwavering as it was whenever they were playing basketball out by the rim nailed to the garage and he was close to losing the game. Of course, he never did. Not to Al Jr. or anyone else on their block. Al Jr. never cared about winning. Hell, he never even wanted to play. And he didn't want to play now. So he went out to the kitchen, hoping Billy would leave and forget about taking him to any parties.

"Oh, screw it," Billy said, getting up from the couch and stamping off to the bathroom. Al Jr. could hear him tossing around his rumpled clothes before coming out and going toward the door with them piled up in his arms. Then Billy started putting everything in a bag. Nothing he did made any sense; he could've packed his clothes just as easily in the bathroom. But the more Al Jr. thought about it the more sense Billy's behavior made. Billy had spent the past several years in crowded gyms, and if he didn't have an audience, his performance would've been a waste of time. Al Jr. laughed. "Where're you going to go now?"

"Anywhere but here and home."

"C'mon, Billy. What difference does it make if I go to your party?"

Billy didn't answer him. He started packing faster, and the showmanship wasn't quite so amusing. He threw the bag over his shoulder and went out to the hallway. Before Billy shut the door, Al Jr. called out to him. "All right, I'll go to your stupid party!"

Billy came back in smiling, as if one of his flops had drawn a charge, and dropped his bag on the floor. He smirked as if he'd been bluffing the whole time; it was probably just another game to him.

Billy sat down on the couch. "This is going to be one hell of a party," he said. "There'll be so many girls there you're going to feel like you're back in school."

"Well, I'm not."

"Yeah, yeah, I know," Billy said, waving his hand at him. "There'll be plenty of beer there, too. Last time, he had at least five kegs and—"

A horn honked outside, and Billy went to the window. "See you later, Al. We should be back around 10:30 or 11."

After the door shut, Al Jr. went to his room and stretched out on the bed. He wanted to take a nap before Billy came back. But the tossing and turning only made him more awake, and his mind kept racing as one thought led to another, until he remembered a time when all four of them had had breakfast together on game day. On those days, their breakfast would come in waves. First the pancakes and then the bacon, eggs and toast. Though he preferred his eggs scrambled, they were always sunny side up because Billy liked to dip his toast in the yolk. Their mother and Al Jr. would always save their pancakes so they could put their eggs on top of the stack. The two of them would eat slowly, while Billy would inhale his food, and their father would sit there merely drinking coffee. Any other day, he would eat, but not on game day. By God, there was too much to worry about — things Coach Randle never thought of — and he wanted to know whom Billy would be guarding and how the coach planned on using him. Billy would shrug as if he were some kind of king or something and pour so much maple syrup on his stack the pancakes would actually float on his plate. When he finished eating, the two of them would leave together.

One morning, after they left, Al Jr. stared at his food but couldn't eat. His mother leaned across the table and tapped him on the arm. "If your face gets any longer, I'll be able to use your chin as a dustpan."

Al Jr. laughed. He began eating his cold food and then washed it down with milk. "I wish I could eat in the front room."

"Eat in the front room?" she said. "I've never heard of such a thing."

"Not every meal," Al Jr. said, shaking his head. "Just breakfast on Fridays."

"Oh, c'mon, Al."

"Really, Mom, don't you get sick of hearing Dad bitch?"

"That's disrespectful," she said. "I don't want to ever hear you say anything like that again."

"Like it'd matter to him," he said. "He doesn't ever mention my name unless he's running me down."

"Maybe you should try harder getting along with him," she said, standing up and gathering the dishes. "Quit leaving the room whenever he comes in."

"So we could sit around talking about Billy?"

And it was still all about Billy. Al Jr.'s head began pounding, until it throbbed with every pulse. How many kids could possibly be at the party that it would take five kegs of beer to satisfy them? A nighttime firefight sounded more fun; at least he'd had allies in the jungle.

He sat up in bed. Everything in the room stood out — the paint-chipped bloody walls, a cluster of trash littered throughout the floor, a wardrobe so small a vagrant would be ashamed of it— heartless reminders his life was more meaningless than it had ever been before. And if Billy hadn't shown up, he could've walked right off the face of the earth without anyone's knowing he had been there in the first place.

•••

Chapter 8

After several shots of whiskey, Al Jr. was ready to step out into the cold weather. His ears rang, and everything was hazy, especially with the cold wind blowing at his back, making everything numb and forcing him to pick up his pace until he was almost running down the sidewalk toward the high school. Waiting for Billy would've been easier. Maybe then he'd have been so soaked Billy wouldn't even have wanted him at his party. But something had begun to nag him, little by little, until he couldn't think about anything else. He had to see his father.

He crossed the Third Street Bridge, glancing over the railing. The water in the twisting river was nothing but a sheet of ice, with cold steam rolling up to the road. Headlights of approaching cars shone through the fog. He hoped the drivers weren't as blinded as he was, and the fear they were made him hurry along the long bridge until he was safely across. He cut through alleys where there were a few burning trash barrels along the way to warm his hands.

He came out of the alley on 11th Street and walked down the long sidewalk leading to the gymnasium. Cars lined the street, moving slowly toward the parking lot, and he fell in behind a group of people going across the crosswalk. An older man came out of the shadows wearing an orange vest and holding a flashlight with a bright red cone covering the light. He feared his father might be in one of the passing cars, and he pulled the hood of his tattered parka over his head.

When he went inside, the smell of hot dogs and popcorn filled the air, making him queasy. The band, on the opposite side of the gym, played the school fight song, their amplifiers so loud his ears rang. Flanking the band were the two upper sections, filled with people kicking their feet on the bleachers. More than likely, that's where his ticket would be — far away from his father's lower-section seat — but he had no intention of sitting down. He waited in line, moving up slowly, until he faced a young girl, no more than 16, who frowned slightly before giving him a faint smile.

"Twenty-five cents, sir," she said, taking his quarter and handing him the ticket.

Sir? Christ, had he aged that much? The girl's face blanched as if she might get sick. The taste of liquor was still in his mouth, though it had been at least a half-hour since his most recent nip, and he turned away from her, hurrying off toward the stairway. The stairs were crowded with people wearing red and black sweaters with Felix the Cat on the front of them and red checkered pants. He waited until there was more space and then went downstairs, maneuvering his way through a group of old men talking about Richland's offense, Rionsburg's defense and, of course, Billy. Just past them was the entranceway his father would have to go through, and he went over there. Al Jr. looked up in the stands, but his father's seat was empty. He froze. He had left too soon and had to get away from there. The sound of balls bouncing out of cadence reminded him of the erratic sounds of a firefight, and he turned toward them.

Billy was juking and jiving, catching balls thrown at him and taking off-balance shots that went in more often than not, while Lonny Green stood a few feet away bouncing a ball. When Billy missed three shots in a row, Lonny took a step forward and slapped him on the back hard enough to make him miss the fourth.

"You've lost your touch," Lonny said, his deep voice rising above the crowd. "I suppose I'm going to have to carry you again."

"Shut up!" Billy said, moving away from him and drilling another jumper. Al Jr. chuckled before a familiar voice approached from behind.

"How're you doing, Cheevers?"

"Fine, Big Al," a gravelly-voiced man said. "You look like a boiled rag."

Al Jr. tried to shuffle his feet, but they wouldn't move. He backed up, almost bumping into several people, who got out of his way to avoid him. When there were enough of them blocking him from his father's sight, he bolted down the long open hallway leading to the restroom. Once inside, he nearly bumped into another huddle of older men. He knew he was an awful sight, but it still bothered him how they regarded him with such contempt. So he went to the last stall, where his stomach began to growl until it made him queasy enough to start retching, which he did till he caught his breath. When he came out of the stall, the four men stopped talking and frowned at him as if he'd interrupted some kind of summit.

He went to the sink and splashed cold water on his face. In the mirror, one of the men — a short, rail-thin man with thick glasses magnifying his eyes, making them look like poached eggs—shook his head and then said to the others, "They've got to do something about these kids coming here smashed."

The tallest of the men tapped the short man on the chest and nodded. "I'll say. Heck, you can hardly tell the boys from the girls anymore."

Al Jr. wiped his hand dry on his coat and hurried off to the open hallway. He let his left arm dangle at his side and smiled over his shoulder at the men until they looked away. As he left, he laughed to himself, and why not? Everyone seemed to think the service members coming home were drug-crazed lunatics wanting to rob and kill anyone who crossed their paths. Coming home, he had been surprised to see people, all of them young, spitting at him as he got off the plane. But what made it worse was when he started noticing older people staring at him as if he weren't quite right— just as the old men in the bathroom had. He tucked his stub in his pocket as he peeked around the corner into the outer hallway for any sign of his father, but Big Al was already gone. Al Jr. headed back toward the entranceway.

But his father's seat was still empty. Then Al Jr. saw him going up the steps, shuffling slowly, wearing the black trenchcoat Billy used to make fun of because it fit so tightly he had to leave the top two buttons unfastened. Big Al used to say he hadn't gained more than 10 pounds since getting married, but the way their mother smiled behind his back always gave him away. But now he was so skinny he had no trouble buttoning it all the way up. And there was something else wrong. His father used to move with a straightforward purpose and the agility of a cat, but now every step he took was plodding. At his row, he walked sideways down the aisle until he reached his seat. Then Al Jr. noticed there was too much space around him and realized he must've bought his mother's ticket, too. His eyes misted, and his chest began pounding as he turned and hurried upstairs past the curious young ticket vender and back out into the cold night.

ooo

Big Al placed his coat on Janet's seat before looking down on the court, where Billy moved with an effortless, fluid motion he couldn't help marveling at. It amazed him the boy could be his. Maybe Janet had been right when she said he was the reincarnation of her brother, Bill, a starter on the Richland teams that won three straight sectionals beginning in 1938. Bill died at Guadalcanal, before they'd ever had a chance to meet. Janet barely spoke as she went around the apartment hanging up pictures of Bill. But her grief eventually passed. She began talking about Bill more often, and when Billy was about 3, she said he must have inherited Bill's spirit because they bounced the ball the same way.

Now Al wondered whether she'd been right. How would she have handled smoothing things over with Billy? There wasn't an answer, because she never would've been in his position. She worshipped her boys, often overlooking things they did that drove him batty. And she'd never have let things get so bad a week would've passed without her seeing one of them. Billy would've never been able to run away without her finding him within hours. And their marriage would've ended the minute he tossed Billy down the stairs. Heck, she acted as if it were his fault for losing his cool with Al Jr. when he stole the car and took it out the night before Thanksgiving. How absurd.

A familiar cackle came from the bleacher steps. Simeon Bledsoe and his mildly retarded son, Mitchell, came walking down the aisle, passing him by on the way to their seats, which were next to his. They were wearing ridiculous black beanies and identical red sweaters. Mitchell was in his early 20s but still lived at home with Simeon and his wife.

They sat down, and Simeon smiled a toothy grin at Big Al. "How you doing, Al?"

"Fine."

"Boy, you should've seen Billy on that last play."

"What're you talking about?" Big Al said. Simeon acted dafter than his son sometimes. "They're just warming up."

"I'm talking about last week," he said, leaning toward him, "after you got mad and left. There were three guys all over him, and he still got his shot off. They should've given him six free throws, because every damn one of those guys fouled him."

Again, Mitchell cackled, and this time he didn't quit until his father shot him a glance. "What's so funny, Mitch?"

"You said the D-word!"

Simeon sighed. "Yeah, that boy of yours sure is something."

Big Al slunk back in his seat and said nothing. Then, as Coach Randle pulled Billy into the huddle, Big Al leaned forward to see him, but there were too many players around him. For a second, he feared Billy wouldn't come out of the huddle — like a scene in a movie he'd seen with Janet a long time ago when one of the passengers disappeared and everyone acted as if she'd never existed — and he'd have to go down there after him. But then the clock ticked down, the buzzer ringing out loudly, and Billy came to the center of the court with everyone else. The team members took their positions against the Rionsburg players, who were standing around lazily like a bunch of talentless thugs.

Of all the teams, Big Al disliked the Rionsburg Kings the most. They were big, rough corn-fed hilljacks still sunburned from working the fields all summer long. All of them played football; all of them acted as if they were still playing football. And they'd been crowing since winning the football sectional last fall, which was something they hadn't been able to do while the big slob Dirk Smith was bowling them over. Now they strutted around, just as they did most weekends when they came to town looking for trouble, trying to find a Richland athlete they could gang up on before getting into their rusty pickup trucks and disappearing back to the sticks.

Finally, the referee threw the ball up, and Lonny, as usual, was outjumped by a kid shorter than he was. The Rionsburg kid reached up and tapped the ball to a guard, who wasted no time running down the court for an easy layup.

"C'mon, guys!" Big Al said, standing up. He sat back down when the young couple behind him grumbled.

Garner threw the ball inbounds to Billy, who ran ahead of everyone else toward the rim. But he stopped and brought the ball back out, waiting for everyone to catch up. Then he passed the ball to Lonny, who cut toward the basket and bobbled the ball. His defender took it away and lobbed it down the court to the toe-headed point guard for another layup. Everyone groaned, especially Big Al.

Richland began protecting the ball better, but Billy was the only one who made a shot, and they were soon down 10-2. Playing like a bunch of ninnies — could there be a better example of Coach Randle's incompetence? — they acted beaten even though the game was only halfway through the first quarter. Big Al squirmed in his seat, and every few seconds or so, Simeon would slap his side and look over at him. But Big Al tried to ignore him; his chest ached, and his heart was throbbing. He could feel his temples pulsating from the folly unfolding before him. When Billy passed the ball even though he was wide-open for a 17-footer, Big Al jumped to his feet and yelled.

"Shoot the damn ball!"

Billy's head jerked toward him as he ran side by side with his defender down the court. Mitchell cackled, and his father smiled at Big Al. "Christ, Al, don't have a stroke."

ooo

Big Al's frantic yell jolted Billy; for a moment, Billy wondered whether his father had any recollection of their fight. Maybe he'd just awakened today and noticed Billy wasn't there. Billy ran toward the basket, holding his hand in the air. The ball came toward him. Once he had it, he lowered his head, drove forward and jumped in the air. His defender slid in his path and planted his feet when the ball left Billy's hand. Billy ran into him, and the referee blew his whistle and called a charge on him. Billy slapped the floor and stood up. The point guard caught the inbounds pass, and Billy trailed a step behind him until he lobbed a lazy pass that hung in the air a little too long. Billy tapped the ball, and it fell behind him. He grabbed it and ran down the court ahead of everyone else, flipping the ball up and watching as it went in.

The crowd roared; up in the bleachers, the standing crowd had consumed his father. Billy hoped the crowd would keep him hidden for the rest of the game. He kept the ball whenever it was passed to him, though Lonny and Terry Glauss, their power forward, stood underneath the rim with their hands up, as did Chad and Garner out on the perimeter. After a few possessions, Terry seemed to realize that the only way he'd get the ball was by rebounding it; everyone else lowered their hands and stood around watching Billy. Coming down the court, Billy saw Coach Randle, his unbuttoned shirt exposing his drenched undershirt, motioning for a timeout. He pulled Billy into the huddle and held on to his jersey.

"What're you doing?" he said, waving his left hand around to everyone else. "Can't you see everyone standing around wide-open?" He paused, his own words pissing him off. "You guys need to keep moving! You're standing around too much! Get aggressive! That goes for you, too, Lonny! For Christ's sake, you're the biggest guy out there, and you've only got two rebounds! Now get out there and play like we practiced all week!"

Out on the court, Billy ran to the side of his defender and took the inbounds pass from Chad. He brought the ball up the court and scanned the floor. Lonny's defender came out toward him, leaving Lonny all alone underneath the basket. Billy gave his defender a head fake and then took a couple of steps before lobbing the ball to Lonny. The pass surprised him, and he nearly bobbled the ball out of bounds before recovering it. Two defenders ran toward him as he jumped up in the air and released the ball. It went up at an odd angle and bounced around on the rim before falling off. Billy timed his jump perfectly, outleaped everyone and tipped the ball up before being pulled backward. He landed hard on the ground. The ball rolled through the net and bounced out of bounds. The referee pointed at Billy's defender and blew his whistle as the crowd began to cheer.

Billy pumped his fists, went to the line and took the ball from the referee. He shot the ball and watched it arc in the air and fall through the net. Before the crowd began cheering again, his father called out. "Keep shooting the ball, Billy! You've got them on the ropes!"

As time was running out in the half, Billy, who'd taken the previous three shots — all of them bricks — hurried down the court and hit the last shot before the halftime buzzer went off. He ran off the court ahead of his teammates toward the locker room, where Coach Randle stood at the door, his arm blocking him from the door. He waited for everyone to go inside before turning toward him.

"Listen," he said, his face red. "I'm coaching this team and not your father. If you can't grasp that, then you can sit on the bench with me and I'll explain it to you."

"But, Coach, I can hear him—"

"I don't care," he said. "Anything else?"

Billy shook his head, and the coach let go of his arm and opened the door. Inside, Lonny and Troy argued, while Garner and Chad just sat there motionless. Everyone else acted spooked, and why not? Rionsburg had never beaten them at home. Billy sat down on a bench, his muscles tightening from the 20 or so shots he'd taken.

Coach Randle came in several seconds later, looking as if he needed those moments to gather his wits. He ran his fingers through his hair and started bitching about everything and everyone. None of them was spared except the benchwarmers. But no matter who was getting reamed, the coach kept coming back to Billy as if he were the one to blame, even though he'd scored 22 points. The coach's face turned a deeper shade of red when he said they'd better start playing the way he'd coached them or they'd spend the whole weekend working on fundamentals. They all sat straight up in their chairs. The whole weekend?

"These guys are feeling pretty cocky," he said, a slight smile forming on his face. "I want you to pounce on them. Cody, Chad, you guys need to attack the rim every time your man leaves you to help out with Billy. And when they do, pass the ball, Billy. You guys got it?"

They all yelled out, "Yes, Coach! Win one for Felix!"

"Well, let's show it then," the coach said. "Send these rednecks home with their tails between their legs."

All the Rionsburg starters were waiting on the court, smiling and laughing as if their 10-point lead meant it was all over. As the buzzer sounded, the coach pulled Cody and Billy aside. "You guys trade places."

"What, Coach?" Cody said.

"Billy's going to handle the ball."

Cody frowned as he ran out to the court. Billy went to the sideline to throw out the pass and smiled as the Rionsburg backcourt switched up. He passed the ball inbounds and then took it back. Chad's defender left him at the half-court line, and he cut toward the rim. Billy passed the ball to Chad, and Chad passed the ball to Lonny for a wide-open chip shot. Soon the smirks disappeared. So did Rionsburg's lead. The strategy worked perfectly, and Billy didn't take a shot until the end of the third quarter. Rionsburg fouled often in the fourth quarter — three of their starters fouled out — and Richland cruised to an easy win, beating them 76-64.

The crowd roared, and students swarmed the floor, jumping and cheering. Once he cut through them, Billy looked up into the stands to see whether his father was celebrating with everyone else. But his seat was empty.

ooo

Enough was enough. Tonight's game painfully reminded Big Al that if it weren't for Coach Randle, Billy would be a Hoosier in the coming year instead of a Purple Ace. His stock with recruiters declined with his scoring average. Big Al had had heated arguments with the coach over his son's role on the team. Billy needed to distribute the ball more for them to be successful, the coach said. But if that was the case, then why weren't they any better than when Billy was scoring less? And why in the hell didn't he say something whenever Garner hogged the ball? Big Al left without saying anything to Simeon or his silly son.

On the floor, Billy stared up into the stands so timidly Big Al wanted to go over and hug him, maybe tell him how sorry he was for what had happened, that it would never happen again. But something held him back; perhaps it was the fear of making Billy satisfied with himself. Then he probably wouldn't even be good enough for Evansville, and everything they'd worked for would be for nothing. Or maybe he was afraid of coming clean, of telling Billy how alone he felt without him at home. If he apologized, maybe Billy would act as if nothing had happened. But Billy gazed around afraid, his chest heaving in and out, and Big Al ducked as he turned his way. Big Al went off to the restroom and entered the last stall, feeling as if he might get sick. His aching chest began to feel better, though, after he took his flask out of his coat and drank a sip of whiskey.

By the time he went back out in the hallway, the crowd had thinned out considerably. He hid in the shadows of a small cubbyhole next to the janitor's closet and waited by the locker room door. Each time the door opened, one of Billy's teammates came out, and Big Al began to wonder whether there was another exit he didn't know about. But then the door opened slowly, and Billy stuck his head out. Afraid Billy would run off, Big Al pulled back and waited. Then the door shut, and Billy's footsteps headed down the opposite end of the hallway. Big Al came out of the shadows and followed him, taking larger strides to make up the distance. His foot came down a little too hard, and Billy tensed up and stopped.

"Why'd you quit shooting?" Big Al asked, and Billy jolted upright and turned toward him. "You had them on the ropes."

"I can't score 75 points a game, Dad," he said. Billy kept his head lowered. Big Al took a step forward, and Billy looked up at him suspiciously but didn't say anything. It was odd. They'd always talked a lot after the games, and not all of their conversations were heated arguments — for example, after the game two years ago when Billy could've broken the school record for points in a game. Big Al was in awe of his boy that night, watching him score 39 points, even though he could've easily scored 50 and Big Al was confused about why he had kept passing the ball when he needed only two more points. Six of his eight assists had come in the fourth quarter, the last of them going to Lonny for his first points on the varsity squad. None of that mattered now. He couldn't care less whether they even talked about basketball. He just wanted Billy to say something, anything at all, or let him have it. Maybe then things would return to normal — or what passed for normal since Janet died.

"Look, son," he said. "I'm sorry about what happened. It won't happen again."

"Won't happen again?" Billy said. "I'm surprised it took that long. I haven't been able to do anything right since Mom died."

"Please."

"No, I don't want to hear it," Billy said. "I can't deal with worrying about when you'll blow up again. I'm through worrying."

"So you've got no use for me anymore," Big Al said, his voice cracking. "What're you going to do now, live on the streets?"

"I'm not living on the streets."

"Well, whoever you're staying with, their parents aren't going to want another mouth to feed."

For a moment, there was hesitation on Billy's face. Then he straightened up. "I'm not staying with anyone's parents. I'm staying with Al."

Al Jr.? The last Big Al had heard, Al Jr. was in the Army. If he was back now, it could only mean they had thrown him out and he was just as irresponsible as ever. If Billy fell under his spell, then everything they'd hoped for was going to crumble. He reached out for Billy, but he was so skittish he backed up further.

"If Evansville—"

"The hell with Evansville," Billy said, his voice rising. "You want me to come home, then Al's coming with me."

"No way," Big Al said, shaking his head. "He's a—"

"He's your son."

Big Al's lips began to tremble. "He'd never say so."

Billy stomped off down the hallway. Big Al called out to him, but he never once glanced back at him as he turned the corner and disappeared.

●●●

Chapter 9

The traffic coming down West Montgomery had been so dead the sound of a loud car pulling up out front made Al Jr. jump up from his seat and go to the window. The passenger-side door creaked open, and a tall skinny man with a mop of hair got out and headed up the sidewalk toward the apartment. At first, Al Jr. didn't recognize Billy, and then it struck him why. Billy moved the way he did after a bad loss. The game had probably gone down to the wire and been lost on a buzzer-beater; after those games, Billy always acted as if the world were about to end. Otherwise, he would be moving with that strutting bounce, taking large strides, and would've already been inside bragging. Al Jr. hoped he'd say that going to a party was the last thing he wanted to do. But the car out front didn't pull away, and a cloud of smoke thickened around the hood. Billy came inside, his head lowered, his body wiry and tense.

"Jesus, Billy," he said. "They must've really stuck it to you."

Billy frowned at him. "Huh?"

"How bad did you get beat?"

"We didn't," he said. "Are you ready?"

"I don't think I can make it," Al Jr. said. "I hurt my feet walking and have a headache. I think I drank too much."

"You said you'd go," Billy said, motioning toward the door. "Now let's go!"

Al Jr. limped toward his chair and glanced over his shoulder. But Billy's face didn't soften a bit, and when he could tell it wouldn't, he sat down and rested his head against his hand. "I went to the game tonight."

"Then how's come you asked if we lost?"

"Because I left after I saw Dad," he said. "Man, he looks awful."

"So you're going to sit around here feeling sorry for yourself."

"Screw you."

"Dad can't stand you."

"I know."

Billy sat down hard on the couch. "Well, if you can't do what you said you'd do, if you're just going to sit—"

"Oh, shut up, Billy," Al Jr. said. "I'll go to your damned party."

"That's all I asked for in the first place."

"Yeah, you never ask for much, do you?" Al Jr. said, standing up. Beer wouldn't settle his nerves — much more was needed — and he went to the kitchen to find a bottle of liquor to take with him. But he couldn't make up his mind; the gin wasn't open yet, but the bottle was a half-gallon, which was just asking for trouble; vodka was perfect for endurance drinking, as long as no one else was around; bourbon, rye and scotch were what he had the most of, but he couldn't decide which whiskey he was in the mood for.

"Christ, Al," Billy said, standing so close to him Al Jr. nearly knocked his bottles over, "quit stalling."

"Hold on," Al Jr. said. He picked up his fullest fifth of rye and started to say he was ready, but Billy was already gone, and he didn't hear anything until the front door closed. Al Jr. put on his parka and went outside on the porch, where Hamlin and Dill sat glaring out at the cloud of blue smoke drifting in the air toward the porch. They looked over at Al Jr., but when Dill spoke, it didn't seem as if he was really talking to him at all. "Damn thing's poisoning us."

Al Jr. went to the car and got in the back. Billy sat next to him, slumped down in his seat as if he might fall asleep. Rich shifted gears, and the engine sputtered, giving Al Jr. hope it wouldn't go any further, but then it revved up, and they were moving down the street.

Rich and Ralph yelled to each other, neither one of them saying
much of substance, and Al Jr. leaned forward. "Hope this thing
doesn't break down. Where're we going?"

"Duke Shell's barn," Rich said, tilting the rearview mirror
toward Billy. "Man, is this going to be one hell of a party or what?"

"I guess so," Billy said.

"You guess so?" Rich said, laughing. "How many girls do you
have waiting for you?"

Billy acted as if he hadn't heard him, but Al Jr. knew better. It
was one of his old tricks. Surely, Rich had seen it, too, but he kept
waiting for Billy to say something, his smile fading to a frown
before he readjusted the mirror. They crossed the Southside Bridge,
going beyond the city limits. The houses thinned out after they
turned left at an empty gas station right before the overpass with a
large RCA billboard.

Al Jr. thought about saying he had to take a leak and then
walking home after Rich pulled over. But too much road had passed
behind them, and he accepted that he was at Billy's mercy for the
weekend. Outside the window, there were rolling hills and endless
waves of snow-covered fields. He drank from his bottle as they went
up a long winding hill. A couple of cars trailed behind them in the
distance. Once they were at the bottom of the hill, several more cars
were coming over the hilltop. Ralph turned around in his seat and
whistled, and Al Jr. sat forward to shield himself from the
approaching bright lights.

"Jesus Christ," Al Jr. said. "Are all these people going to the
party?"

Billy sat upright and leaned toward Rich, shaking his seat.
"Slow down. It's the next left."

"I know," Rich said. "Jesus, I've been there before."

The car slowed down, and they made their turn. Soon they
were bouncing around chuckholes the size of craters. Rich cussed
and tried to veer around them, but the car continued bouncing around
until it turned onto a narrow road lined with sycamore trees that had
been run into so many times the bark on them had been knocked off.
What was left looked like naked skin against the backdrop of their
headlights. Then Rich went off the road through an opening where
bright pole lights shone on one of the biggest barns Al Jr. had ever

seen. The kids in school had called it The Palace. He used to laugh at them, thinking it was probably just some caved-in dive everyone talked up. But now he could hardly take his eyes off it. The barn was as white as snow. The light from the poles made it glow, and there were three levels of lofts and a shiny red metal roof.

Around back, at least 100 clunkers were parked off the dirt driveway. They pulled up to an empty spot near the tree line, and a loud cry came from Al Jr.'s side of the car. A blur came running toward them, a lanky boy leaping through the air and landing on the hood. He peered into the car, his head swiveling around at all four of them. Rich and Ralph laughed so loudly it made Al Jr.'s ears ring. He clutched the neck of his bottle, but Billy continued to sit, seemingly neither annoyed nor humored. Rich laid on the horn until the kid jumped off the hood and ran, disappearing into the woods.

Al Jr. tapped Billy's arm. "What kind of freak show did you bring me to?"

Billy didn't flinch or say anything. Why in the hell did he want him there anyway? To snub him as usual? None of it made any sense. Billy had talked about this party as if it were one of the biggest deals ever, and now he was pouting. Maybe he could be persuaded to turn back and they could hurry to Garry's to get a pizza. Of course, Rich had the keys, and Billy leaned forward, hit the seat release and pushed on the seat until Ralph was smashed against the dashboard, bitching instead of laughing.

Billy got halfway out before turning back around toward Al Jr. "Are you coming?"

It was such a stupid question. Where the hell else did he think he'd go 5 miles from town, especially when the snow was falling and the temperature was dropping? And that's what he had been about to say when Billy started walking away from the car. Ralph mumbled something before pushing the seat back and leaning out the door. "Christ, Billy, I was about to get out."

But his irritation didn't last, and he was soon laughing. Al Jr. waited for the brothers to get out and then followed them as they walked arm in arm like a couple of drunken sailors smirking identical smiles. They broke free from each other and hurried to catch up with Billy, who'd already gone inside the sliding barn door.

Al Jr. drank from his bottle. The Blynners were already inside, and he walked forward in the hard, crunching snow. Once he reached the door, he took a deep breath and slid it open. Several kids turned to look at him, and he tucked his left arm in his coat and then looked away, their voices mingling together as they carried on their separate conversations.

Then he imagined them doing the things they'd soon be doing, whether they liked it or not: digging foxholes and bunkers, sometimes carrying buddies to an awaiting chopper. He tried to wipe the image from his mind, and once he did, he was able to see them for what they were now — cocky kids laughing at everything, content to live in the moment, which was something he envied and pitied. Some of them were mildly buzzed; others were plain shit-faced, much more so than he was.

A short fat kid stumbled around and bounced off several people before nearly tripping into him, but Al Jr. stepped back as he fell harmlessly into the arms of a couple of big kids, who dragged him to the corner of the room and sat him down. Al Jr. went out to the large bay with several empty horse stalls.

The tough-guy types strutted around in leather coats and thick-heeled boots. Nothing in the world scared them. They were talking tough, some of them mocking Charlie, trying to intimidate whomever they could. Some of them probably were tough. Mostly, though, they were all gut wind, saying things they couldn't back up. They'd wilt once they realized how faceless and well-hidden Charlie really was. That's one thing everyone suffered over there, sitting up at night wondering whether the jungle sounds were real and harmless or imitations bringing death. Here, these guys were comfortable with cigarettes dangling from their lips. They didn't care much for the timid kids walking around in packs more sober than anyone else.

The wallflowers were comfortable in their science labs, but here they were squares talking timidly among themselves, wearing loud colors and trying in vain to fit in. Their future was on a college campus, and none of them seemed to realize how lucky they really were, that slumming it with these Neanderthals was the closest they'd ever come to the jungle. But the pot-smoking hippies hiding in the corner would. Some of them might run and hide in the Southwestern communes or Canada. Most of them would go to

Vietnam, though, even though their heavily lidded eyes made it obvious that fighting a war was the last thing they wanted to do. He had served with quite a few of them, kids who probably had peace posters hanging on their walls at home. Those guys always took as many drugs as they could get their hands on and freaked out every time a bullet came whizzing by from nowhere.

In the middle of the crowd, flanking everyone and acting as if no one in the room mattered but them, the athletes wore their letterman jackets on their barrel chests, and Billy, as usual, was right in the middle. They tilted their chins in a cocky manner, their silly jackets with Felix the Cat clapping his paws together while they clogged up most of the space. Probably very few of them were going to college. Always coddled in class, they weren't any better in school than he'd been. Just luckier — for the time being, anyhow. Once they got over there, they'd be the most pathetic of all, sitting around camp, whining about the days when they used to be something.

Billy stood back, ignoring the circle of jocks holding a conversation around him. Every time one would say something to him, he would shrug. Then he looked toward the door and smiled. Their eyes met, or so Al Jr. thought, and the flirtatious expression on Billy's face made him think he'd lost his mind. Someone brushed by Al Jr., pushing him aside, and he started to say something, when a beautiful blonde wearing her hair in a beehive, a blue miniskirt and white ankle-high boots hurried by and hugged Billy. Al Jr. took a few steps closer until he could hear what they were saying.

"Billy," she said breathlessly. "I was afraid you wouldn't make it."

Billy pulled her closer, his face smug. His smile was a line of privilege Al Jr. couldn't cross, and Billy kissed the top of her head. "I wouldn't have missed it for the world."

Al Jr. wondered what a girl would do if he said something so witty to her. Would she cling to him as this girl was clinging to Billy? He doubted it. Then Billy smiled at him knowingly and winked before whispering something in her ear. She giggled, and Billy took her hand and led her to a stairway across the room. Once they were gone, Al Jr. searched the room for refuge. Being alone with a bunch of weirdos wasn't what he'd expected. He felt people looking at him, their lingering stares lowering to his left arm. He pushed his arm down as far as it would go in his coat, but it was too late; they'd already spotted his deformity.

Some wallflowers banded together with a couple of reed-thin hippies with dirty hair falling down their faces like a couple of sheepdogs. They took turns pointing at him. Al Jr. headed to a dark corner partially hidden by a horse stall. He put his bottle down and stood next to an open space. One of the hippies pulled a joint out of the cellophane of his cigarette pack as a wallflower boy, a heavyset kid with thick glasses, waited for a turn. The hippies walked away, leaving the kid standing there dejected. Then he turned and walked away.

Al Jr. came out of the shadows and scanned the room for any further threat. A girl flanked by two boys stood across the room smiling at him. Though there was nothing hostile about them, he still felt that they were acting as if he were some kind of monkey in a cage. When he met the girl's eyes, there was an eagerness he couldn't understand, especially given that he was wearing clothes he had bought at a church flea market and his hair wound around his head in uneven tangles. He waited for her to walk away and was surprised when instead she came into the shadows after him. Her friends followed closely behind.

As she came closer, the overhanging florescent light made her features clearer. She wore platform shoes, bell-bottom jeans and a checkered coat with a matching purse hanging from a shoulder strap. Her hair was pulled back in a ponytail. And though he found her to be very pretty, there was a sadness on her face that made her seem a lot older than she was. He felt that he should've recognized her but couldn't figure out why, even as she came closer, smiled and held out her hand for him to shake. He shifted around and offered her his hand, and she took it.

"You're Al Hennessy, aren't you?" she said, frowning slightly. "Do you remember me?"

Where had it been? Everything was foggy, and he shook his head. "I'm sorry."

"Last year, first period," she said.

"U.S. history," he said. "You sat next to me. Sara Silverston. I guess I cut class so much I almost forgot."

"I'm surprised you're here," she said, laughing. "I never imagined you coming to a party like this."

"Me neither."

"I heard you dropped out and went in the Army," she said. "Why?"

"I'd have ended up there anyway," he said. "So I figured I might as well get it over with."

"That's a funny way of looking at it," she said, stepping closer. "Are you here alone?"

"No, I came with my brother," he said. "Actually, he made me come."

"Billy Hennessy?" she asked. "The basketball player?"

His heart sank. How could he be so stupid to think she would come up and talk to him just because they'd shared some stupid class? So he stepped back, realizing only then that she still had ahold of his hand. He pulled it away, jerking so abruptly she frowned.

"Billy's booked up."

"Excuse me?"

"He's already got a girl for the night," he said.

She said nothing. Then her blushing face became a deep shade of red. "You think I'd want to be with that pig?" she said. "My brother's been missing in Vietnam, and I thought maybe you'd help me... Oh, forget it."

Then she turned away, her hand coming so close to his face he wondered whether she had meant to slap him. Her ponytail bounced from one shoulder to the other. She reached her friends and turned back around. Her lips moved rapidly, and her friends began laughing.

He picked up his whiskey and lifted the bottle toward her. Then he tipped his head back and drank until he couldn't tolerate any more.

ooo

Even though the loft was cold, Billy pulled away from Carla and sat up against the wall.

"What's wrong with you?" Carla asked.

Under other circumstances, Billy would've found her confusion funny. He had worshipped Carla since the eighth grade. But she was Karen's best friend and had been with her boyfriend, Chip Dawkins, a pitcher, for as long as he could remember until they broke up after Christmas. And though Chip had moved on easily, she hadn't. So he was surprised when she came upstairs with him; being with her was a dream he never dared to have. But after they finished making love, he was filled with an emptiness he didn't want her to notice. Now that she had, though, there wasn't any reason to keep quiet.

"What's Karen say about me?"

Her lips turned down, and her shoulders slumped. When she recovered, she let out a bitter laugh and got dressed. "She doesn't say anything about you. She's got Brian now."

"You're lying."

"Guys are all alike," she said, pulling her boots on. "You screw around with every girl you can get your hands on and mope around when you get caught."

"Maybe," he said, "but I don't believe she never says anything about me."

"Used to, hotshot, but not for a long time," she said. "She's moved on."

"What's—"

"Oh, shut up," she said. On her way out, she looked over her shoulder. "I knew I was making a mistake with you."

ooo

His bottle was running low. Al Jr. tucked his left arm in and went to the keg room in time to see the beauty Billy had gone upstairs with hurrying downstairs. He waited for Billy to come down, but he never did, so he went to fill up a cup he'd found with beer. The kids by the keg moved away when he filled up his cup. Then he scurried back to the safety of the shadows. Once he was there, the two hippies came his way. The taller one smacked his buddy on the arm. "I wonder how many babies he's killed."

Coming closer, the other one pointed down at his tucked-in arm. "Serves him right."

Al Jr. chased them away, but their mocking laughter only got louder. Once he looked back out, his eyes met Sara's; her face — so pretty and sad — made more of a point than anything she could have possibly said. She would find her brother one way or another; whether he helped her or not didn't matter. When he stayed at the opening a little too long, she looked at him reproachfully, and he went back to the shadows.

• • •

Chapter 10

"Have a good night, folks," Big Al said to the elderly couple as they waved going out the door. He had gone to the bar after the game because he hadn't felt like going home.

Eric turned toward Big Al and said, "I've never seen a deader Friday night." He picked up their mugs and tossed a couple of dimes in the air. "The last of the big tippers, huh, Al?"

"I'm surprised they left anything," Big Al said. "Must've felt sorry for us."

"Twenty cents," Eric said, laughing. "They must still think it's the '30s."

"Did you see the one guy trying to leave without paying his tab?"

"Do you think he forgot like he said?"

"Yeah, right," Big Al said. "The crummy bum thought he could slide out with a freebie."

Eric blew the dust off the lid of the tip jar. Big Al told him to put it down. "Keep the change. You're the one who waited on them."

Eric put the change in his pocket. "Yeah, they sure kept me busy."

Then he washed the mugs and wiped the bar. "I wish I could think of something else to do. I feel like I'm just taking up space."

"Why don't you close down by yourself tonight, the way you usually do on a Friday. Would you mind?"

"I don't mind, Al," Eric said. "Besides, you could use some rest. This is your night off."

"Oh, I'm rested enough," Big Al said. "I think I'm going to see Nick."

Eric frowned. "At Ripton's?"

"That'd probably be the place to find him."

Eric wiped the counter for what had to have been the fifth time already, the motion of his hand slow as he moved from one end of the bar to the other. Then he turned around, started to say something and put the towel down.

"What?" Big Al said.

"Do you think Nick still wants to buy this place?"

"Why would he want to buy this dive?" Big Al said, laughing.

Eric seemed offended, maybe even a little angry. "We've always done OK until lately."

Big Al put on his coat. "Well, lately counts for a lot."

He waved over his shoulder on his way out, but Eric had already gone back to wiping the bar. "See you later, Eric."

"Be careful, Al."

Outside, a cold gust of wind kicked up, making it hard to close the door. Big Al pulled his coat up around his head and ran to the car. Once inside, he started the engine and waited for the heater to warm up. He wondered whether he really wanted to go to Ripton's or not. It had been several years since he'd last been there with Janet. Maybe it had been a Christmas party or, no, a New Year's party, right around the time everyone was talking about putting bunkers in their yards. Nick kept joking that they might as well live it up because the whole world would probably be nothing but Swiss cheese soon, and Big Al got drunker than a skunk and had to be helped out to the car by Janet and Nick. The next day, she told him that would be the last time she'd be seen in public with him when he was being a drunken fool. He never went over his two-drink limit whenever they went out again.

But tonight there was no limit. The heater began putting out hot air, and Big Al noticed how dead the streets were; all the diners closed around 9, but it was barely 8:30. Everything seemed to be over there these days, and he wasn't surprised that he didn't see another car until he crossed the bridge on East Market. There were only a few cars parked at the theater; the Chinese man in the restaurant across the street pulled the blind down over the picture window and flipped his sign around to the "closed" side. Traffic picked up toward the outskirts of town, most of the cars headed in the same direction, beyond the large empty lot announcing, "The future site of the Richland Mall." Past that were only a few businesses: a bowling alley, a car dealership and Ripton's — named after Nick's late Great Dane, a dog that had weighed more than Nick and, according to him, been smarter than most of his patrons.

Big Al parked in the last row of the lot. When he got out of the car, he heard a ruckus coming from somewhere far off. There were three longhair boys, none of them much older than 20, slapping one another on the backs and laughing in a strange way. Other voices in the distance sounded less playful; some of them were downright confrontational and boozy. Everything was so different from what it had been just a few years earlier, and even though the crowd then was much younger than he expected, the people were more respectful and not so disruptive as these kids.

Music blared out from an outside speaker he couldn't remember being there before, a lively song about a brown-eyed girl that reminded him of Janet, overwhelming him until he was momentarily oblivious to everything. All of a sudden, an old Chevy sedan came flying around the corner, and the driver laid on the horn. Big Al jumped out of the way, and the tail fin brushed his coat. Whirling around, he raised his hand in the air and pumped his fist.

"Watch where you're going, you idiot!"

The car came to an abrupt halt. The driver rolled down his window and stuck his head out. Laughter spilled out from inside the car, and the pipsqueak driver craned his head around, yelling, "Hey, old man! The nursing home's on the other side of town!"

"Old man"?! He doubled up his fists and walked toward the car. The laughter intensified, and the driver rolled up his window and tore off, kicking up gravel and snow that hit Big Al on his pant legs. He started to yell but caught himself; they would've just laughed louder, thinking he was jealous of their youth. He bent over and brushed off his trousers before walking toward the bar.

When he was inside, heads turned his way and lingered. He searched out the table where Janet, Serena and Trini had always would sit so many years ago. His eyes misted up thinking about how hard it had been to gain a spot there.

Janet had made clear that she wasn't impressed with his efforts in life, even though each passing day at Beta Die was marked by a new burn or cut. Her new worry was he couldn't cut it and would soon quit. She showed him scratches of her own from the ribbon factory, implied they were comparable and said a man should be able to take the pain. What did she know about having blistering-hot particles burning their way through clothes until they seared skin?

Life had been so much simpler going from one day to the next without worrying about pleasing anyone but himself—especially someone whose first impression of him was so damning. Once he began to lose hope, he daydreamed about simply walking out the door without a word to anyone and never coming back.

Then, after two months, the thought of spending the next 30 years doing a job he despised became so unbearable it outweighed his desire to win Janet over. Maybe if she had cared — or even noticed — he would've stuck around. But she hadn't acknowledged anything, and what was worse, she acted as if he was intruding whenever he came to her table. The last day at Beta Die was a bad one. Dick kept throwing his damn trash in the molten metal and complaining to Abel about the parts not being clean enough. Big Al didn't walk out during his shift, but when it was quitting time, he asked Stan whether he wanted to go get a few beers. Stan said he was short on cash but told Big Al there was a place, called Clawson's Saloon, where the owner, old man Clawson, sometimes let him slide by with an IOU.

"Don't worry about a tab," Big Al said. "I've got plenty of cash."

Big Al hurried along the sidewalk with Stan, wanting nothing more than to drink beer until Janet was out of his mind forever. But once they were inside the cozy bar, his somber mood lifted. The lights were dimmed, and the shade from the surrounding trees kept the place much cooler than he'd expected.

After getting a couple of drafts, he went to the table in the back of the room, where Stan was fanning himself with his hat. He sat down and pushed one of the mugs to Stan. Stan dropped his hat on the table and drank half his beer before setting the mug back down.

"I wish the missis would get off my back," Stan said, belching. "There's plenty of work out west. My uncle Joe bought a bunch of land in California dirt-cheap 20 years ago. He sold it off a couple of years back and made a fortune. I told the missis we should go down there. With a little luck, a guy like me could get rich."

"I hear you, Stan."

"But no, she don't want to leave her folks," he said. "She'd rather see me dry up like an old prune in that dive." He paused and looked beyond Big Al for several seconds, and then a frown came across his clownish face. "She'd better watch out, or I might just up and leave her. Hell, we don't own anything."

Big Al grunted yet said nothing. Stan stared at him curiously. "Are you married, Al?" Big Al shook his head. "No."

Stan smiled and slapped him on the shoulder. "Smart man!"

Big Al recoiled, but Stan's smile reminded him of a marquee poster of the cowardly lion, and he couldn't help but laugh. He took a drink of his beer and put the mug back down. "There's a girl named Janet I thought I could impress if I held a steady job," he said. "But I don't think I ever will, so I'm done."

Stan seemed taken aback, maybe even a little sad, but then he continued his rant about his unjust and demanding wife. Big Al watched the old man working behind the bar. He was moving like someone who was doing exactly what he was meant to be doing. When a burly patron got up and left, Big Al saw a "help wanted" sign right by the register.

"You need another beer, Stan?"

Stan winked at him. "It might be a bit cheaper if you just got a pitcher."

"Well, what the heck?" he said, standing up. By the time he reached the bar, the old man had already moved on to another set of customers. Big Al stood by the cash register, waiting. Finally, Mr. Clawson came back toward the register, sorting the bills in his hand. "Can I get you something, pal?"

Big Al tried to speak but couldn't. Mr. Clawson's deep-set eyes were close together, like a hawk's, and his bulbous nose made him look very unfriendly. But it was his mouth — tight and impatient — Big Al found the most intimidating. Another customer came to the bar.

"Can I get you something?" Mr. Clawson said, walking away.

Big Al cleared his throat. "I'd like a pitcher of beer," he said, "and an application."

Mr. Clawson turned around and came over to the register. "So you think you can bartend, huh?"

"I'd like to give it a try," he said, holding up his reddened, cut-up hands. "It'd have to be better than what I'm doing."

"I'm not offering anybody an office job, buddy."

Big Al let his hands drop. "I've never bartended before, but I've bounced."

"For who?"

"Joel Lydon."

Suddenly, the old man smiled. "And you are?"

"Al Hennessy."

"If that don't beat all," he said, laughing. "I've heard all about you, young man."

Big Al felt hot, as if he'd never left the factory. He turned to walk away, but Mr. Clawson called out to him.

"You still want the pitcher?"

"Yes."

"And the job?"

He laughed, and Mr. Clawson smiled even wider. "When can you start?"

"As soon as possible."

From there on out, Big Al couldn't decide what made him happier, having a job he could keep or never having to stand next to that crummy cauldron of molten metal again. But Mr. Clawson hadn't been lying; working in the bar was no office job. The old man told him that he'd never hired anyone before and that he only did so then because he was too old to keep running the bar by himself.

The hours were long, and it seemed to take forever for Sunday, his only day off, to roll around. When it finally did, he listened to the occasional game on the radio or went to the Laundromat, but the day always flew by. Before long, he opened a checking account, and without any time to spend his money, he soon had enough for an efficiency apartment a couple of blocks away from the bar. A smart double-breasted flannel suit came next, and then he replaced his straight razor with a new one he found at the Sears downtown. He was almost ready. Sitting in a barbershop on 17th Street, he came up with a plan so foolproof Janet would have to see how sincere he was and how hard he had worked to change for her.

The missing link was literally the missing link — a man Charles Darwin would have pointed to as proof he had been right. Clyde Rogers, a gangly ape of a man with a crude sense of humor and a foul disposition. Clyde made sure everyone around him knew he was there, often picking fights with guys who wanted nothing more than a fun night out on the town. When Big Al had gone inside Joel Lydon's Lounge for the first time, he'd noticed the big ugly man right away. He made everyone so uncomfortable they shied away from him. But Big Al waited for him to start picking a fight with him, and then he smiled. A flicker of doubt, just like every flicker of doubt he had ever seen in a bully's eyes, came across Clyde's scrunched bovine face. But Clyde still followed Big Al to the alley behind the bar, where they fought for several minutes. They battered each other pretty badly, but neither could claim he'd won. Afterward, both were hired as bouncers, but they hated each other so much Mr. Lydon ordered them to stay at opposite ends of the lounge. And they'd kept their distance, until the night Big Al approached him with his plan, right after he had his haircut.

Clyde stood up from his stool, towering over Big Al, his fists balled up. Then he regarded Big Al with curiosity — taking in his suit, his clean-shaven face, his haircut — before bursting out in mocking laughter.

"Are you for real, Hennessy?" he said, holding his stomach. "You look like a sap."

"I need to talk to you," Big Al said, wiping his forehead with a handkerchief. "There's 20 bucks in it for you." Big Al laid out his plan: "I want you to pick a fight with me on Saturday night so I can back down from you."

Clyde, who'd started to slouch, stretched out to his full height. "Are you trying to catch me off guard, Hennessy?"

"No," Big Al said. "There's a girl I'm trying to impress."

Clyde shook his head slowly. "By being a coward?"

Big Al cleared his throat. "She doesn't think I can change."

"You make me sick," Clyde said, cupping his chin with his long fingers. "But I could drink all weekend on 20 bucks."

"When she gets a load of me, I doubt we'll even have to go through with it."

Clyde's head shot back as he held his stomach and laughed. His toothless mouth twisted in a hideous leer, and his earlobes jiggled around like bells. "You goddamn clown," he said. "I'd do it just to watch you fall flat on your face, but for 20 bucks, I'm going to really enjoy myself."

Big Al fled the bar and didn't return until the following Saturday. The night couldn't have been nicer. Even though it was the end of November and very cold, the wind calmed him as it blew against his back while he walked down Market Street. Not one hair had been left out of place. Still, he couldn't stop wondering whether he'd spent enough time on everything.

Approaching the door, he straightened his coat and made sure his shirt was tucked inside his trousers neatly. Inside, he glanced over at Janet's table, where she was sitting with Serena and Trini, laughing as she twirled a straw in her drink. At first, he was afraid she was laughing at him, but then he realized she didn't even recognize him. So Big Al worked up the nerve to go over to her table, his head suddenly light and his chest pounding. Their eyes met, and the radiant smile faded from her face. Janet's lips moved, but he was too far to away hear her. Whatever she was saying had to be bad; Trini and Serena turned around in their seats, frowning at him.

He had come too far to weasel out. So he sat down across from her, flanked on each side by her friends. They scooted away from him, but Janet looked away, acting as if he weren't there.

"Hi, Al," she said, finally meeting his gaze. "Did you roll some drunk?"

"No," he said, attempting to smile but only managing a twitch. "I've been working for over four months now."

"You're still at Beta?"

"Well, no."

"Where then?"

"Clawson's Saloon."

Janet leaned back in her chair. "So you're still loafing."

"I'm bartending," he said. "I'm on my feet from 3 to 12 six days a week."

"Then why aren't you working tonight?"

"Because Mr. Clawson was nice enough to let me have the night off," he said, pausing, "so I could ask you out again."

Trini giggled again, and Serena remained silent. His face felt hot, his palms clammy. He felt stupid sitting there in his suit trying to be not only something he wasn't but something everyone else knew he wasn't. Janet picked up her purse and nodded toward the door. "Can we leave now?"

All three of them got up, but Janet stopped, staring above Big Al's head. From behind him, footsteps approached and then stopped.

"Hennessy!" Clyde said, his voice so loud several people turned toward him. Big Al turned, too, and smiled up at him. Clyde looked at him with drunken hatred before shifting his gaze toward Janet. Then he smiled, licked his lips and whistled. "I'd sure like to see her in between the sheets."

"Damn it, Clyde!" Big Al said, twisting around in his chair until it made a cracking sound. "She's a lady and wouldn't even be in the same room as you."

"She's in the same room with me now."

"This is a bar."

"Well, Big Al," he said, drawling his words out slowly. "If you've got a tumblerful of manhood left in you, we can discuss this outside."

Twenty dollars be damned, Big Al wanted nothing more than to punch Clyde in that big mouth of his and knock the remaining shards of his teeth right out. Clyde backed up, and then Big Al caught a glimpse of Janet's face, which showed a mixture of reproach and sadness and told him she knew he'd never change no matter how much he wanted to. He stood up.

"I won't bother you anymore," he said to Janet, turning toward the door. "I'm sorry I…"

He nudged his way through the crowd, avoiding a group of drinking buddies calling out his name. He began feeling sorry for himself; everything in his life had been a sham. Even as a child, people had assumed he was the Stevenses' grandson, showing him respect until they found out he was just some tramp the old couple had pitied. Then they acted differently toward him, just as these people were doing now. He'd never wear this clown suit again. And he'd never spend another night tossing and turning while coming up with schemes to win Janet over, schemes that were sure to fail and cost him money he didn't have.

At the door, he felt a slight touch on his shoulder, and he turned around to find Janet. He figured she was giving him the dignity of brushing him off face to face, so he had no reason to lie. He told her everything and was surprised when she said she'd known the whole time.

"How?"

"The creep's been buying drinks left and right and telling everyone he got the money from you."

"Well, one thing wasn't phony."

"What?"

"I wanted to go out in the alley with him," Big Al said. "I didn't think he'd take it so far."

"See? It doesn't pay to be dishonest."

"I guess you're right," he said.

"We're going to a movie next weekend," she said. "*Casablanca*. Would you like to tag along?"

"Yes," he said, laughing. "Yes, I would."

And tag along he had, for nearly 25 years. But everything was different now. His once-starched shirts were wrinkled and stained, and all he had to do was look in a mirror to see how much more slovenly he had become. Ever since Janet died, he wondered whether some of the things he remembered and cherished had happened at all. Even the nightclub had changed. Today three longhair punks sat at her table. The one with freckles and fat lips kept making obscene gestures toward Big Al and then laughing with his friends.

A group of tough-looking young men stood next to the bar and watched the crowd. As Big Al approached, they turned and regarded him with bemused wonder, as though he were a lost traveler trying to find the right path.

"Is Nick around?" Big Al said.

The biggest of the four — a huge Samoan Eric always talked about — nodded toward an office at the end of a hallway. "He's in there."

"I'd like to have a drink with him if he can find the time," Big Al said, holding out his hand. "I'm Al Hennessy. You must be Chi-Chi. Eric Rolston says you're the best bouncer in town."

Chi-Chi's face softened, and he smiled a toothy grin. He engulfed Big Al's hand and pumped so hard his arm began hurting. These roustabouts would have to be a fool to mess with someone like Chi-Chi.

"Nick says you and Clyde used to rule this place back in Mr. Lydon's day."

"Oh, I don't know," Big Al said, taking his hand back and shaking it around. "Everybody wanted to fight me back then. I'll bet a guy your size doesn't have too much to worry about."

"You'd be surprised."

The movement of the kids in the crowd was so bizarre Big Al couldn't help but notice how strange they were. They twisted their hips and rolled their shoulders around. Just watching nearly made him dizzy.

"What's wrong with these kids?" he said, waving his hand out toward them. "Why are they acting so weird?"

"They're all tripped out on acid," Chi-Chi said.

"Tripped out?" Big Al said, frowning. "Acid?"

The young man smiled at him. "They take acid."

"Like, battery acid?"

Chi-Chi laughed so loudly that some of the kids turned toward him, their panic-stricken faces weirdly exaggerated.

"My job would be a lot easier if they were taking battery acid," he said, pointing to a kid staring at a strobe light. "It's a drug that makes them act dumber than shit. Oh, yeah, this place is a real freak show."

"I had no idea," Big Al said, looking at the kid. The boy had deadened eyes, which were almost covered by his flowing bangs. Why anyone would want to be so out of it was beyond him. Eventually, the light began to give Big Al a headache, and he had to look away.

"I'll go tell Mr. Dooley you're here," Chi-Chi said, turning and going down the hallway, where he knocked on a door before going inside. After several seconds, he came back out and motioned for

Big Al to follow him to the bar. "Mr. Dooley says anything you want is on the house."

"Is he going to join me?"

"In a while," he said. "He's hurrying, but he's got a ways to go yet."

"OK, how about a rum and Coke?"

Chi-Chi made the drink. Big Al thanked him and took a sip; the drink had more rum than cola, and he smiled. Chi-Chi went back over and stood by the other bouncers.

The only available booth was the one where Nick always sat. Even though he didn't think Nick would mind if he sat there, it didn't seem proper. So he went down a small set of steps to the billiards area. Three of the tables were occupied with seedy young men, taking their time scoping out their shots, and he went to the cue rack and picked the straightest stick there. Then he went to the only open table and put a dime down on top of it and started to chalk up the tip of his stick.

"Hey, old man," a young man behind him said, his voice harsh and disrespectful. "Are you ready to get whipped?"

Big Al turned. The kid was a little older than most of the people there, a dirty ponytail hanging over his leather jacket. His build was slight, but the other men moved out of his way whenever he came near them. His head stuck out of a yellow turtleneck sweater that made his face look small and cold.

"We'll see, won't we?" Big Al said. "You break?"

"Nah, I'll let you," he said. "That's if you can do it without breaking your wrist."

Big Al tried to force a smile. He waited for the young man to rack up and step away from the table before lining up and aiming right for the center of the cue ball. The tip of the stick hit the cue ball hard, and the balls scattered all over the table. A couple went in.

"Not bad," the young man said, smirking.

Big Al wondered whether he himself used to be so rude. The young man gestured for him to hurry. But being patient was how Big Al had always approached the game, and he scanned the table for his best shot, chalking up his cue. There were so many options. He could run the table whether he picked stripes or solids. The nine ball sat next to the side pocket; it was an easy shot, maybe too easy. The cue ball grazed it softly, and the nine ball barely went in. But it did. And he was about to run the table, never coming close to missing, until the eight ball rimmed out of the corner pocket.

"My turn," the young man said, nudging him out of the way and taking his first shot. He was lucky. Though he took almost no time at all, his first three shots went in. But when he missed his last shot, the cue ball rolled a couple of inches away from the eight ball, and he cussed.

Big Al made the shot easily. He went to put his cue back on the rack, but the young man stood in his way. "Where the hell are you going?"

Big Al went around him. The young man mumbled something and called out to him. "You got lucky, old man!"

Big Al whirled around. "Yeah? Maybe you're not as good as you think you are."

The young man put his dime in the coin slot and pushed the gully release. "Get over here. Let's see who's as good as they think they are."

"I've had just about enough of your company, son."

The young man threw his stick on the table and turned toward him. "Call me that again and I'll rip you limb from limb!"

The young man started walking toward him. Big Al hadn't come to his friend's place to get in a fight, to start trouble, but the young man's ego and bad manners needed to be dealt with. Walking away was something he had never been good at, but now he had nothing to prove, nothing to lose except his pride, and he smiled. A doubtful frown came over the young man's face, almost as if he wouldn't have minded turning back himself. But they were too close to each other by then.

Someone yelled, and heavy footsteps came running from behind. Big Al almost turned around but knew he risked a sucker punch if he did. So he took a step back and glanced over his shoulder. Chi-Chi came cutting and veering through the crowd. He stood between them, and the young man leaned back and slouched against the pool table. Then he tried to lunge around Chi-Chi, but the bouncer grabbed hold of his jacket and pushed him back against the table. "You'd better settle down, or I'll throw your ass out for good."

The young man stretched around Chi-Chi's side. "He just saved your ass, old man."

Chi-Chi smiled at Big Al and laughed. Soon the room was filled with the weird laughter of the freaks. Many of them, Big Al thought, probably didn't even know what they were laughing at. The young man stood straight up and glared around the room. Chi-Chi led Big Al away. "Nick's waiting on you."

Along the way, Chi-Chi kept glancing over his shoulder. Big Al found himself doing the same thing, even though he didn't know why. But after bumping into a young girl and nearly knocking her down, he asked Chi-Chi, "What's wrong?"

"Probably nothing," Chi-Chi said. "But let me know when you're leaving so I can walk you out to your car."

"Because of that punk?" he said, cocking his thumb over his shoulder. "Why would I need protection from someone like him?"

"Because Ronch Laroy is dangerous," Chi-Chi said. "I wouldn't put anything past him."

"I'm not afraid of a bum like him," Big Al said.

"I'm not saying you are, but he'd never jump both of us."

"Oh, piss on him."

Chi-Chi started to say something but hesitated for a second. "The police think he killed a couple of his friends."

"What?"

"Yeah, Don Stingley, the kid they found in the alley behind Maple Street last summer."

"With his throat cut?"

"Uh-huh. This is the last place anyone saw him alive," he said. "The cops came in here asking questions. Mostly, they wanted to know about Ronch."

"Why? The guy's all talk. Hell, he was about to crap his pants before you showed up."

"The word around here was Don ripped him off."

"Who else do they think he killed?"

"The retarded guy they found hanging in the tree outside of town," he said. "Just so happens he was the one who came in and got Don out of here that night."

ooo

"Whatever happened to Serena and Trini?" Nick said, leaning forward. "I haven't seen them in ages."

Big Al tried to remember. Trini had married — he was sure of it — a serviceman right after the war. But that was the last he'd heard; if she stayed in the area, he couldn't ever remember running into her. And he knew even less about Serena. She'd simply moved on a couple of weeks after they had all gone to see *Casablanca*. Neither had been too fond of him. He'd overheard them talking about how he only got a chance because there weren't many men around to pick from. So he wasn't too broken up when they drifted apart from Janet. Without their constant bad-mouthing, she actually began acting nicer toward him.

And that's when they got to know each other, talking nonstop for hours. She pried things out of him he had long forgotten — the old doctor's nervous twitches, his kindness toward others and Mrs. Stevens' belief that dishonesty was never acceptable — memories, he was ashamed to say, he had forgotten the day he walked away from the empty farmhouse.

Nick was still waiting for an answer, and Big Al offered an apologetic shrug. "I haven't seen either one of them in over 20 years. God, it makes me tired just thinking about it."

Nick patted him on the shoulder. "Are you OK, Al?"

"I'm fine," he said, looking over at her table. A new group of longhair kids was sitting there now. Their sickening presence made him forget everything but the need to flee. "I'm going home. Good night, Nick."

"Good night, Al."

Big Al stood up and went to the door. Chi-Chi was talking to a young man who was insolent and very drunk. Big Al waved at him and went outside. The parking lot was mostly empty now. No one was outside except him; even the speaker hanging off the building was silent. The snow crunching underneath his feet echoed as the front door opened behind him, spilling out the sounds of the bar. He turned around to see who it was, but no one was there. A moment later, the side door hidden in the shadows opened and closed, and he heard trash being thrown in a dumpster.

Once he was close to his car, a cold breeze blew tiny snowflakes up the back of his neck, making him shiver. He stopped next to his car and fished around in his pocket for his keys, but the sound of crunching snow continued for a couple of seconds. Then it stopped.

Big Al took a deep breath and smiled. Soon he would be free of all his worries and mistakes. He'd never have to agonize over Billy's future or spend another sleepless night wondering where he had gone wrong with Al Jr. Maybe Janet would explain it to him—explain everything. Maybe she'd be wearing the blue crepe dress she wore when she was dancing by the jukebox or the harvest sweatshirt she loved to bake in during the holidays.

He shrugged slightly, put his palms up and spoke without turning around. "Hello, Ronch. What a wonderful night to die."

"Don't move," Ronch said, his voice wavering. "How'd you know my name?"

Big Al dropped his arms and turned around. "I guess it just came up."

"I told you not to move."

"Why?" Big Al said, tilting his head. "Do you feel better looking at a man's back?"

"I've got a gun," Ronch said, bringing his hand up in the air until the gleam of the streetlight reflected off the end of the gun barrel.

"And that probably counts for something somewhere," Big Al said, nodding his head. "Go ahead and shoot."

"Who says I want to shoot you?" he said, taking another step forward and looking around. "I just need a ride."

"Why? So you can cut my throat or leave me hanging from a tree?"

Ronch's gun hand twitched. It was too dark to see his face clearly, but Big Al wanted to know whether his eyes had finally come alive with guilt, so he took a step forward. Ronch was puzzled, maybe even felt like a fool for coming up with such a silly plan, which was really no plan at all. Then he waved the gun at Big Al. "I said let's go. I'm not going to tell you again."

Ronch steadied his hand and pulled the revolver's hammer back. When Big Al spoke, his words came out measured. "Go ahead, son."

Ronch cupped the handle of the gun before taking a deep breath. Heavy footfalls came crunching through the snow, and Ronch turned around as a large hand pulled his arm up in the air. The gun went off before the man could take it away, and the bullet whizzed past Big Al's ear. Chi-Chi came into the light and threw the gun on the ground, wrapping his arm around Ronch's neck until he began to slacken.

"You'd better stop fighting, or I'll break your neck."

Big Al walked forward. "Let him go. I want to see how tough he is without his gun."

Chi-Chi let go and pushed him. Ronch had enough fight in him to come charging forward, throwing his fists about and wasting his energy by yelling as loudly as he could. Big Al stood to the side and put his foot out, tripping the young man forward, where he landed facedown in a snowdrift. Big Al laughed; it looked as if Ronch had been embedded there. But he finally pulled himself up, shook the snow off and charged again, throwing an awkward punch above Big Al's ducked head. Al landed a punch of his own in Ronch's stomach.

Ronch gasped and doubled over. There wasn't much fight left in him. Big Al put him in a headlock and punched him in the face three times before letting go.

Ronch fell to the ground, sniveling. Big Al said, "I can see why you need weapons."

Chi-Chi cackled as sirens, ringing in the distance, approached. Big Al waited as two squad cars came sliding onto the lot. The officers got out, drawing their guns. They lowered them when they recognized Big Al. Officer Strand, a tall man with receding hair and a puzzled face, frowned.

"What're you doing here, Al?" he said, his eyes lowering to Ronch. "Aren't you a little old for this?"

"Well, yeah, I am, Herb," he said. "But I'm not too old to teach a kid manners, especially when he's trying to slap me around."

The other officer — a plump kid who looked as if he had a serious case of indigestion — came forward. "We're here because someone reported hearing a gunshot. Care to tell us about it?"

Chi-Chi knelt over and dug the gun out of the snow. "I took that away from him, and it went off in the air."

Officer Strand turned Ronch over and smiled at the other officer. "Recognize him, don't you?"

"It's Ronch Laroy," the young officer said. "The punk's finally got himself in a jam."

The young officer picked up the gun with a pencil and put it inside his car, while Officer Strand helped Ronch up, handcuffed him and led him to the squad car. Ronch shuffled his feet while they walked, almost causing both of them to fall. Officer Strand opened up the door and threw him in the back seat. Officer Strand pulled a small notepad from his coat pocket and started writing. When he spoke, his pen kept moving.

"We'll need you to come to the police station with us so you can press charges."

"As far as I'm concerned," Big Al said, "he's been punished enough."

"Punished enough?" the young officer said. "He's a suspect in a double homicide."

Officer Strand stopped writing. But Big Al shrugged. "Then why don't you lock him up for that?"

"We would if we could," Officer Strand said. "Sooner or later, we will."

"And in the meantime you want me to waste my time in court with this screw-up?" Big Al said. "Sorry. If this clown wants more of my time, he'll have to come to me. I've got a business to run."

"A business?" Officer Strand said. He started to get into his car and then paused. "Remember this, Al. If he kills again, it'll be on you."

•••

Chapter 11

Al Jr. had watched Billy from a distance for most of the party. Billy was walking from one person to the next with a beer in his hand, as if nobody was interesting enough to waste too much time on, even when a couple of pretty girls tried to corner him. And even though Al Jr. would've just sat around the apartment drinking all weekend, being at the party Friday night still seemed like such a waste. All he'd managed to do was upset a girl wanting to talk about her missing brother.

As the night drew on, Billy began acting even more weirdly; he kept going over to the barn door and staring out at the barren field beyond. Billy was always hard to figure out, though he always did the right thing, said the right thing, flashing his perfectly dimpled smile. But there was a private side of him only the family knew about; he'd even kept it hidden from Karen. It was the side of him that holed up in his room, pouting if things didn't go his way, if the ass kissing got a little old or if their father had criticized him a little too much. Al Jr. had never seen him act that way outside the house. So it was puzzling to see him brushing kids off, and even the jocks, as self-centered as they were, seemed to notice his distance.

Al Jr. was convinced he'd seen such a change in someone somewhere else, but he couldn't place who.

When Al Jr. finally came out of the shadows, no one bothered him. Maybe he'd just imagined the two hippies tormenting him. He went to the keg room and peeked inside; four kegs were lying on their sides while a couple of boys tried pumping beer from the last one. Nothing but foam came out of the tap.

"I hope they get back with those kegs soon," one of them said.

Al Jr. walked toward the barn door for fresh air. A large group of kids passed by. A jock brushed against him and knocked him off balance, and Al Jr. grabbed hold of a beam to keep from falling on his face.

"Watch where you're going," Al Jr. said. But the jock had already gone out the door, and all Al Jr. could do was cuss under his breath. Sara went past him, and before she could get too far, he reached out and grabbed her arm. She jerked away. "Get your hand off me!"

Al Jr. cringed and let go. After a few seconds, she turned and began walking away. He called out for her to wait and moved toward the door, blocking her from leaving.

"What do you want?" she said, her voice so low he could barely hear her.

"I, uh, wanted to—"

"Quit stammering."

Finally, he cleared his throat. "I'm sorry about... What I mean is, I hope you find your brother, alive."

His words sounded so stupid and plodding that he broke out in a sweat despite the coldness of the barn. Sara smiled slightly as if she found his awkward apology amusing. He started to walk away from her, probably back to the shadows of the corner wall, but she reached out and grabbed his arm. He could only manage a feeble glance over his shoulder, but a warm smile formed on her face, and he turned back around to face her.

"Maybe," she said, letting go of his arm and holding out her hand for him to shake, "we could start over."

He tried to find any signs of deception. But there weren't any, or at least none he could find, so he took her hand and shook it lightly. He wanted to say something to make up for his behavior, maybe something smart or clever, but he had never been either. So he just smiled and nodded like some kind of loon, but he didn't care.

"I was hoping you'd help me," she said.

"Anything you want," he said, "anything at all."

"Would you write some letters and send some pictures of my brother to the guys you served with over there?"

"Sure."

She thanked him, began to cry and then rested her head on his chest. He wanted to warn her — to tell her what kind of odds they were facing and that over there, missing was as good as dead. But instead, he said, "Don't worry. We'll find him."

She noticed the dampness on his shirt and wiped at it with her gloved hand. "I'm...sorry. I don't—"

"Quit stammering," he said.

She giggled and lowered her head against his chest again, where she seemed to be resting from an exhaustive trip. When she finally pulled away, she looked down at her Mickey Mouse wristwatch. "I'd better go home before my dad calls the cops. Do you need a lift?"

He wanted to say yes, but Billy came downstairs with an odd blankness on his face. "I'd better stay here."

"Suit yourself," she said. She opened her purse and found a pen and a piece of torn paper. Then she wrote her number on the paper and handed it to him.

"Thanks," he said.

"Call me tomorrow," she said as she turned and walked out the door. He stuffed the paper into his coat pocket and zipped it shut. Billy was across the room, talking to two unlettered jocks. The taller squirmed around as he spoke, and Billy turned away from him, sipping from his cup. And then, while the kid was still speaking, Billy walked off, leaving the kid confused.

Al Jr. rushed to catch up with him. They walked side by side before Al Jr. said his name and made him jump. "Don't sneak up on me like that," Billy said.

"I've been right by you all across the room," Al Jr. said, laughing and slapping Billy on the arm. "I've got a date."

A sickened frown came across Billy's face. "Who?"

"A girl named Sara."

"Sara who?"

"Silverston."

Billy rolled his eyes and looked away.

"What?"

"Oh, nothing," Billy said. "She's kind of a nutcase."

"Huh?" Al Jr. asked. "Why?"

Billy smiled, but his mouth barely curved upward and didn't affect the rest of his face. "Did she say something about finding her brother?"

"Yeah," Al Jr. said. "What's wrong with that?"

"Because he's dead."

Al Jr. shook his head. "Missing."

"What's the difference?"

"They have POW camps over there," Al Jr. said. "I'm telling you, I've heard some pretty wild stories."

"Why don't they go in and get them then?"

"Because they keep moving."

"Sure," Billy said. "So you think you can help her?"

"I don't know. Probably not."

Billy slapped him on the back. "But it's worth trying if you can get her in bed, huh?"

"Christ, Billy. I wasn't even—"

"C'mon, Al," Billy said, winking. "You might as well get something out of it if you're going to play her nutty games."

"You just don't know how important it is to her."

"Oh, yeah," Billy said, nodding his head, "it's real important."

"What's that supposed to mean?"

Billy tipped his cup up to his mouth and frowned as he poured the remaining foam onto the ground. Then, without another word, he walked off to the keg room. Al Jr. was glad he walked away. Who the hell did he think he was? And who the hell was he starting to act like?

Al Jr. had a headache, and he wished he'd left with Sara. He made his way through the cluttered partitions until he found the last room. There was not anyone in there, just junk. Pieces of broken chairs, tables and other mangled fixtures were strewn all over the place, littering so much of the floor he nearly tripped going across the room. On the other end of the room, a legless couch rested against the wall. The sparse light filtering in through the thin blanket covering the door was bright enough for him to be able to see springs sticking through some of the cushions. It would be better than lying sleepless on a concrete floor. He stepped over and around everything and collapsed onto the couch. A rodent scurried out of one of the cushions. But that didn't bother him at all. One night in the jungle, he had awakened to see a snake crawling over his legs. He went back to sleep once it slithered off. Just like then, his eyelids felt so heavy he couldn't keep them open, and as he began to drift off, a face began to form, taking shape so clearly it made him sit upright.

The face belonged to Chuck Ogilvy, a strapping young man from Alabama whose words always rolled out in hypnotic syllables. Many nights, Al Jr. had fallen asleep listening to him talking. And Chuck wasn't just some scrub there to fight someone else's mess because he didn't have anywhere else to go. Al Jr. heard Chuck had turned down a football scholarship from Alabama to join the service. Al Jr. would've probably guessed something along those lines. Though Chuck was a big man — well over 6 feet tall, with wide, broad shoulders — he moved like a cat. He reminded Al Jr. of Dirk Smith, except Chuck wasn't a jerk Al Jr. would want to fight; he had a pleasant way about him. Chuck said his grandfather and father were disappointed he didn't go to college, but he wanted to be like them and serve his country during a war.

The whipping wind blew a tree limb against the barn so hard Al Jr. jolted back. His chest throbbed. He took several deep breaths and waited for the pain to go away. Chuck's optimism had carried him through every skirmish, at times carrying them all. Nothing was ever hopeless to Chuck, and his life would be perfect once he went home, where his beloved Sally waited for him. He'd looked forward to his August discharge and September wedding. He even had names for his unborn children and spoke about them as if they already existed. Before supper each night, he prayed for everyone— including his enemies.

On a hot, sticky day in July, a letter came for him. Chuck went off by himself to read it. Al Jr. waited for him to come back so he could listen to Chuck tell them about the letter from home in his Southern drawl. But after a half-hour, Chuck was still gone, so Al Jr. went out in the brush to find him. Al Jr. kept walking until he heard gasping coming from underneath a tree. A twig snapped underneath his feet, and he froze, afraid Chuck might think he was a VC sneaking up on him. But the sounds continued. Someone back in

Anniston must've died, one of his grandparents or his dad, maybe in an accident, just as his mother had. Chuck looked up at him, scowling, and held the letter in the air before throwing it on the ground. Then he stood up and stepped on it, twisting his boot around until the paper was torn to pieces.

"Sally says she met someone," he said. "Someone she can't live without."

Al Jr. tried to speak. Birds and insects chirped, and Chuck began to squirm around. "I've got to get out of here," he said, grabbing hold of Al Jr.'s shirt. "Will you help me?"

"We'd never make it," Al Jr. said, trying to pull away from him. "They'd throw us in the stockade. Even if they don't, what about Charlie?"

"The hell with those slopes," Chuck said. "We'll shoot our way through them."

"C'mon, Chuck, you've only got six weeks left," Al Jr. said. "She'll forget all about him once you're back."

Chuck began picking up his letter, piece by piece, and when he was done, he sat cross-legged and lit up a cigarette — something Sgt. Tucker would've raised hell over. "She's getting married next week."

Al Jr. turned away from Chuck's sad face and stood there for a few more minutes before heading back to base camp. He thought about telling Sgt. Tucker about the letter. But he kept his mouth shut, even after Sgt. Tucker asked whether anyone had seen Chuck. Eventually, Chuck came walking out of the woods.

Later in the evening, before they ate their rations, everyone waited for Chuck to say a prayer, but he just lowered his head and ate silently. But nobody really seemed to care about hearing Chuck's prayers. Maybe they never had.

A week later, while they were out on reconnaissance, Chuck and Al Jr. were on point, well ahead of everyone else. They heard raspy breathing, like a death rattle, coming from behind the thick brush. Chuck cut a swath with his machete, and they passed through the clearing, where a VC sat against a tree, his blood-drenched hands holding his stomach. He was young, probably no more than 14. And he was small, much smaller than any soldier Al Jr. had ever seen. His skin was waxy pale. He reached for his rifle several feet away and then stopped, closing his eyes and lowering his head. He started mumbling in Vietnamese.

"Go get Sgt. Tucker," Chuck said, his voice soft.

"No way, Chuck," Al Jr. said, his voice rising. Chuck motioned for him to be quiet, and they listened for movement. When they didn't hear anything, Al Jr. said, "For all we know, there could be more of them out there."

Chuck aimed the barrel of his gun at Al Jr.'s stomach, his finger wrapped around the trigger. Al Jr. felt a new kind of fear. Had all the time he had lain awake worrying about booby traps and snipers been a waste? He waited for the rifle to fire, but Chuck was waiting for him to leave. So Al Jr. backed up and turned toward the trail. He caught a glimpse of the boy's fearful face, which was almost pleading for him not to leave. But he did. He had to. At least that's what he told himself as he hurried down the trail. He plodded the whole way, and twigs snapped underneath his feet. He came to an opening, where Sgt. Tucker stood against a tree, aiming his rifle at him. Once Sgt. Tucker recognized him, he cursed and lowered his rifle.

"Hennessy, I could've blown you…" he said, looking beyond Al Jr. "Where's Ogilvy?"

Al Jr. pointed down the trail. "We found a wounded VC."

"What?" Sgt. Tucker said. "Let's go!"

Al Jr. followed behind Sgt. Tucker, who moved with so much stealth nothing cracked underneath him, until they made their way back to Chuck. When they found him, Sgt. Tucker asked, "What're you doing baby-sitting a corpse, Ogilvy?"

"He just died."

"Let's get back to the others," Sgt. Tucker said, whispering, "in case they decide to come back and get him."

Sgt. Tucker went back down the trail. Al Jr. could finally see through the brush, and he gasped when he saw a few gouges on the young soldier's shirt around his rib cage. A couple of them weren't there when he left. It didn't seem possible Chuck would've stabbed a soldier already so close to death, but what else could've happened? Al Jr. couldn't move past him; the humility was gone from Chuck's once friendly face. What was left was nothing but a cold, vicious hatred. Al Jr. must've looked like a frightened child, because

Chuck's face softened for a moment as he motioned for him to go ahead down the trail.

Al Jr. forced himself to stare straight ahead on the trek back to the others. The walk felt like miles instead of meters, hours instead of minutes, and when they finally made their way to the clearing where everyone waited for them, Al Jr. collapsed on a tree trunk. He shook off the incident the best he could, making jokes about getting lost. Later on, he even tried to convince himself nothing had happened.

Yet he couldn't stop thinking about the boy, lying where they had left him, rotting away in the jungle without a marker of any kind. Did the boy have parents worrying about him, wondering whether he was OK? If so, would they spend the rest of their lives guessing about what had happened to him? Al Jr. hoped he was an orphan. And he worried about Chuck.

One night, about a week later, he found Chuck out by a tree, smoking a cigarette. Al Jr. asked him what had happened after he left.

Chuck's face was still hidden in the darkness. "He just died. That's all. You saw him. He was already a goner when we found him."

"Did he do something?" Al Jr. said. "I didn't see any…"

Chuck's hand slipped down to his side, where he kept a knife. Al Jr. took a step back and brought his hands up to his chest. "I'd never say anything."

Chuck came up with another cigarette and lit it; the glowing match shined on Chuck's smiling face.

"What're you afraid of?" Chuck said. "You don't think I'd hurt you, do you?"

"Yes," Al Jr. said, wiping away sweat from his forehead. "I'd never say anything to anyone."

"But you think I should, huh?"

"Don't you feel…?"

"Damn it, Al," Chuck said, his voice so low it sounded like a growl. He took another step toward Al Jr. "Why should I care about these pukes?"

Then Chuck reached out and grabbed hold of Al Jr.'s jacket and began to breathe heavily. After a few seconds, he let go and walked away, running his hand through his hair and propping himself against a tree for support.

"I'm tired of this crap," he said. "I lost my life; I lost my Sally."

Chuck gasped in the same way he had when he read Sally's letter. Al Jr. wanted to walk away from him, but no matter what, he was still his friend. So he put his hand on his shoulder.

"Maybe I could accidentally shoot you in the leg," Al Jr. said, feeling feeble and stupid, "and get you out of this hellhole."

"Why?" Chuck said. He slouched and rested his cupped hands on the barrel of his rifle. "I haven't got anything to go home to."

"You'll find someone else."

Chuck laughed, only it didn't sound like laughter; it was bitter and hateful. "She had me underneath her fingers like some kind of sap," he said. "'I'll wait for you, honey,'" he went on in a high-pitched voice Al Jr. would've found funny any other time. "You think I could go home and watch her running around with another man?"

Al Jr. couldn't answer him. The pain on Chuck's face was so intense there was nothing he could've said. "That's right, Al," Chuck said. "I love her so much I'd kill them both."

They barely spoke to each other thereafter. Al Jr. didn't want to alienate him, but he couldn't get past the frightened child he had left behind. How could Chuck have done something so cold? Maybe it was the first time in his life he had ever been rejected. If so, it was a hell of a time for it to happen, and now he was lost, probably for good. After a while, everyone in their squad began sidestepping him with awkward glances along the way, all of them wondering what had happened, none of them knowing. Except Al Jr.

Al Jr. leaned forward on the couch, jerked upright by a long-forgotten twinge of guilt. He'd wanted to help Chuck, but nothing short of getting Sally back for him would have helped. Even then, knowing the man Chuck had become, Sally would've never been safe, yet Al Jr. would've done it if only he could've.

A month later, going through a deserted village, their platoon came across two VCs coming out of an underground bunker and running toward the tree line. They chased them out toward an embankment, where the two men were cornered, with nothing more than a few small trees to keep them covered. It would've been easier just to kill them, but Sgt. Tucker wanted to take them alive. So the platoon dug in, up above on a ridge, and fired shots nearby, hoping they'd give up. It paid off; one of the soldiers threw out his rifle and stood up with his hands in the air. The other soldier tried to hold him back by grabbing his arm, but then he finally tossed his rifle out, too.

Someone laughed. Al Jr. felt like laughing, too, now that everything was safe. More than once, someone in the squad had been killed by a displaced VC, and the danger was always higher when there was more than one and they started shooting and slithering off in different directions.

Chuck slid down the embankment, holding a grenade in his outstretched hand, and ran toward them. Sgt. Tucker yelled Chuck's name. The VCs jumped toward their rifles and fired at Chuck as he threw the grenade. It fell in front of them, and the squad returned fire, sending round after round at the soldiers while both huddled near the same tree. The grenade exploded, filling the air with smoke and debris, and everyone kept firing until the smoke cleared to a thin fog.

Everyone in the squad went down the embankment with his rifle aimed forward, finding the two VCs' shrapnel-torn bodies. And then Al Jr. saw Chuck lying on his stomach. Chuck's shallow, labored breaths began to come less frequently. Then they quit coming at all.

The platoon went down the trail as the helicopter carrying Chuck's body flew away in the distance and disappeared. They mumbled to one another, trying to figure out what Chuck had seen to make him do something so crazy.

They came back to the base camp a week later. Nobody wanted to pack Chuck's stuff up, including Al Jr., but he volunteered anyway. Chuck had been a tidy man who'd kept everything in order; his T-shirts were neatly rolled, and his pictures were stacked evenly in his foot locker. The only thing out of place was a stack of unopened letters that had piled up on his bunk while they'd been in the field. Once everything else was packed in Chuck's duffel bag, Al Jr. began putting the letters away, one by one, trying not to think about the words inside. His hands began to shake, and the letters fell on the ground. He gathered them up, separating family from friends, and toward the end of the stack, he found one from Sally.

He looked around the barracks, and when he didn't see anyone around, he stuffed it into his pocket and went to a stall in the latrine. The stench of lemon and urine had drawn a swarm of flies, but he barely noticed as he ripped the envelope open and began reading Sally's neat writing. At first, he was angry that Sally had enough nerve to write to someone she had driven insane. But then, as she reminisced about things only Chuck should've read, he felt guilty. And then he was confused as to why a newly married woman would've written such a letter. Was she so evil she felt that Chuck hadn't been tormented enough? Halfway through the third page, she fell apart. Not only did she want forgiveness but also she wanted them to start all over; she hadn't gone through with her wedding, because her fiancé, Ben, walked out on her saying he could tell she loved Chuck and not him and he'd be damned if he was going to be married to a girl who spent all her time talking about another man.

At the end of the last page, she said she'd be eagerly awaiting his return, and Al Jr. couldn't help thinking Chuck's homecoming was going to be a lot different from what she had in mind.

•••

Chapter 12

All the freaks were closing in on him, and Billy couldn't handle it any longer, especially because he had only had one piece of pizza since lunch and was so queasy he had to lean against the wall several times to keep from falling. Outside a side window, the sun was starting to rise. It cast an orange glow against the snow, and he nearly gagged at the smell of hay and cow shit. He'd go nuts if he didn't leave soon.

Though his mind was fuzzy, he remembered everything about the previous night. Rich had gone upstairs with a girl he could've sworn he'd seen upstairs with another guy earlier. And right before that, he had nearly been hit by vomit when Ralph puked all over the front of the barn. Worst of all were all the petty fights egged on by the same kids who always acted as if a party just wasn't a party unless somebody got beaten up so they could stand around and laugh at the loser. It was the lamest party Duke had ever had; it'd be a wonder if he ever had another party again — or at least any time soon.

Ralph was still lying on the floor next to a stall. Al Jr. had disappeared shortly after saying he had a date with that weird girl, Sara Silverston. Maybe he'd left with her, but Billy doubted it. Al Jr. wasn't smooth enough to get a girl's number and go home with her on the same night. So he had to be around somewhere. He was probably propped up against a wall sleeping.

Billy went upstairs as quietly as he could and peeked in each of the partitioned rooms before he found Rich and the girl in the last one lying underneath a blanket. Rich stirred and woke up as Billy was about to shake him.

"What the hell?" he said, sitting up.

Billy put his finger up to his mouth and whispered. "C'mon, we've got to go."

The girl moved slightly, and Rich waited until she settled before looking back up at Billy. "Can't we stay awhile?"

"No," Billy said. "I've got to get out of here now."

Before Rich could say anything else, Billy let go of the blanket and went back downstairs to where Ralph was slumped against the stall. Billy leaned over and shook him until he started moaning.

"Where'd Al go?" Billy asked.

"How the hell would I know?" Ralph said as he began to retch.

Billy searched the barn. The corner Al Jr. had hidden in all weekend was now occupied by a couple of passed-out hippies. But his capped bottle was on its side near them, and when Billy saw it, he figured Al Jr. had to be around there somewhere. He was probably off past the keg room. He found a dark room filled with so much trash he could barely find a path. He whispered Al Jr.'s name and listened; after several seconds, he heard someone snoring. He crossed the room, nearly tripping along the way, until he finally did trip. He fell forward onto the sleeping person. A hand reached up and grabbed hold of his jacket.

"I'm sorry," Billy said. "I tripped."

"What the hell are you doing?" Al Jr. said.

"Quit freaking out!" Billy said, pulling Al Jr.'s hand away from his jacket. "We're leaving. I could've just left you here."

"You probably would do that."

"Oh, you're crazy," Billy said, standing and going back out to the large bay where Rich was trying to get Ralph up. Al Jr. came up behind him, kicking things out of the way. Billy went outside and looked across the field, where a doe was standing next to three fawns. As he walked toward the car, the deer ran off, their hoofs crunching in the snow, and they disappeared in the woods. Ralph came stumbling out of the barn as if he were still asleep or drunk or both, followed by Rich and Al Jr. None of them seemed too happy to have been awakened so early, and Ralph made several retching sounds, which killed Billy's appetite. It was irritating Ralph was such a weakling when it came to booze. Billy had hoped to talk Rich into stopping at the diner on the bottom of Jefferson Hill, but now he just wanted to stretch out on the couch and sleep until Sunday morning. So he slumped down in the back seat, trying to ignore the cold chill.

Rich nearly flooded the engine starting up the car. He kept turning toward Al Jr. as if he wanted to ask something. "Can we stay at your place awhile?" he finally asked, pointing at Ralph. "I can't take him home like this."

"I don't care," Al Jr. said. Rich flashed a relieved smile before gunning the engine and sliding through the snow until they were finally on the road. Al Jr.'s face was as red as a tomato. Everything sucked; nothing was cool. The whole night had been a waste of time. Billy had hoped their father would give Al Jr. a chance, for once, maybe even let him move back in with them. But watching their dad in the stands acting as if everything were all right and nothing had happened was enough to make Billy think he'd been fooling himself all along. And Carla? She'd bitched and bitched and bitched about Chip and then gotten pissed at him for asking one little question. After all, how could Karen be happy with Brian Keeler? He was just some science nerd who would look out of place with her, with his ink-stained vinyl pocket liner. Now Billy knew that Karen was through with him. And as it sank in he'd finally screwed something up so badly he couldn't change it, his stomach felt sick and sour. He gagged to catch his breath.

Rich pulled up in front of the apartment. The two winos were already outside drinking their breakfast. Billy reached over Ralph to get to the door handle, but Ralph reclined the passenger seat, slumping down deeper until Billy's legs were pinned down in the back seat and he was wedged down against Ralph's weight. Finally, Billy glared at Rich. "Will you get him out of my way before I have to climb over him?"

"We're here, Ralph," Rich said, and sighed when Ralph didn't move. He killed the engine, got out and went around the other side of the car. He tried to lift Ralph up out of his seat by his arm, but Ralph pulled away, and he had to grab him by his ear. Ralph cursed before getting out and walking with his brother, the two of them moving as if they were about to get tangled up with each other. Then, when they were halfway up the sidewalk, Al Jr. got out, hurried past them and opened the door. Billy waited until they were all on the porch before getting out.

Once inside, he had to step over Ralph on his way to the couch. Rich was messing with the TV antenna, but the picture didn't get any clearer. The sound of bombs and machine-gun fire mixing with static unnerved him so much he almost told Rich to shut it off. But then he saw Al Jr. standing in the doorway of his room, his mouth slightly open.

"Holy shit," Al Jr. said, coming back into the living room. "It's the embassy."

"The embassy?" Billy said. "Where?"

"Saigon," he whispered. "But it doesn't make any sense."

"Why?" Rich said. "They're at war, aren't they?"

"Yeah, but they've never attacked during the Tet."

The image shifted to a couple of fallen soldiers at the feet of three others wearily looking above a wall. One of them had a cigarette dangling from his lips as rounds came crashing into the ground around him. Rich's face was pale, and he started to turn the dial, but Al Jr. told him to wait.

"Jesus, Al," Billy said, lying down on the couch. "Can't we watch something else?"

Al Jr. sat down on his chair and continued to stare at the television set. Before Billy drifted off, he heard Al Jr. mumbling.

"They don't fight like that," he said. "That'd be like us attacking at Christmas."

ooo

Al Jr. sat upright in his chair; the front door opening and closing had woken him up. The Blynners were gone, and their jalopy's engine was revving. Billy became restless and turned over, snoring. The television had faded to nothing but static, and even though Al Jr. went over and adjusted the antenna, the picture never came back. He kept trying, thinking maybe something new had happened while he was dozing off, but when he couldn't get anything better than the static outline of a man walking, he shut the television off.

Maybe he'd imagined everything he'd seen or only been dreaming. How many troops had been caught off guard, toasting one another, enjoying a short-lived moment of peace? Maybe the war wasn't going to end in victory as Sgt. Tucker used to say it would in his Southern drawl. His face was usually hidden against the bright glare of the sun, but Al Jr. always imagined him smiling. God knows he said it with a lot of confidence. Maybe the gung-ho, hurrah bullshit was just for show so he wouldn't lose them. Al Jr. would give anything to talk to Sgt. Tucker now, just for a couple of seconds, so he could study his face for lies. But he knew the truth without asking; the slopes had sneaked up and blindsided everyone.

His stomach growled, and he didn't give a damn anymore about the whole rotten mess. He searched through the kitchen cupboards for any food he might've forgotten about, but there wasn't anything, not even a package of crackers. The refrigerator held only a can of moldy corn, hidden behind several beers. He threw the can out and put his coat on. When he opened the door, Billy stirred and asked him where he was going. Billy started snoring again before he had a chance to answer.

Outside, the sun had melted most of the snow on the ground. He unbuttoned his coat and walked down Maple Street, where an old couple named Beasler ran a small grocery. The place smelled of mothballs and analgesic rub, and Mr. Beasler watched him through thick bifocals. He wore an old suit and a fedora hat, which matted the thin wisps of white hair hanging over his ears. Mirrors hung in every corner, and Al Jr. saw him staring at him through them as he went from aisle to aisle, picking through dust-covered cans. Up above, the old woman shuffled around the apartment they lived in. Living where they worked was probably the only way they could survive. They were probably lucky to make a couple of bucks a day.

Finally, Al Jr. had everything he needed — a pound of hamburger for later, a dozen eggs, a bottle of ketchup and a loaf of bread. He hoped Sara liked burgers; other than eggs, they were all he had ever fixed.

He put his stuff down on the counter, and Mr. Beasler craned his neck to see Al Jr.'s tucked-in arm. Kids used to brag about how easy it was to go in there and shoplift stuff, and it appeared the man had finally caught on. So Al Jr. smiled and let his arm dangle. The old man blushed and started ringing up the groceries.

"Sorry, young man," he said, nodding toward his arm. "Been back long?"

"A couple months," Al Jr. said, smiling. "I'd just now be getting out if this wouldn't have happened."

"That's too bad."

"I don't know," Al Jr. said. "After watching the news this morning, I think I got out at the right time."

"Maybe so," Mr. Beasler said, taking the money and giving him his change. "I'm proud of you boys. The hell with what those damned hippies think."

Al Jr. took the sack and thanked him. The door opened, and the old man eyed two young boys who came in and went down separate aisles. Al Jr. wondered whether his father was like that, scrutinizing every young person coming in the bar. He didn't want to think of his father as an old man, but he couldn't deny he was aging. Their mother had often joked about his gray hair and receding hairline, making smart remarks that would send him to the mirror, where he'd try to manipulate it until his hair didn't look as if it was thinning. Only then would their mother — trying hard not to laugh — go over and hug him, saying she was just joking. Maybe he had been self-conscious about being older than she was, especially after they came home one night and he was grumpy because a younger man had asked her to dance. Al Jr. was saddened to think that memories of his family were all he had left to remind him that not everything had been bad, and now what was there? His mother was gone. His father hated him. And Billy couldn't let go of the past.

But in a couple of hours, he'd get to see Sara again. He couldn't wait to call her. And after eating a couple of scrambled eggs and toast, he would.

Inside the apartment, Billy was still sleeping, his long arm hanging over the side of the couch. Then he stopped snoring, and his unfocused eyes stared at the grocery sack through his sheepdog bangs. He mumbled something, and Al Jr. put the sack down on the counter. He washed the skillet and lit the stove with a wooden match. The springs on the couch uncoiled, and Billy came out to the kitchen and stood over him.

"What've you got going?" Billy said, flipping his hair back. "What're you doing?"

"What's it look like?"

"I know what you're doing," he said, hovering even more, "but I thought we were on a hunger strike."

His stringy hair dangled a bit too close to the skillet, and Al Jr. crowded him out of the way. "C'mon, Billy. You can fix your own when I'm done."

Billy grabbed a plate from the cupboard. Then he rummaged through the grocery sack. "Why'd you get burger?"

"Because Sara's coming over."

"That's an awful lot to go through for someone like her."

"What're you talking about?" Al Jr. said.

Billy folded his arms and leaned against the counter, smiling smugly. Al Jr. recognized the look — a painful reminder that Billy was better, smarter and more successful than he'd ever be.

"You should've grooved on her at the party," Billy said, laughing. "But you were way too soaked by then, weren't you?"

Al Jr. pointed the spatula at him. "I've got friends over there, and once we send letters around, they'll find him."

"Sure, Al."

"Why are you staring at me like that?"

Billy nodded toward the skillet. "Your eggs are burning."

Al Jr. turned the stove off. "I asked you something."

"You should have a drink first."

"I don't want one," Al Jr. said. "Just spit it out."

"She comes on to every guy who comes back," Billy said. "Then she dumps them when they can't help her."

The eggs smelled good, and sunlight shone through the kitchen window. But Al Jr. felt like an idiot for tricking himself into thinking there was anything beautiful in the world. People never came as they were; everyone was phony, even a girl like Sara. Why did they say you can't trust anyone over 30? Hell, you couldn't trust anyone period.

He sat down hard on his chair, and Billy came out and sat on the couch. Why couldn't Billy let him find out for himself about Sara? To spare him? What a laugh. The arrogant prick didn't spare anyone, especially him. It wouldn't have killed Billy to let him have one measly day to believe he could make a difference and — silly as it sounded — be someone somebody could care about.

Billy's sneakers tapped so annoyingly out of cadence with each other Al Jr. wished he could've beamed his old drill sergeant, Sgt. Mateo, a foul-tempered son of a bitch with a vicious contempt for anything out of rhythm, into the room and then back out again along with Billy. But he couldn't. Hell, he couldn't even throw Billy out himself. Billy frowned. "What?"

"You're saying she's just some slut out to use me."

"I didn't want to see you get all bummed out," Billy said, his voice a putrid whine.

"Oh, please," Al Jr. said, slumping back in his chair. "You don't think I can handle anything on my own."

"She probably just likes you and—"

"Oh, shut up. Just shut up, will you?" Al Jr. said. "Don't go talking her up after running her down."

"Oh, c'mon—"

"You're a phony—"

"I didn't want her—"

"Like you care," Al Jr. said, his words catching in his throat. "Saint Billy."

Maybe he had been foolish to believe he could fit in a world with normal people. Sara probably would've hit the door before the glue on the envelopes dried out, leaving him wondering why she was in such a hurry to leave, none of it sinking in until later. And then where would he have been? All alone and drunk. Maybe he'd have ended up on the porch, swigging the cheapest wine he could find with Hamlin and Dill and hoping his mind would be so sopped up he'd never think of Sara again.

Billy had probably done him a favor. Sara was probably on the phone in her perfect house, talking to one of her friends and laughing about the silly sap she'd met at the party, wondering how she'd let him down easy. No matter how she would have done it, the pain would have been unbearable.

He drank from the bottle of rye, grimacing from too much all at once. He'd be damned if he'd ever speak to Sara again.

ooo

Billy had ruined what could've been the first normal day since Al Jr. got back. The tension was so high he could barely move. Al Jr. sat in his chair, drinking from his bottle of rye; it was the damnedest thing Billy had ever seen. Half the bottle was gone before Al Jr. went to his room and closed the door.

How could he be so upset over a girl he barely knew? Although, Al Jr. had always been weak when it came to girls. Jealousy always ruined everything for him. He would pull away from a girl whenever he thought he might get hurt. And that's why he had to be warned — just to make sure he knew what he was getting into so he wouldn't end up all crushed.

Billy turned on the television set and sat back down. The reception cleared and then faded back to static. The wind outside picked up and blew against the picture window, combining with the static to make an eerie whistling sound. He went out to the kitchen and ate the cold eggs. Then he put his coat on and went outside. He hoped to find a basketball game somewhere to help him forget everything. But the gym was closed, and he didn't have a basketball. Across the bridge, he might find a game at Riverside. Most kids there didn't have a chance at playing organized ball, and they rarely went out for the team. If he was lucky, none of them would recognize him. Although, they'd notice his jacket. Maybe they'd believe he was a runner or a football player.

He walked along a path on the Eel River and came out close to the carousel. A ball bounced in the distance. But he moaned when he came around the corner. There were four kids — three of them runts — chasing after whoever had the ball and forcing one another into taking off-balance shots. While he watched, none of them came close to making a basket. Even the big kid, who was at least a head taller than his friends, could hardly sink anything. Billy sat on a bench, facing away from them. But nobody came down the road to kick the squirts off the court.

The ball quit bouncing, and one of the little kids yelled, "Look out!"

As he turned around, the ball sailed past his head. He stood up. The smallest runt, a carrot-topped freckle-faced kid, came running toward the ball and then came to an awkward halt that almost made him fall on his face. The boy recovered and smiled up at him.

"You're Billy Hennessy," he said, turning toward his friends. "It's Billy Hennessy!"

He was about to bawl the kid out, but the boy was tongue-twisted even as the other kids came over and stood next to him. The biggest kid, who was all of about 5'6", looked Billy up and down with a cocky smile.

"Do you want to play 21?"

Billy laughed. "I'd wipe you out, kid."

"You're just afraid one of us will beat you."

"Beat me?" he said. "None of you guys can even hit a basket left all alone."

All of them groaned and argued about who could shoot and who couldn't. After listening for a while, Billy whistled and cut them off. "OK, I'll tell you what. We'll have a free-throw contest, and if any of you beat me, I'll spot you all the first 15 points."

The small boy waved his hands in the air, forgetting he had the ball underneath his arm. It rolled away. "I can't shoot from that far out!"

"What?" Billy said. "Who nearly hit me with the ball?"

"Me," he said.

"So you can throw the ball clear over here, but you can't hit a free throw?"

The boy shook his head.

"If you use your legs to get some lift on your shot, I'll bet you could hit one."

The tall boy laughed. "He doesn't know what he's talking about. You shoot with your arms."

"Oh?" Billy said. "How many points a game do you score?"

One of the other kids, a fat boy with long shaggy hair, pointed at him. "He got cut from the team."

They all laughed except the tall boy, who lowered his head and started walking toward the court. "C'mon, let's go."

"I want to see if he's right," the small boy said, looking back up at Billy. "Will you show me what you mean?"

"I'll do even better," Billy said. "If any one of you mutts beats me, I'll buy you all a pop."

The three small kids cheered and ran past the tall kid, who shot Billy a dirty look. It was the same look Lonny had given him when they first played together in the fourth grade and Lonny thought he was the best player because he was twice the size of everyone else. Back then, they all stank; listening to the coaches and practicing drills was what helped make Billy better than everyone else. As time passed, Lonny kept moving farther and farther away from the coach on the bench. Finally, he learned to practice, but Billy always thought he would've been better if he had taken the game more seriously when they were younger. This kid wasn't any different. Billy stood at the free-throw line. The small boy tossed the ball to him, and he bounced the ball three times before aiming and releasing it. The ball arced in the air, looking as if it would drop right in, but then it hit the front of the rim and bounced back to him.

"Great shot, superstar," the tall boy said.

Billy ignored him — the only thing to do with a trash talker. He'd learned that when he was a freshman and played Kokomo for the first time. Kokomo's point guard, Tyrone Strong, talked a lot. Some of the older players on Richland tried to get him off balance by doing the same thing, but Tyrone only got better and tore them up even more. So Billy imagined they were playing a game and trailing by 8 points with hardly any time left. In Billy's fantasy, Tyrone had talked so much trash the referees decided to let Billy take free throws until he missed one.

Back on the court, the tall boy was waiting for the ball to bounce out so he could make another remark. The next two rolled around on the rim, but they went in. And when Billy started swishing one shot after another, the cocky smirk disappeared. After the last one went in, Billy smiled at the kid. "Well, there you go. All you have to do is hit 10 in a row."

The tall boy went to the line, a serious frown on his face, and aped his form perfectly; he even bounced the ball three times before shooting it. But each time he released the ball, there was a slight twitch, just enough to make his shots slightly off. Still, he hit five out of 10, which was better than the others. The fat kid and the rail-thin one, who hadn't yet said a word, only hit two apiece. The runt, who jumped in the air, throwing the ball instead of shooting, was even worse. Billy told him to straighten his arm, and once the kid started to listen, he came close to hitting his last shot. And in the next round, the little kid actually got a couple of shots to go in. The others did a little better, too, and the tall boy almost hit eight out of 10; his last shot bounced in and out of the rim.

The sun had begun to lower along the tree line, and it was getting too dark to play. Billy turned toward the trail. "I'd better get going."

"Yeah, me, too," the small boy said. "We're here about every Saturday, if you want to play again."

Billy smiled. "We'll see, kid."

The tall boy came up to him and stretched. "I think I'll be able to beat you by then."

"It'll take more than your mouth," Billy said. He reached in his pocket, pulled out a handful of quarters and handed them to the small boy.

"Thanks, Billy."

Then they were off running toward the pop machines by the pavilion, laughing all the way. They disappeared in the shadows, and Billy heard the pops hitting the bottom of the machine's tray. He kept waiting for them to come back, but they didn't reappear until they came out the other side. The small boy turned around and waved before they all went down an alley off 15th Street, their laughter fading until there was nothing but silence.

•••

Chapter 13

Al Jr. cursed at what was left of his egg sandwich on the floor. It had fallen out of his hand for no reason and splattered ketchup all over the bell of his jeans on its way down. He picked the messy sandwich up and threw it in the trash. His hand wouldn't quit twitching, and his head was throbbing. What little he had eaten made his stomach roll. There had been a tense silence all day Sunday, and that had unnerved him, and now that he was finally alone on Monday, it was worse. He wanted to sleep until Billy went to school the next day, maybe even change his hours around so they'd never have to be around each other. A car pulled up outside as he headed for his room. Two car doors opened and shut. It was only 3:30, and Billy wasn't due for an hour and a half. But then the screen door opened and closed. A pair of footsteps, one much heavier than the other, came down the hallway.

"Al," Billy said through the door. "I brought someone with me."

Al Jr. cursed, thinking Billy must have one of the Blynners with him, but the footsteps were too quiet, and he hadn't heard the car halfway down the block. Then a girl spoke in a soft voice. Was there ever an end to Billy's boldness? He probably wanted to use Al Jr.'s bedroom for another fling just so he could rub Al Jr.'s face further in the dirt. Al Jr. thought to himself that maybe he'd keep the door locked until Billy went away and then put Billy's clothes outside for him to pick up later. But he wanted Billy to know how much he'd worn out his welcome before he finally threw him out and he could ignore Billy's bitching with a clear conscience. He opened the door.

"Why aren't you at practice?"

"Because, Dad," he said, cocking his thumb over his shoulder, "I brought someone to see you."

He waited for one of Billy's cheerleaders to come in the room, someone who would probably spout off about how run down the place was, but when Billy stood out of the way, Sara came in behind him.

"Hi, Al," she said. She raised her head until their eyes met. "I waited all day yesterday for you to call."

Al Jr. quickly lowered his head. The pain on her face convinced him Billy had already had a talk with her, probably about their ugly conversation yesterday. Everything was making him dizzy — her sad, timid frown and the uncharacteristically humble smile on Billy's face. He wanted to barricade himself in his room and hide under his blanket. He began to turn away, but Billy grabbed his arm.

"What's wrong?"

"I don't want anyone here," Al Jr. said, his voice hoarse.

Sara stood in between them. "Would you quit acting like I'm not right here?"

"I can't help you," Al Jr. said. "I don't think anyone can."

"I don't understand."

"I don't know, Sara. Maybe your brother's in one of their camps, but the jungle probably opened up and swallowed him."

At first, she just stood there, uncomprehending, almost as if she hadn't heard him. Then she put her hand up to her face to wipe away tears.

"You're just being hateful," she said. "One of these days, Stu's going to…"

Each word was weaker than the one before, until they finally caught in her throat and she couldn't say anything else. She ran down the hallway and out the front door. The screen door thwacked several times before stopping.

Billy stood still until the sound of her car starting up forced him to jump. "Oh, shit," he said, hurrying out the door as she sped away. Then he threw his arms up in the air. "Now I've got to walk."

Al Jr. said nothing. Billy said, "You screwed this one up all by yourself, so don't blame me."

Then he was gone. Al Jr. shut the door and locked it. He ran to the bathroom and vomited on the floor, not quite reaching the toilet. He cleaned up his mess and splashed cold water on his face. His head was still hot when he put his hand up to his forehead. He felt so low it took him several seconds before he could even look at himself in the mirror. Red dots had broken out on his face. He was getting sick.

Sara's devotion to her brother was powerful yet simplistic. She seemed to believe she could will him alive whether he or anyone else believed her. Outside of God — which his mother had pounded into his head for as long as he could remember — he believed in very little. He knew winter lasted longer than any other season, and summer would become so hot and miserable by August that he always wished it would just end. Other things were easy to believe, too, as long as he had seen them over and over. But Sara? Her strength was something he'd never had. He hoped that she'd soon forget his ugly words and that sooner or later, he'd just be a faded memory. She'd keep on writing letters. Whatever her reasoning was, he shouldn't have tried to destroy her faith just because she might've hurt him down the road. Besides, what the hell did a drunk like him know anyhow? How to pour a shot of whiskey maybe, but not much else. And hell, Stuart still could be alive. Hadn't Sgt. Tucker often preached against wandering too far by asking them how they'd like to spend the rest of their lives shackled, being moved from camp to camp with nothing more than a small amount of rice and a little bit of water to keep them going? Once, he'd told them about a prisoner they'd found in an abandoned village whose mind was so far gone he couldn't even tell them his name. Al Jr. realized Sgt. Tucker would take her letters seriously — he might even have some ideas — and decided to write to him.

His closet door bulged open from the overstuffed duffel bag hanging on a hook. He removed the bag, barely able to hold it in his hand, and lowered it to the floor. The clasp was tight and rusty, and when he opened it, several letters fell out. He picked up the one on top, from Pfc. Doofenhaus. Old Doofus never got tired or relaxed until everything was done. Things never got completely done in the field, which seemed to suit him. On the dairy farm where he was raised, somewhere in Wisconsin, his father worked him from sunup to sundown. So he never complained about work, even if it was something as tedious as digging trenches or filling sandbags. Often, he would finish digging his own foxhole and then help someone else with his. Just seeing his name made Al Jr. feel guilty for not opening his letter sooner. There were specks of blood on the inside of the envelope, and the paper had dirt smudges, making the words difficult to read.

> *Dear Al,*
> *We got hit pretty hard today and something bad happened, buddy, something really bad. I feel like I'm in a fog. For some reason they sent us to the border and Charlie's real thick down here. Snipers are everywhere, taking shots at us all day and night. Just this morning they got lucky and killed Sgt. Tucker and Cpl. Sullivan and we had to wait all morning for the chopper to come and get them and we just loaded their bodies.*

The letter fell out of Al Jr.'s trembling fingertips. Those specks of blood had to be from Sgt. Tucker or Cpl. Sullivan. What kind of fear had everyone felt watching those two die? Sgt. Tucker — a black man from Mississippi everyone looked up to — and Cpl. Sullivan, a big burly Irishman from the Bronx, killed on the same day. How was it possible?

Then he opened more of the letters; one after another, they were all the same. Junior Selby, a member of his basic training class, had been blown in half bumbling through a tripwire. Carey Pat, the lanky kid from Catalina who smiled all the time, had been killed by friendly fire. Sam Drake, the little guy they called the chicken hawk, had gone down in a helicopter crash. And they kept coming, all in all reporting the deaths of eight soldiers he had served with — eight men he had thought of as alive until then.

He sat back on the bed, too numb to move. Could it be possible there were more letters piling up in the mailroom of the hospital?

Were these men who were writing about dead men dead themselves now? Maybe the letters had stopped coming; maybe there wasn't anyone left to write them. Maybe he was the lucky one. He slipped in and out of sleep until the memory of his last day there overtook him.

Rain had been coming down for days, and VC movement had picked up around them, when Capt. Morris sent them to a village to gather information from the town elder, Vu Tran, a little old man so well-known for his hatred of the VC they'd already had to protect his village several times from being attacked.

So they went out through the muddy trail, all of them tense and jumpy. They traveled through the night, reaching the village at daybreak, thinking the pounding rain was the reason they didn't see a single person.

They went straight to Vu's hut and knocked on the door. When there was no answer, Sgt. Tucker motioned for silence and opened the door slowly. He whispered for Selby and the rest of them to follow him. Al Jr. went in last and gasped when he saw Vu, his head resting on the table, a bullet hole through the top of his skull.

They went through the other 11 huts; all were empty and had bowls of rice sitting on their tables, as if everyone had just gone for a walk and hadn't yet returned. Outside, Cpl. Sullivan knelt down beside a southern road that went about a hundred yards before disappearing in the tree line. He called Sgt. Tucker over, and before long they were arguing. Cpl. Sullivan pointed down the road, while Sgt. Tucker patted his shoulder and motioned for the corporal to follow.

"You mean we're not going after them?" Cpl. Sullivan said.

Sgt. Tucker shook his head, a look of fear on his face. The sergeant was a brave man, braver than most, but whenever he got that look, something bad happened. Never failed.

"We're getting out of here," he said. "We came here to ask Vu a question, and I don't think he could've answered it any better."

Cpl. Sullivan stamped his foot in the mud. "Those people might still be alive!"

"No," Sgt. Tucker said. "They're dead. Charlie wants us to come after them. Hell, they're probably down there waiting for us. If we hurry out of here, we might make it back before they realize we're not coming."

None of them wanted to leave the villagers, but they retreated, the sounds of the jungle becoming more intense once the rain stopped coming down. A couple of miles away from the base camp, someone said something about movement in the jungle behind them, and a shot rang out — and then another. Soon, bullets came whizzing in at them from almost every direction. Al Jr. ran ahead of the new guy, Pope, who gasped and screamed. Al Jr. went to help him up, when Al Jr. left arm jerked backward and his hand exploded. At first, he felt nothing — the shock had been a blessing — but then it was as if his whole arm were on fire, and he fell to the ground.

He was about to pass out, when he felt someone pulling him up. Sgt. Tucker dragged him over a hill. He began to drift off again, thinking it odd he was going to die in a muddy ravine with his hand blown off. But he didn't die. He woke up on a chopper, a tourniquet on his wrist, the pain so unbearable he passed out again. When he woke up again, he was in a hospital bed with so much morphine in him everything seemed like a waking dream.

Just as he had then, he drifted off to a dark, dreamless sleep. When he woke up, he jumped to his feet, thinking the letters had been a boozy hallucination. But they were lying on the floor where he had knocked them.

He went out to the living room, looking for a dime. He ransacked the drawers and pulled the cushions up. And there, where Billy slept, Al Jr. found one in the couch. He put his coat on and went outside to a phone in front of several empty stores. He reached in his pocket and found Sara's number. The phone rang several times, making him think he had misread her number. Then the ringing stopped, and Sara's voice was on the other end.

"Hello?" she repeated. "Is anyone there?"

"Sara," he said. "Please don't hang up."

She sighed. "Is this Al?"

"Yes."

"I don't have anything to say to you except goodbye."

"But I want to help."

"Why?" she said. "As far as you're concerned, my brother's a bag of bones rotting away in the jungle, right?"

Sweat drenched his hand until the phone nearly slipped out. What could he say to smooth things over? Nothing, that's what. Would she really care if he told her he'd had a revelation that this was his last chance to do something important? No, she'd tell him to go straight to hell because he'd already blown more chances than he deserved.

"So you've got nothing to say for yourself?"

He took a deep breath and rested his head against the booth's glass. "Please, Sara," he said. "Yesterday I was watching the news about the embassy getting overrun—"

"What's that got to do with the way you—"

"Nothing. You're right," he said. "After you left, I opened the letters I had from the hospital. I'd have never opened them if it wasn't for you, and I wished I hadn't, because a lot of the guys I knew over there are dead."

"Now I'm supposed to feel sorry for you after the rotten thing you—"

"Damn it, no," he said. Then, in a softer tone, he said, "I need to help you."

"I'm not sure."

"Please, Sara, just let me help you," he said. "After that, you'll never have to see me again."

"If it wasn't for Stu, I'd tell you to shove it," she said. "But you'd better not be drunk. I swear, if you act like a horse's ass, I'll, I'll…"

"I won't. I promise."

"I'll be there after school tomorrow."

"Good. I'll see you then," he said. He listened for a moment, thinking he might hear her speak again or hear her breathe. But the line went dead, so he hung up and went home. Despite the night's cold breeze, Hamlin and Dill were sitting on the porch drinking their wine, and he said hello, even called them by name, but they ignored him, looking away as they sipped from their paper bags. He laughed as he went back inside. He noticed how messed up everything was. Litter cluttered almost every square inch of the carpet. Cobwebs wound around the ceiling corners, so thick they looked like banners. Beer cans were arranged in a carefully constructed pyramid. Then there was that god-awful stench. Where was it coming from? Maybe everywhere. And if so, Sara had surely noticed earlier.

He opened the kitchen closet. A new stench, dank and musty, came from a mop head that had been in there so long it was stuck to the floor. He peeled it up off the floor and soaked it in a bucket full of hot water and Ajax. Then he gathered the rest of the closet supplies — a rusty can of Lysol, an old broom and dustpan, and a half-empty box of trash bags — and got busy.

He picked up the trash on the floor and threw away his empty bottles. The apartment began looking different to him, and the air didn't seem so stale. It wasn't anything his mother — who'd kept their house spotless — would have been satisfied with, but a half-hour in, all the trash had been picked up, and the only thing left to do was mop the floors and spray the toilet down with Lysol. Once he was close to being finished, Billy came in, looking at him as if he'd lost his mind.

"Damn it, Al. Coach Randle made me stay over," he said. "Why are you cleaning?"

Al Jr. sat down on the chair and smiled at him. "Sara's coming over tomorrow."

Billy laughed and spun his long index finger in circles around the side of his head. "You been smoking dope, or are you crazier than I thought you were?"

"I called her," Al Jr. said. "She's not happy with me, but she still wants my help."

Billy slumped back on the couch and pouted. Oh well, there wasn't any reason to argue with him now. More than likely, Sara would trip over her own feet getting out of there the next day, but so what? What did Al Jr. have to lose? He wasn't going to be any worse off for trying than if he just sat around sloshed. And who could tell? Maybe their letters would make all the difference in the world. And that's what Al Jr. told Billy. If Billy didn't like it, then so be it.

"Jesus, Al," Billy said. "You don't think much of me, do you?"

"Well... I don't... I mean..."

"Why would I bring her here if that's how I am?"

Al Jr. took the mop out to the kitchen and mopped the floor. And then he mopped the bathroom and sprayed the toilet down with

Lysol. As he poured the water in the toilet, Billy came down the hallway.

"C'mon, let's go grab a sandwich."

Al Jr. put the pile of moldy clothes in a trash bag. There were still cobwebs to sweep, and his room was still a mess.

"Oh, c'mon, Al," Billy said. "It wouldn't kill you to walk a few blocks."

"Why? If you're hungry, go fix yourself an egg sandwich."

"Whoever heard of eating eggs for supper?"

"Fix a burger then," Al Jr. said, opening up his bedroom door. "But just one. Sara might want one, too, tomorrow."

Billy moaned, and Al Jr. went inside his room. There weren't any trash bags left, so he had to start putting trash in his closet. Once finished, he sprayed Lysol in the air, found a pen and paper, and went out to the table. He thought about what to write, how he would word his letter and who, besides the guys he hoped were still alive — Doofus, Pvt. Roth, Cpl. Temple and Capt. Morris — might help them the most. The brass at the battalion would probably throw out anything sent to them from a private, but he wouldn't know one way or the other, so he decided to at least send them one, maybe another from Sara, and hope they'd land on someone's desk who still cared.

"I'll buy you a beer," Billy said, leaning over him, his hair draping down over the paper. Al Jr. jumped and nearly knocked his pen off the table.

"Christ, man," he said. "If I wanted a drink right now, I wouldn't be messing with this."

"You've got all day tomorrow to write," Billy said. "It wouldn't kill you to come out for a while."

Jesus, Billy never let up. Al Jr. began gathering his stuff; maybe if he went to his room and shut the door, Billy would finally get the message. But Billy looked so down Al Jr. felt a strange kinship. It was as if for the first time, he could see how they were brothers and not just two kids who'd grown up in the same house. So he set his stuff back down on the table and put his coat on.

"Did you change your mind?" Al Jr. said, opening the door. Billy smiled and hurried out the door. By the time Al Jr. locked it, he had to run to catch up with his brother.

"Where're we going?" he asked. "And where're you going to be able to buy a beer?"

"Crayton's," Billy said. "They don't ever card anybody."

No, they didn't, but there was more to worry about than the police. Erie Avenue was where most of the bikers lived, and Crayton's, the smallest of four bars sitting catty-corner from one another, was across the street from the Eagle's Nest. Some of the roughest people in town hung out there, and some of the most shiftless hung out at Roy's, the place on the corner across from it. The barflies there were known to work for the owner doing odd jobs and then drink their earnings away. But it was winter, and there weren't any yards for them to mow or trees to shear. And sure enough, as they walked toward Crayton's, a man sitting on the steps at Roy's shot up, took off his derby hat and ran across the street toward them.

They were standing in front of Gabe's, where the hippies hung out. It was a rundown building whose roof tiles had fallen on the sidewalk. The last thing Al Jr. wanted was to hand the old man money there. Billy, who'd yet to even acknowledge the old man, went inside.

But Al Jr. gave him more than a passing glance. His face was weather-beaten, the lines there as deep as trenches, but there was something strange about it, as if it had once been a happy face. The man had probably learned a long time ago that nobody was going to give anything to a bum with a happy face. Before he spoke, the man lowered his head.

"Could you spare some change?"

Al Jr. was about to say no, that he didn't have any change, which was true, but couldn't. Instead, he reached down in his pocket and found a couple of crumpled-up dollar bills. He handed over the money. The old man smiled, did an exaggerated bow and put the hat back on his head. "Thank you, sonny!"

Then he was gone, running across the street faster than a deer and opening the door at Roy's Place. Through the window, Al Jr. saw the bartender pointing toward the door before the old man held the money in the air.

The door opened behind Al Jr., and Billy was hanging out of the doorway. "You never could resist a sob story, could you?"

"No," he said, turning around and going up the steps. "That's why I'm stuck with you."

Billy laughed. Inside, a bunch of old men sat lined up at the bar; none of them even glanced their way as they sat down. The bartender, a big man with greased-back hair and a face so fat his thin-slit eyes were barely visible, waited for their order.

"What can I get you?"

"A pitcher of Hamm's and a cheeseburger," Billy said, swiveling around on the stool toward Al Jr. "You want anything to eat?"

"No, I've got food at home."

The bartender filled up a pitcher and sat two frosted mugs down in front of them. After he walked away, Al Jr. looked over at Billy, who'd already filled his mug and gunned down his beer. "What's eating you?" Al Jr. asked.

Billy filled his mug again. "Coach Randle got all over me for being late."

"I'm sorry," Al Jr. said. He wanted nothing less than to forget the afternoon. The more he thought about the way he'd acted the more he dreaded seeing Sara. He took a sip of beer and put the mug down. "You didn't tell him why you were late?"

Billy let out a harsh laugh. "He wouldn't have cared."

The bartender brought out Billy's cheeseburger. He looked at their pitcher, saw it was still half-full and walked away. Billy crammed half the burger in his mouth so forcefully Al Jr. thought he might bite off one of his fingers. He said something with his mouth full, and Al Jr. had to ask him to repeat what he'd said. He waited until the last of his sandwich was gone and he had taken a gulp of beer.

"I'm not so sure I'm going to play next year."

"Something happen to your scholarship?" Al Jr. said.

"Nothing happened," he said. "I'm just tired of being told what to do."

"Nobody likes that," Al Jr. said, "but it's better than being told what to do and shot at."

"I don't think they'll shoot me for not playing."

"I'm not talking about here," Al Jr. said. "I mean over there."

"I don't need basketball to go to school."

"Dad can't afford to send you."

"Then I might put it off awhile," Billy said, drinking the last of his beer and belching. "The hell with it."

"Yeah, well, I opened my letters."

"What letters?"

"From Vietnam." Al Jr. swiveled around toward Billy. "You have to read them before you do anything."

"Why?"

"Read them and you'll know why."

"My grades are good enough to get into school," Billy said. "Maybe I could get a part-time job."

"Your grades are good because Dad always got on you. He knew you'd only get there with a scholarship. Now you're saying you can make it on 30 bucks a month?"

Billy frowned, a look very much like the one their father always had. Then he whispered something Al Jr. didn't quite hear.

"What?"

"Maybe I should go."

"Back home?" Al Jr. said, relieved. Billy seemed to be coming to his senses. But Billy's somber expression never changed.

"What makes me any better than you, Stu or your friend Freddy?"

A chill ran down Al Jr.'s back. He still had the Hopalong Cassidy watch Freddy had given him before he shipped out for basic training. Freddy was a tall black kid with hardly any friends at all. There'd been something haunted about him when he handed the watch over. And when his mother came in right afterward to hurry him along, Freddy looked around his bedroom — stopping on posters of Otis Redding, the Four Tops and Marvin Gaye — and wiped away tears, saying he'd never stand in the room again. And he never did, either. He lasted a couple of weeks over there. Dead when a child came up to the jeep he was in and detonated a bomb. And Stu? They'd probably never know what happened to him. "You know I'm the only one who came back, don't you?"

Billy winked. "But you're going to save Stu, aren't you?"

"I hope so."

Billy poured the rest of the beer in his mug and motioned for another pitcher. Al Jr. felt tired, and he could hardly stay awake. "I'm going home," he said. "I'll leave the door unlocked."

"Wait, Al." Billy grabbed hold of his arm. "Just one more."

"I've got things to do," Al Jr. said. "What about you?"

"What about me?"

"Are you going to school hung over?"

"I could care less."

"Well, I'll see you tomorrow," Al Jr. said, pulling away from his grip. Outside, walking down the sidewalk, Al Jr. heard running footsteps approaching. It was Billy catching up with him.

"You could've at least waited for me."

They walked along the sidewalk in silence. A light snow began to fall, and Al Jr. smelled trash burning in the distance. The odor grew pungent enough to make his eyes water. They came to an alleyway where a fire flickered in a barrel. The flame jumped and fell as it shone on three old men surrounding the barrel. The old panhandler from the bar smiled and held up a light-green bottle like a trophy.

"Bless you, sonny!" he said, his friends smiling with him. "God knows about your kindness!"

● ● ●

Chapter 14

Morning sunlight spilled through the window, shining on Billy's face and waking him up. He sat up and massaged his temples, but the dull ache in his head wouldn't go away. He would have given anything for a couple of aspirin pills but knew from searching in Al Jr.'s medicine cabinet that there weren't any. Then he realized everything was too bright and looked up at the clock; it was well after 9. He started to hurry out the door, worrying about being on the absence report, but then stopped. Late was late. So he took his time getting ready — the bathroom was so clean he didn't mind being in there — and by the time he left, the sun had warmed things up and there wasn't any wind at all.

At school, the hallways were empty; third period was already halfway over. He went into Mr. Stringer's classroom. A few kids started mumbling, and then he saw why. Mr. Stringer had picked up a piece of paper, pointed down at it and looked over at Billy.

"You're on the absence report," he said, his timid voice barely audible. "You'll have to go to the office and get a tardy slip."

Billy slumped in his seat before standing up. As Billy was making his way to the door, Mr. Stringer pushed his glasses up and smiled at him. "Sorry, Billy. School policy."

He headed toward the office, blocking out the voices coming from the classrooms he passed by. Getting sent to the office didn't bother him; if they wanted to make a big deal about his being late for the first time ever, then so be it. He'd just walk right out the door and go back to the apartment. But the sight of Miss Jones, the receptionist, made his stomach turn. Her beady eyes followed him to the desk, but she didn't say anything. Billy cleared his throat and sat down in the chair across from her.

"I, uh, overslept this morning," he said. "Mr. Stringer said I needed a pass."

"I'll give you one, but your parents will need to excuse you."

"Why?"

"Because, young man," she said, drawling in a cold tone, "as far as I know, you could've been doing just about anything."

She took a yellow slip out of the top drawer and began writing, but then she stopped. She looked at him for a long time, pretending she didn't know who he was and waiting for him to tell her.

"Billy Hennessy," he said. "My mother's dead, and I'm not staying with my father."

She put her pen down and folded her hands. "Your father called regarding your attendance."

"When?"

"Last week," she said, leaning forward. "How old are you, William?"

"Billy," he said, his tone harsher than he meant it to be. "And I'm 18."

"Your father still has to excuse you."

"Oh, c'mon."

"That's the rule."

No wonder no one liked dealing with her. A kid ought to get a break the first time he screws up, Billy thought to himself. But grown-ups always had to kick kids around, just to show they could. Worse, Miss Jones enjoyed watching him squirm; a slight smile twitched on her face, and he almost walked out of the office. The only thing keeping him from doing so was that she'd surely call his father then.

"Don't bother," he said. "What now?"

"Detention until 4 o'clock," she said, filling out the slip. She handed the paper to him without looking up and then noticed him writing on it. "You'd better not be changing it to an excused absence."

He held the slip out to her. "I told you, it's Billy."

The third-period bell was about to ring, and Billy walked slowly to his locker and put his books away. The woman had some damn nerve pretending she didn't know who he was. How couldn't she? Her office sat across the hall from the display case with all the school's athletic achievements, pictures of him on every shelf.

The smell of Brussels sprouts and boiled chicken from the cafeteria lingered in the air and made him woozy. He headed for the narrow table where the rest of the team sat. Turning the corner, he jumped back in the shadows. Coach Randle sat at the table. He was talking to them, his hands flailing all over the place as Lonny, Chad and the rest of them sat quietly. It didn't make any sense. Coach Randle should've been watching over a study hall on the first floor. When Coach stood up and looked around, Billy ducked out the door to the smoking area. Coach Randle would never think of trying to find him there. The kids out there took deep drags off their cigarettes, blowing smoke toward him. He had no more business there than they had at a basketball game.

Through the window, he saw Coach Randle disappear around the corner of the stairway. Billy went back in, slouched down and hurried off in the opposite direction. He looked around a pillar to the table. Lonny ranted and raved, his hands flailing in the air exactly as the coach's had. Billy walked away toward the stairs.

He should've stayed at Al Jr.'s all day. Coach was going to let him have it, maybe make him run a little more, a little harder, until he bent and broke. But that'd have to wait a few hours. Nobody would bother him in study hall, where the shop teacher, Mr. Morrison, a man who'd lost more fingers than he still had, usually sat at his desk reading Popular Mechanics. He blocked kids out so well he never noticed when someone was being a little loud or fell asleep.

Billy walked toward the large hall as the fourth-period bell rang. He felt as if he could sleep standing up if he wanted to. But he nearly backed out of the room when he saw Coach Randle sitting at the desk. His face was strangely cagey, as if he really wanted to rip him good and could hardly control himself. Coach Randle motioned

Billy over to the desk, and as he approached it, Billy saw the strain on his face in his tightly drawn lips. Coach Randle's shirt was soaked in the way it was when they were in a game he knew they were going to lose. Then the coach unbuttoned the top button of his shirt and cleared his throat.

"What's this I hear about you running away from home?" he said. "And not showing up this morning until after 10:30?"

"I overslept."

"And running—"

"That's none of your business."

"None of my business?" he said, his mouth twitching. "Is anything anymore? You were late for practice yesterday, and I let it slide. What's next? Are you going to show up at halftime Friday night?"

"No, Coach," Billy said, looking away. "I just overslept."

"I don't like what I'm seeing here," Coach Randle said, stiffening up. "I can smell booze on you from here. Who're you staying with? Nobody seems to know, or they aren't saying."

"I'm staying with my brother."

The coach's eyes widened, and he scowled. "You stayed up all night drinking with your brother, huh?"

It made Billy sad, always had, the way people mentioned his brother with such contempt, especially the teachers who — as far back as the sixth grade — always acted strangely toward him whenever they found out they were brothers.

"Boy, nobody's going to be happy until I admit my brother's a piece of trash."

"I never—"

"It doesn't matter anymore," Billy said. "I think I'm going to quit playing after the season's over anyway."

Coach Randle acted as if he hadn't heard him, but his look of authority faded to stunned anxiety. For a moment, Billy thought he might even cry.

"Quit?" he said. "Did your brother—"

"Stop it, Coach," Billy said. His voice was so loud the other students coming through the door stopped and glanced their way. When he spoke again, he whispered. "Al doesn't have anything to do with it."

"But—"

"I'll turn my uniform in today if you want me to."

"No," Coach Randle said shortly. "I want you at practice when you're done with detention. Is that OK with you?"

Billy sighed and looked down. "Yes."

"All right, go have a seat," he said. Then he went to the door, his footsteps fading down the hall until they were distant clip-clops. Billy sat down in the back row, and Mr. Morrison came into the room and started reading a magazine he pulled from his back pocket.

Billy opened his history book and pretended he was studying, but his lids became heavy, and he rested his head down on the desk. Until last night, he had no idea how much booze Al Jr. had tucked away. He found out, all right, getting Al Jr. to drink even though he didn't want to, arguing back and forth about everything. Pretty soon, Al Jr. was pulling out bottles from all his different hiding spots. Once they were both soused, he went to his room and came out with a handful of letters. Specks of blood and dirt covered the first one, a horrible story about two men getting killed by a sniper. Some letters were written in such shaky handwriting the guys writing them must've been out of their minds. Certainly, the horror in their letters was enough to drive anyone insane. A shame overcame him for attending Andy Cross's student rally, especially because most of the guys Al Jr. had served with had been drafted. Everything seemed so unfair. Why did so many people take it out on kids forced to serve when the politicians were the ones causing all the trouble?

Voices in the classroom and the hallway mingled like a swarm of hornets surrounding him. Then a voice cut through the sound, calling out his name and filling him with a crippling fear that made it impossible to do anything but sit there and wait.

"Billy! Billy, where are you?" his father said from the hallway. Then there was an argument; maybe one of the teachers had asked him to leave. But his voice kept getting louder and louder, until he was standing in the doorway. Billy expected him to be angry, but instead, he looked hurt and confused. Then — as if he had unfinished business with Billy — Big Al straightened up, lowered his head and barreled forward toward Billy. Billy tried to stand, but his body was helplessly immobile as his father came closer, with his outstretched hands ready to snag him up from his seat.

The hands jerked Billy around, but he was able to stand up, his fists balled up. Once Billy awakened, his father disappeared, and a timid redheaded kid with a cowlick stood in his place holding his hands out defensively.

"I'm sorry," the kid said frantically. "I didn't think you'd want to miss your next class."

Everyone had left except for the two of them. Billy smiled and nodded at the kid. "Thanks."

He picked his books up and headed toward his locker, where a group of loafing kids stood around laughing. He cut through them, opened up his locker and tensed up when he heard Karen's voice nearby.

"That's no surprise," she said. "That's why I dumped him in the first place."

Billy hunched down, hoping he could get low enough to avoid her noticing him. But he turned around, and she was standing right in front of him.

"I can't get away from you," she said. "Do you know how many kids have come up to me since that damned party?"

Her badgering never had an end, ever. She didn't want him back, and even if she did, he'd never be forgiven for screwing up, which was something he'd give anything to take back. She'd cornered him before a couple of times; now he couldn't take it. So he tried to find an escape route, but she had him blocked in completely. He put his hands on her arms to move her, but she shook him off.

"What?"

"Quit it," she said, her voice cracking. "How could you — I mean, my best friend."

He began to ask her why she always had to make a scene whenever she heard about his being with someone; it could've been Carla or a girl she didn't know or would never know. But before he could say anything, she turned around and hurried down the hallway.

ooo

Back at Al Jr.'s place, Billy went straight to the couch, and the small living room was soon echoing his snores. It would've been nice if he would've done that last night before their drinking carried on until 3 in the morning. Al Jr. could barely keep his coffee down. Worst of all, Sara caught him every time he massaged his temple or grimaced in pain. Right when she'd walked in two hours ago, she'd crinkled her nose and acted as if she might get sick.

"I didn't notice yesterday, but this place smells like a barn."

"What're you talking about?" Al Jr. said. "I mopped the floor yesterday."

"With what?" she said. "Dirty toilet water?"

"I'm sorry."

She let out a groan and sat down at the table. Then she organized her things in an amusing way; her envelopes and paper flanked each other in their own neat piles. She took a pen out of her purse and began writing, her hand moving with a purposeful fury. The absurdity of it all struck him. How could a young girl and a shellshocked hermit find someone who'd gone missing in the vast, chaotic jungles of Vietnam? When she looked up at him, a cross frown coming over her face, he worried she could sense his skepticism. He started to massage his forehead before picking up his mug off the table.

"Would you like some coffee or maybe a hamburger?" he asked timidly.

"There's no way I'd eat anything out of there," she said, pointing out to the kitchen. "Why don't you get over here and do something?"

"Hold on," he said, going out to the kitchen and filling his cup. When he came back to the table and set it down, a little coffee spilled, landing several inches away from Sara's envelopes. She pulled them toward her and shook her head. "Watch what you're doing."

He wiped up the drops of coffee with his shirtsleeve. "I wish you'd quit snapping at me."

Her irritated frown faded to a merely peeved one, and he tried to smile at her, but his mouth twitched. To his surprise, she started laughing — a hearty, girlish laugh — and it made him laugh, too. She was much prettier when she smiled. There was a glint to her eyes, and her dimples were larger. Soon, his hand quit shaking, and he forgot about his hangover. He sat down and picked up the letters he'd begun writing earlier.

She went through her purse, and her hand came out clutching a manila envelope. She took out several pictures and slid them across the table carefully, so as not to smudge them. Several seconds passed before she let go.

"Do you remember him?" she said, her voice a sad whisper.

"Yes," he said, studying them, becoming more and more certain they had shared a class, maybe wood shop or music appreciation or some other jerk-off course the counselors always offered kids like him. But he'd never seen Stu dressed as he was in either of his two pictures. One of them was his senior picture, in which he was wearing a three-piece suit his boyish grin made him seem much too young for, and the other was a basic training graduation picture, in which he was subdued and wearing his government-issued dress blues.

"What is it?" she said. "Why are you looking at his picture so strangely?"

"I don't know," he said, mesmerized by Stu's Army picture. But he did know. There was a deer-in-the-headlights quality underneath the tough facade. And fatigue. As a teenager, Al Jr. had always struggled to get up at 7 in the morning, when their father would yell up at them from the bottom of the stairs. But having someone doing the same thing at 4 in the morning was pure hell, especially when you'd had fire duty at 2 and there'd been no way of getting back to sleep. It wasn't unusual to have someone fall asleep in formation; it had happened to him more than once. When he looked back up, Sara was studying him, so he smiled at her. "I haven't thought much about boot camp."

"But you are now?"

"Yes."

"Where'd you go?"

Al Jr. shivered as a cold draft forced a chill down his back. "Fort Jackson. Old Tank Hill. Man, it'd be 35 in the morning and warm up to 90 by noon. Where'd Stu go?"

"Fort Leonard Wood. He hated the place. Nothing but woods for miles."

"Nobody likes where they go," Al Jr. said, laughing. "I've never met anyone who did."

Sara smiled, her eyes lighting up again. "Do you have any pictures?"

"Yes," Al Jr. said, rising from his chair. He went to his room and dumped everything out of the duffel bag and onto the floor. Sifting through the mess — all the notebooks, clothes and trinkets— he found a crumpled-up manila folder. He found a wallet-sized picture in better shape than the others. He brought the picture out to the table and handed it to her.

She took it from his hand, put it up close to her face and laughed. "This doesn't even look like you."

"Well, it is."

"Don't you look tough?"

"I didn't want them to see how scared I was," he said, reaching for his picture.

"Do you mind if I keep it?"

"Why?" he asked. "Have you got some mice you want to scare?"

"That's a good picture," she said, a frown coming back to her face as she picked up her brother's pictures. "The day his notice came, I don't think I quit crying until I went to bed."

Al Jr. said nothing; he wasn't sure she wanted him to. And then her stare went through him to another time, another place. "I sat next to him on the way to the bus stop," she said. "I cried so much my eyes hurt."

Al Jr. had felt all alone when he left. The only tears shed were by him, and they weren't for him. At the time, he wondered why God had even bothered putting him on earth. Was he meant to be a fool who didn't know how to do anything but screw up? Now he was glad there hadn't been any such fanfare when he left.

"He kept talking about all the things we'd do when he'd come back," Sara said. "Can you imagine? He's going off to war, and he's got to comfort his little dingbat sister."

"I'm sorry, Sara," Al Jr. said. "Stu sounds like a great brother."

At first, she said nothing. "The Christmas before he left, I'd lost my baby-sitting money — a whole 50 bucks — and he heard me crying in my room. He asked what was wrong, and I told him, and he smiled and said, 'Boy, I knew it was too good to be true.' Then he went to his room and came back and gave me 50 bucks!"

"Boy, did you luck out."

"Yeah, that's what I thought. But he gave me all tens. My money was all fives and ones."

"What'd he say?"

"Oh, he's real clever," she said, laughing. "He said he'd put all my money in the bank."

"Sounds reasonable," Al Jr. said, nodding. "Maybe that's what happened."

"Yeah, I thought so, too," she said, pausing, "until after he left. I was cleaning my room, and when I started vacuuming my chair, something caught, and I'll be damned if it wasn't the money I'd lost."

"Wow."

"I used Stu's money to buy my parents a grandfather clock for Christmas. Now every time I hear the stupid thing chime, I think about Stu."

Sara put her head down onto her folded arms. Al Jr. wanted to say something, something smart, but his throat tightened, so he took a deep breath and reached out to her instead. Once she felt his touch, she leaned over and buried her face in his shoulder, crying as he massaged her back, and he felt guilty for having thought he had the right to judge her.

Then, as if nothing had happened, she sat up and began writing again. Once she was finished, she handed her letter to him. It spoke of Stu's habits, his favorite foods, the things he wanted to do in the future. None of what she had written would be very useful to anyone who could help her; the Stu she remembered would be a lot different from the one she was trying to find. Yet writing the letter soothed her, and she was a lot more relaxed than she'd been when she got there. They talked about their favorite movies and shows. He preferred *I Spy* and *Star Trek*, while she loved to watch *Laugh-In* and *Bewitched*.

Everything was going great until Billy came in and went to the couch, ruining the moment with his snoring. Sara hurried to finish her last letter and handed them to Al Jr. to include with his short, apologetic letters promising to write more, and he sealed the addressed envelopes. With nothing left to do, Sara gathered everything up and put her stuff back in her purse. Al Jr. followed her to the door in a daze. This lovely girl, if only for a moment, had given him a chance to make a difference, to crack his shell and rejoin the human race. Now she was off, maybe to find someone else who might help, in a different direction, in the darkness of night, and out of his life forever.

"Thanks, Al," she said, turning around and frowning. "You seem so sad. I'm sorry if all this brought back bad memories."

"It's not that."

"What is it then?"

"I'm sorry I said such awful things to you," he said. "I hope you find your brother."

She reached out and touched his arm. "Al?"

"Yes?"

"You'll call me tomorrow, won't you?"

A small laugh escaped him. "I sure will."

She stood on her tiptoes and kissed him on the cheek. Then she walked down the hallway, out the screen door and down the sidewalk, her purposeful stride never once breaking until she got in her car and drove off.

•••

Chapter 15

The numbers never lied, especially after they'd been gone over three times, and Big Al knew a fourth wasn't necessary. The truth was right there in black and white: He'd spent more money than he'd made in the previous month. The most recent time that had happened, Al Jr. was a toddler and Billy was barely 6 months old. Back then, Jack was running things, and Big Al had worried about getting let go. But Jack was loyal, and Janet kept telling Big Al everything would be all right and they'd make it even if they didn't have anything at all.

His worries then proved to be wasted. Jack had money squirreled away, and they rode out the storm. A new bar had opened across the highway, but after a while, the customers came back, and the old man embraced them as if they'd never left. Throughout it all, Jack had Big Al and Janet over for supper every Sunday. They'd listen to the Cubs on the radio, more often than not disgusted, and they'd argue about whether Handy Andy Pafko could hit enough homers and Dutch Hiller could win enough games for the Cubs to get out of the cellar and back to the top of the division, maybe even the World Series.

Those days had been so simple. Big Al figured he'd always be OK with Jack and Janet beside him as they took on everything together. Of course, the feeling didn't last the summer. One muggy night in August 1950, when they were about to close for the evening,

Jack's face became as white as a sheet, his skin clammy, and he said his stomach ached. Big Al pleaded with him to go to the hospital.

"I'm all right, kid," he said breathlessly. "The day I can't close down my own place is the day I ought to get out of the racket."

Then he staggered, falling to the ground like a stone. Big Al ran to the phone and called the hospital. But it was too late; it would've been too late no matter what. Just like Big Al's father, Jack had a damaged heart. Losing Dr. Stevens had broken Big Al's spirit for years, but losing Jack meant he was going to lose the only job he'd ever loved.

As he grieved, Big Al began to feel guilty and selfish, as if his true colors were finally showing and he was more like his father than he cared to admit. His routine became monotonous. He'd spend his days with his boys, Billy sleeping in his crib and Al Jr. trying to get into every drawer, and then he'd go to work waiting for the inevitable. Maybe a lawyer would show up. Or a banker. No matter what, someone would come and tell him to shut down and be on his way.

So he was surprised to go home one slow afternoon to find Janet smiling.

"Jack's lawyer called," she said. "He's got some papers for you to sign."

"Papers? What papers?"

"Jack left you the bar."

"What?" he said. "I thought Jack would leave his bar to his son. Why wouldn't..."

Jack had always talked about his son, Everett, but Big Al had never met him. Leaving the bar to Big Al didn't make sense. Unless Jack had made Everett up.

"Jack's son died of pneumonia as a child," she said, leading him to the table. After they sat down, she took hold of his hands and cupped them. "His wife died around then, too."

"What?" he said. How had it been possible to work with someone for eight years and not know something like that? And then he realized he'd never really told Janet much about his own childhood other than his time with the doctor and his wife. Before he knew it, everything was coming out, and he couldn't have stopped himself even if he'd wanted to. The whole time, he looked away from her, fearing she might consider him weak, as damaged as he felt. But when he was finally able to meet her gaze, tears had streaked her mascara in black lines down her face.

Now the bar was meaningless, as the numbers in front of him were hopeless. There was only one customer, a man drinking the same beer he'd bought almost an hour ago. Once finished, the man stood up, put a quarter on the bar and left, tipping his hat on the way out. Big Al turned, retrieved his ledger from the office and brought it out to the bar. He motioned Eric over and showed him the numbers.

"Things will get better," Eric said. "We'll bounce back once the tournaments start."

"Yeah, if the lights are still on by then."

"C'mon, Al," Eric said, his voice soft, as if he were soothing a scared child.

"It's not just last month," Big Al said. "Last year was one of the worst we've had in years, maybe ever."

Eric wiped off the countertop, as if he had to keep busy to earn his keep, but he remained silent. The silence didn't bother Big Al; there wasn't anything Eric could've said to make him feel better anyway. So he took the ledger back to the office and placed it in the top drawer, where, he hoped, the damn thing would stay hidden. Deep down, he wondered why he hadn't worried about the bar — or Billy — more. But worrying was for people who cared about the future and had a place there. Him? He'd lost Al Jr. a long time ago, and Billy was slipping away from him, a distance that'd grown wider since Janet died. What was left?

He thumbed through the Rolodex cards until he found the number for Ripton's. He dialed it. The phone rang several times, and he was about to hang up, when the sound of soft jazz came through on the other end.

"Ripton's, Chi-Chi speaking."

"Hello, Chi-Chi, this is Al Hennessy," he said. "Is Nick around?"

Chi-Chi hesitated. "Hold on."

He imagined Nick standing in the background, waving Chi-Chi off, telling him there was no way he was going to talk to a nut like him. He was about to hang up again, when the music came back.

"Hi, Al," Nick said cheerfully. "What's on your mind?"

"I'd like to drop by," he said. "I want to talk to you about something."

"Sure, Al. Come by whenever you want. I'm always here."

"It'll be a business call."

"OK, same goes."

"I'll be there in 10 minutes."

ooo

Ripton's parking lot had only a few cars parked there now — a purple Pinto station wagon, an old Thunderbird and Nick's Cadillac. Big Al parked away from them in the front row and went inside, where the lighting was dim and the atmosphere was much calmer than it had been the previous time. Nick sat at his booth with his feet up, stirring a drink with a cocktail straw. Big Al thought about backing up and leaving, but before he could, the closing door caught Nick's attention.

Nick took his feet off the seat and pointed at it. Big Al sat down, fidgeting, and Nick smiled. "What's on your mind?"

"Well," Big Al said, clearing his throat. "I was wondering if you're still interested in buying my place."

At first, Nick kept stirring his drink. Then he stopped and frowned. "I'm still looking around. I've seen a couple of places, but they aren't as nice as yours. Honestly, I've kind of put the idea on hold. Are you serious?"

"Yes."

"How come you didn't say something the other night?"

"I just wanted to unwind," Big Al said. He paused. "To get away for a while."

Nick laughed. "Coming here made you want to sell your bar?"

Big Al thought of making something up. But he said, "We're not doing so hot, Nick. I think the place needs some new ideas. Sorry if I didn't mention it the other night, but I really just wanted to come here and talk to you, maybe even relive some old times."

"From what I heard," Nick said, "you sure did."

Big Al's face felt hot. He unbuttoned his coat, and Nick called out for a drink. He asked Big Al whether he wanted a rum and cola. Big Al nodded, and they remained silent until after Chi-Chi brought their drinks over and set them down. Big Al took a drink, and the nervous feeling went away.

"Thanks," Big Al said. "I wasn't looking for trouble the other night—"

Nick held up his hand. "I'm sorry for what happened. I've wanted to call you." He paused. "Chi-Chi says you're still pretty tough. Looks like nothing much has changed."

"Do you need any more help?"

"What?"

"If you buy my bar, I could work here as a bouncer."

Nick kept a straight face. Big Al feared he had already made up his mind and was thinking of a way to let him down easy. Big Al hoped he wasn't; otherwise, the young punks had been right the other night when they let him know he was just an old man getting in their way. He almost stood up to leave, when Nick laughed again. He asked Nick what was so funny.

"Imagine that," Nick said. "Who'd have ever thought you'd end up working for me?"

Big Al felt much better knowing Nick wasn't mocking him. They both laughed.

"I don't know why you'd even want to work here," Nick said. "These kids act like they can spit in your face as long as they're leaving good tips."

"I'm just tired of worrying about everything," Big Al said. "Sooner or later, I'd have to let Eric go. That's why I don't want to sell to just anybody. I know you'll give him a shot."

"I find your idea pretty interesting."

ooo

"But I've never worked anywhere but here," Eric said, his chest heaving. "This place's all I know."

Big Al patted Eric on the back and told him everything would be fine. But if anything, Eric acted sadder, just as he had when he came running through the door for the first time 17 years ago, when he couldn't have been much more than 10. The child had been trying to find his father, a shiftless bum if ever there was one, a customer

Big Al had inherited along with the stool he was always perched upon.

The boy was so thin Big Al doubted he'd eaten in a while. And though it was raining and cold, he was only wearing a white T-shirt, drenched and clinging to his ribs. When he spoke, his voice rattled with congestion.

"Mommy's gone! Mommy's gone!" he said, running to his father's side. "Nobody's seen her…"

Herbert Rolston's eyes widened with the same kind of contempt Big Al had always seen from his own father. He backhanded the boy to the ground and smiled cruelly.

"She's not coming back, you whiny little brat!" he said, getting up off his stool and drawing his foot back. Big Al jumped over the counter and pushed him backward.

"What do you think you're doing, Herb?"

Herbert gave him a tough scowl before sitting back on his stool. Then Big Al leaned over the boy — who kept mumbling— and helped him to his feet. The boy pulled away from him and ran out the door, leaving a watery trek of mud behind.

Ten years later, while sleeping, Big Al woke to the phone ringing downstairs. He ignored it, thinking it had to be a wrong number or some drunken fool. But Janet stirred and started to get up.

"I'll get it," Big Al said, putting on his robe. He hoped the phone would quit ringing before he got there, and when it didn't, he picked up his pace, ready to unload on whoever it was. But when he answered, a police sergeant with a tired voice told him Eric Rolston had been arrested for breaking in to the bar. They had caught him coming outside with a couple of bottles tucked away in his coat pockets.

"Will you come down and press charges in the morning?"

Why would Eric Rolston steal from him, a guy who had never done anything to him and had to work 16-hour days? Then he wondered whether Eric blamed him. Many men came into the bar, spending more money than they had any right to, and Herbert was worse than most. Many of their wives would call to yell at them or come down to the bar and haul them off. How much contempt would a kid like Eric, with no one to watch out for him, feel for someone liquoring up his dad and then sending him home? It really wasn't any wonder the boy had turned out to be a petty thief. And it wasn't news, either. Herbert had come in the bar a few years earlier all happy because the boy had been caught joyriding in a stolen car and was sure to be sent away.

But Herbert had died walking home one night when he had fallen off a train trestle and landed in the river, and the boy was probably sitting in his jail cell worrying about spending a couple of years in prison. So Big Al told the officer he'd be down there shortly to talk to Eric and then he'd decide.

Upon arriving, he was led to a room off a hallway adjacent to the jail, where Eric sat at the end of a long table. The room's air was musty, and the overhanging lights were dimmed low. But it wasn't dark enough to hide the smug arrogance on Eric's face or his disheveled appearance.

"I can see you still remember me," Big Al said.

"Yeah," Eric said quietly. "You're the do-gooder who was in the bar when my dad tried to kick me."

"I'm glad to see you're still grateful."

Eric blushed. "Nothing personal."

"Nothing personal?" Big Al said, his voice rising. "Those bottles might not mean much to you, but they're my livelihood."

The officer behind him tapped Big Al on the shoulder and pointed at his wristwatch. "Are you ready to press charges now?"

"Not yet," Big Al said. He sat down across the table from Eric. "I want to know why you picked me to steal from."

"I just wanted a drink," he said. "Simple as that."

"You're willing to go to prison for a couple of bottles of whiskey? Why not work for it like everyone else does?"

"Nobody will hire me."

"Well, I could use somebody to help clean up around the place," Big Al said. The officer behind him grunted. "Maybe clean the toilet."

"Uh-uh," Eric said, pushing as far away from the table as his manacled hands would allow him. "I'm not scrubbing any toilets."

"I know you're not," Big Al said, standing up. "It's a lot easier sitting in jail feeling sorry for yourself."

Eric brought his hands up as high as they would go and slammed them down on the table, his face a little less arrogant. He tried to stagger to his feet before falling back down on the chair. "I've had to steal ever since I was a little kid. Never any food. My clothes never fit. How would you like that?"

"You're going to sit in jail saying no one ever gave you a chance when you're really just too lazy to work." Big Al said. "You'd better make up your mind, because once that door shuts, I'm pressing charges."

Eric said something in a mousy voice, and Big Al turned toward him. "Excuse me?"

"When can I start?"

Hiring him had been a gamble. Many times in the beginning, Big Al had thought Eric was too far gone to salvage. But he grew up, started taking classes and met a young girl studying to be a nurse. Now he was a father close to getting his degree in business management, but today, to Big Al, he didn't look much different than he had as a child.

"It's not that bad, Eric."

"It's not that good."

"You're going to be the new boss."

Eric stared at the desk. Big Al sat back down and waited until he looked back up. "You're not even 30 yet, and you're going to run this place."

"It's your place, not mine."

"And it was Jack's place before."

"You're not that old," Eric said. "What're you going to do?"

"I'm going to be bouncing at Ripton's."

"That's nuts," Eric mumbled.

Big Al fixed a couple of rum and colas and handed one to Eric. The front door opened, and the bells jingled as a man called out to ask whether they were open. Eric stood up and went to the office door. He opened it, hesitated and then turned back around. "You're just hoping Ronch Laroy or some other derelict will kill you."

"That punk didn't do too well the last time he tried."

ooo

The morning had been so warm he'd turned the thermostat all the way down, not expecting the temperature to drop to 20 degrees.

When Big Al opened the door, a cold draft greeted him, making him feel as if he were walking into a mausoleum. And it wasn't just the cold; the air had lost all scents of Janet. Neither Billy nor he had done more than halfheartedly clean up after himself. After she died, he wanted all traces of her to go away, because just smelling her scent made him think she'd come back. But once they did finally fade, he would spray her perfume in the air every now and again. Sometimes Billy would notice and look at him as if he were batty. But the perfume had run out a long time ago, and he hadn't wanted the short old man at the drugstore where she had always bought her perfume to think he had a girlfriend.

On the mantel was a picture of her. Her happiness always made him feel that he had been a good husband and father, which— honestly — he became only after the photo was taken.

She had been waiting up for him after the bar closed one night. "You're going to be a father."

A father? He hadn't been able to speak, and Janet's smile faded to a distressed frown. He feared for how the child's life would be and broke out in a cold sweat. Finally, he forced a smile. "That's great, honey."

"Are you sure?" she said. "You don't act like it's great."

"Yes," he said, pulling her closer. "I can't believe it."

Never again did he show her anything but delight. Through many sleepless nights, he kept his fear to himself and did everything he could to dote on her. But it wasn't easy. Janet would cry over the damnedest things. One time, she got all weepy because he had forgotten to put the empty jar of milk out on the porch for the milkman. Afterward, he tried to stay on top of things.

Yet when the time came for her to have the baby, he came apart, and she was the one telling him everything would be all right. He stayed away from the delivery room until a nurse came and got him so he could hold his boy, a chubby cherub in whom he could already see his own likeness. His arms weakened, and he had to hand Al Jr. to the nearest nurse before collapsing on a chair.

Now, the still silence of the living room was interrupted by a blustery wind rattling against the window, and Big Al's heartache intensified as he went over to the mantel, picked up Janet's picture and went to the couch, where he plopped down so hard dust came up in the air and made him cough. Then he placed the picture on the table facedown and went to the study to make a stiff drink.

•••

Chapter 16

Lonny and Chad barely spoke to Billy, and every time he approached them, they walked away. Then Billy realized it wasn't just them. Coach Randle could barely stand to be around him. And throughout practice, the team blocked him out of the huddle. He had to stand on the outside. Afterward, everyone went to the locker room in silence.

"OK, guys," Coach Randle said once they were dressed and seated. "We're really going to have our hands full with Kokomo."

Kokomo had three starters headed to the Big Ten. Billy gazed over at the locker room door and the sanctuary beyond it. When he turned back, the coach was studying him as if he could read his mind. Coach Randle pointed out their mistakes, a number of them Billy's, rambling on for another half-hour, his flat voice reminding Billy of an argument he'd had with Al Jr. a couple of years ago. Billy had said everyone would like him better if he joined some clubs and worked harder to get his grades up. Anything would be better than sitting up in the garage smoking dope all the time.

"You think people like you?" Al Jr. said. "Just drop off the team and you'll see how many people like you."

Maybe he had been right; it certainly seemed so now. Everybody always slapped him on the back after a win, but when the team lost, everyone gave him the cold shoulder. He couldn't wait to get away from his teammates, and he was glad when the coach caught himself repeating himself and finally dismissed them.

Billy hurried ahead of everyone else and dressed without showering. On his way out, Lonny came around the corner of a locker and blocked the exit.

"What's wrong with you?" he said, poking Billy in the chest with his finger.

"What're you talking about?"

"You've stunk it up all week," Lonny said, lowering his voice to a whisper. "Damn it, Billy, don't you want to beat those guys? Just once?"

"Hey, I'll do what I can. But they've got one hell of a team."

"So do we."

Billy laughed. "Oh, yeah? How many scholarship players do we have?"

Lonny's eyes widened before a dull, hurt look came over his face. "So what? Nobody gives a damn about your scholarship. Everything's wrapped up for you, and that's why you don't care about us anymore."

Then Lonny disappeared around the corner, and Billy left the locker room without saying anything else. Outside, the cold wind blew against his face until his cheeks numbed and his body stiffened, making the walk unbearably long. Most of the stores were still open, and he ducked into every third or fourth one, trying vainly to warm up. But the suspicious clerks forced him back outside before they could ask him what he wanted. And when there weren't any more stores, he hurried as fast as he could, crossing the bridge in moments.

A block away from the apartment, an orange station wagon drove slowly down the street. The car stopped at the stop sign, and he saw the driver was Eric Rolston, slumped in his seat. As he pulled away, Billy flipped him off and hurried to the apartment.

Al Jr. sat on the couch wearing corduroy slacks and a turtleneck sweater. Stranger yet, he was sober and somber. Billy sat down on the chair and laughed. "What's this? Are you getting ready to go to church or something?"

"No," he said. "Just a movie."

"You'll never guess who I just saw."

"Eric Rolston."

"How'd you know?"

Al Jr. shot him a quick glance. "Where'd you think he came from?"

"Here?" he said. "Why?"

"Because Dad's flipped his lid."

"Huh?"

"He got in a fight last Friday night at Ripton's with some guy named Ronch Laroy."

Everyone in school knew who Ronch Laroy was and what he meant: bad news. Ronch would sell drugs to anyone, regardless of age. And not just pot, either. One kid overdosed on heroin. Another just wanted a hit of acid but made the mistake of showing his wad of bills to Ronch, who convinced him he could make his money back and more if he bought 20 hits and sold them for a little more. But the kid took them all, lost his mind and had to go to the nuthouse for nearly a year.

But their father wouldn't even know what most drugs were. And why would he go to Ripton's, a place so seedy bad things happened all the time? Before Billy could ask, Al Jr. said something else, something that didn't make sense, and he asked him to repeat it.

"Eric said Dad's selling the bar."

Billy rested his chin on his folded hands. "Eric's lying. We're going to take it over someday, and Dad's going to show us how to run things."

"Why would Eric lie?"

"Why wouldn't he?" Billy said. "You know what Dad said."

"Yeah, 10 years ago."

"But he said it," Billy said, sitting back. It wasn't fair. When their father had said they'd run the place someday, he was showing them around the bar, pointing out where the kitchen would be and, once it started making money, where the new dining room would be added on. He talked about how they'd all work together as a team. Everything he said had been nothing but a bunch of lies. Billy wished he would've been there earlier to ask Eric why. Then there was a knock on the door. He went to the door before Al Jr. had a chance to stand up. He hoped Eric had finally realized how troubled their family was and how much they needed his help, but it was only

Sara. She glanced up at him, looked beyond him and then smiled. "Hi, Al."

Al Jr. walked out, and they hugged. Billy sat back on the couch. They both gave him strange glances before Al Jr. shut the door and headed out. Billy was alone there for the first time while being awake, and the sounds of the house settling and a train whistle blowing in the distance made him skittish. He jumped when the wind rattled against the picture window.

Being alone had always made him nervous. When he was a child, his mother would leave his door open so the hallway light could spill through the crack of the door. But she never understood that it wasn't the darkness that frightened him; it was the sounds he heard when no one else was around. He was watching *One Step Beyond* one night. The episode was about a man accused of killing his wife, but the weird thing about it was that their house made her disappear after they'd been in a fight. Billy was so frightened he wouldn't go upstairs by himself, thinking something just as scary could happen to him, even though his mother said it was just a television show.

He went to the TV now and turned it on. Through the static, he saw the outline of a man pointing a snub-nosed revolver at another man and then pulling the trigger, hitting the man point-blank. But it wasn't like a television show, in which the guy getting hit always fell backward; this guy crumpled to the ground, and a pool of blood grew around his head. Walter Cronkite appeared, sitting at his desk, and Billy almost vomited knowing that what he'd seen was real. He shut the TV off and went out to the kitchen to make a hamburger. Eating always took the edge off. But so would the rye. He filled a cup and then drank the liquor. Immediately, his nerves settled down, and he took the bottle and cup to the table, where he had several more drinks. After the fifth one, he wasn't worried about the sounds the apartment made anymore.

ooo

At Wong's, Al Jr. ate his chicken dinner and watched the people lined up along the sidewalk to get into the movie theater, while Sara tried to pick up her water chestnuts with her chopsticks.

Every time she would get the food inches away from her face, it would fall right back down onto her plate. Finally, she started using her fork. He looked away out of fear she might be reading him too easily. She reached out and touched his hand.

"What's wrong with your brother?" she said. "He seemed lost. Why is he always at your apartment?"

Her question caught him off guard. He'd been so worried about making her think he wasn't a creep they hadn't even talked about Billy. He told her everything, how everything started when he'd missed his bus home from school and been too lazy to walk, prompting him to call his mom for a ride — something his father had told him never to do because she wasn't a very good driver — even though the roads were slick. She had ended up dying in a wreck, and that's why he'd joined the Army. His words trailed off.

"That's what this is all about?" Sara asked. "I remember your mom getting killed, but I never heard any of that other stuff."

"Probably because I went away right after," Al Jr. said. "Now Dad's selling the bar. I wish Billy would've never showed up."

"Don't say that. Are you sorry we ran into each other?"

He tried to smile but couldn't. "No, it's just, well, I know Dad wouldn't be selling the bar if Billy would've let their fight slide."

"He sounds like a real jerk to be blaming you for everything," she said. "I'm sure it wasn't the first time she picked you up."

"No, it wasn't."

"What a—" she said, stopping when she looked down at her wristwatch. "We've only got a few minutes before the show starts."

Outside, the line for the Paul Newman double feature, *Cool Hand Luke* and *Hombre*, was still long. They ran across the street.

"Which one are we seeing?" Al Jr. said.

"I think I'd like *Cool Hand Luke* better," Sara said, shivering as they moved slowly toward the window. Al Jr. opened his coat, and she pulled herself inside and smiled up at him.

"Better?" he said.

She hugged him. Being with her made him feel as if he were in one of those great dreams he'd wake up from and try to return to by attempting to go back to sleep.

"What is it, Al?"

"Everything feels weird, like I'm not really here."

She pinched his side and laughed when he jumped. "See? I'm real."

"Yes, you are."

They made their way to the window, where a kid with red glasses took their money and gave them tickets. Inside, a line of soda jerks, boys with pimpled faces, worked behind a glass display case filled with candy. Popcorn popped and filled the air with a buttery scent. Al Jr. started to get in line to buy a tub, but Sara pulled him away.

"I don't want to miss a second of this movie."

He followed her through the red swinging doors, and they found seats in the back row. A seemingly endless series of singalong cartoons with the bouncing balls went on and on. Then the theater got really dark, and the movie began. Al Jr. soon felt again as if he were being hypnotized.

Luke was a loser through and through, much like him. But Luke not only embraced it but also ran all the way up and down the warden's nerves every chance he got. And the other inmates loved him, even when the big guy stomped him in the boxing ring and he kept coming back for more. When Luke ate the 50 eggs, Al Jr. had no doubt he could've done it, maybe even had, and that's why he seemed so real, because he was. And when the warden finally broke him, just tore him down in front of the rest of the convicts, Al Jr. could hardly watch. Al Jr. was as stunned as the convicts — all of them acting as if they wouldn't have been broken — until Luke stole the truck keys and drove away, fooling everyone in the movie and the theater. Yet he could tell Luke was doomed. It didn't surprise him one bit when the creepy guard wearing sunglasses at night shot him. And even though the big convict got hold of the guard and choked him out, Al Jr. couldn't cheer with everyone else in the theater; his hero was dying, and that's all he could see. The mocking smile on Luke's face as they were driving away made him feel better, though. It was the perfect ending. If death couldn't beat you, then nothing could — at least nothing on this earth.

Everyone in the crowd seemed to be mumbling together. All those babbling voices made Al Jr.'s ears ring. He looked over to see whether Sara was ready to leave and was surprised to see her crying. But if she noticed him smiling, she didn't seem too bothered. Then, just as she had the other night, she wiped her eyes and acted as if nothing had happened.

"How can you cry for some rich movie star after all you've been through?"

"I guess it's silly," she said, laughing. "But that was such a great movie."

"Well, let's go," Al Jr. said, wiping away a tear, "before they think I did something to you."

She laughed and took hold of his hand. Then she led him through the swinging doors, where two Chinese masks — one of them smiling, the other crying — were mounted on the opposite wall. He laughed at them, and Sara turned around and jabbed him in the ribs.

"Knock it off," she said. "I know you're laughing at me."

"I'm sorry," he said, "but this is the best night I've ever had."

She smiled at him as they went through the glass doors, where a blustery wind made them run to her car. Sara started the engine and blew into her cupped hands as the heater warmed the car. She talked nonstop about the happier times in her life — many of them revolving around Stu — until, finally, she frowned over at Al Jr. It was too dark to see much of her face, but something was troubling her, so he asked her what was wrong.

"Where's your life headed?"

"I don't know. I try not to think about it," he said. "Probably nowhere."

"That doesn't bother you?"

"No. Maybe a little. I guess I've never thought about it, but I always thought I could end things if I couldn't take it anymore. God would forgive me."

"I wouldn't," she said.

"You're the one who asked," he said, smiling at her. "Besides, that was before I met you."

"What do you mean?"

"I can't think about anything but you," he said, his words sounding so stupid he turned away from her.

"We don't know each other very well."

"It's a miracle we know each other at all," he said. "Why'd you keep giving me chances?"

"I needed your help," she said. "But last night, you seemed so lost when we said goodbye."

"What?"

"I don't know," she said. "You must've been so unhappy to say the things you did." She paused, and he suddenly noticed how hot the car was becoming. "Like you've been sad your whole life."

He wanted to defend himself, to tell her that she was wrong and that he'd had a lot of happiness in his life, but the more he thought about it the more he realized he hadn't. He wouldn't have been able to say anything she'd have believed anyhow. The lights in the downtown stores began shutting off.

Then she put the car in drive and drove off, across the bridge and railroad tracks, where a billboard of Robert Kennedy smiled a toothy grin. Neither of them spoke until she pulled up in front of the apartment and glanced down at her wristwatch.

"Oh, God, Dad's going to kill me."

Al Jr. leaned forward to kiss her, but she nudged him away. "Do you want me to stop by tomorrow?"

"Yeah, what time will you be here?" he said, opening the door.

"Around 4."

He got out and watched her speed off. Liquor fumes wafted out of his apartment. Billy was passed out, his legs still on the couch while his torso hung off and rested on the floor. An empty bottle of rye lay nearby.

There was a letter on the coffee table, and Al Jr. picked it up. Billy's writing was so neat; everyone always said he wrote like a girl. But the letter was sloppy, barely legible, and what he could read, he wished he couldn't. It was to their father — just as Al Jr. figured — accusing him of betraying them both. Al Jr. put the letter back down and lifted Billy up to the couch. Once he caught his breath, he went to his room and closed the door behind him.

• • •

Chapter 17

Big Al had spent the whole morning trying to find the tax records from 1962, the only year missing from his files, and worrying Nick might think him an incompetent businessman if he showed up without them. Every other year was in his file cabinet in the office, lined up in perfect order. He tried not to panic; Nick had told him to take his time. But he wanted to impress his old friend, who, though nearly 10 years younger, he had always admired. He'd rather not even go through with the sale if it meant admitting to losing a full year's worth of records.

It struck him the file had to be in the cabinet in a spare room at the end of the hallway upstairs. When he opened the door, a musty draft, which seemed like a long-held breath, blew out at him. He had to go to the middle of the dark room to turn on the hanging light. He fumbled with the switch until it caught just right, and the light stayed on, shining on the remnants of time, most of it junk Janet had meant to get rid of. But the discarded stuff wasn't all meaningless—outdated toys, the boys' matching cap guns, Billy's chemistry set, old records, dusty photo albums and, most painful of all, an old tricycle, once red, now rusted, leaning against the wall on a broken axle. Everything reminded him of his happiest years, when both of his boys were young and they played together, hardly ever fighting. Even when they had done something wrong, he couldn't stay angry with them for long. He wished he could've frozen time, making them small forever, so he could've had a month of Sundays just standing on the porch, lean and strong with a full head of hair, while they took turns riding the tricycle around in circles.

He looked away from the tricycle, focusing on the metal file cabinet across the room, underneath the window. He grabbed hold of a pipe running the length of the room and walked along the narrow aisle he was barely nimble enough to navigate. Once there, he knelt over to open the top drawer, but the damn thing wouldn't budge, and he almost lost his balance. He cursed. He and Janet had often argued about the way she stuffed things in drawers; of course, Janet said she wouldn't have had to stuff things if he weren't such a pack rat. What could he have said? You couldn't ever have enough paperwork when Sammy came around.

He gave the drawer one more hard yank, breaking it free from whatever had been holding it in place. Then he began tossing stuff out of the drawer, panicking the closer he got to the bottom, until he finally found the file. He fled from the room without bothering to turn off the light or shut the door and ran down the stairs, not stopping until the front door closed behind him. He knew that if any of the neighbors, especially the nosy spinster across the street, had seen him, they'd be talking about how he'd lost his mind. But ever since Billy left, he felt as if the house was angry with him and made noises he'd never heard before. But soon the house would be on the market, and he'd find a small apartment and never think about the place again. Otherwise, he really would go nuts.

He drove to the bar, hoping Eric would be in a better mood, especially after thinking things over, but he was still moping around, cleaning things he'd already cleaned. Big Al said hello and asked whether they'd had any customers.

"A few guys from the graveyard shift," Eric said. "They had a couple of beers and left."

"I'll be in the office if you need me."

Eric looked at the folder under Big Al's arm. "I doubt we'll get too flooded."

"Yeah," Big Al said, closing the door behind him. At his desk, he put the folder in place with the others and started going through all his paperwork. In '51, his first year running things, the numbers had dipped quite a bit. He hadn't really known how to order, and it showed on paper. One time, Stan called him out.

"Beer's OK, Al," Stan had said after being told the Seagram's was all gone.

"Are you sure?" Big Al said. "I've got bourbon."

Stan made a gagging sound. "The stuff's stinko, makes my stomach turn."

Similar complaints from other people made him a better listener. Easing into the mid-'50s, he'd been able to pinch his pennies well enough to get a loan for their house. It was a big house, much bigger than the two-bedroom sardine can they'd lived in since getting married. And the files from '62 lit up his memory, and he knew why he'd stashed the file someplace special. That was the first year they'd made over $10,000! Never before had Janet looked at him with so much pride. Things had changed so much in six years. He put the folder, along with the others, in his briefcase.

He heard a knock on the door. "What is it?"

Eric stuck his head in the room. "I found this in the mailbox," he said, placing an envelope sheepishly on the desk. "There's nothing on it but your name."

He hurried out the door, and Big Al tore open the envelope, finding Billy's sloppy writing. He nearly fainted when Billy accused him of betrayal, of not honoring Janet's wishes. Billy wrote that Janet wanted him and Al Jr. to take over the bar. And there was more. He said Big Al was a liar and a jackal before rewording it, saying he was worse than a jackal because at least jackals would take care of their young.

By the time Big Al finished reading the letter, the paper was crumpled up in his hand, and he threw it down on the desk. As if Al Jr. had shown any interest in anything besides smoking pot and sneaking the car out for a joyride! He couldn't even catch the bus, and now Janet was gone. And Billy? Couldn't he see all the sacrifices Big Al had made for him? Didn't Billy know how many times he'd taken a sack lunch to work, boiled eggs or bologna, instead of going home to have lunch with Janet so he could attend every basketball camp, in some cases as far away as Indianapolis? Now Billy was going to throw everything away. For what? What made Billy think he had the right to question, to approve or disapprove of, every one of his decisions? But when Big Al read the letter again, something wasn't right, and then it struck him. Only three, maybe four, people knew about the bar. He went out to the bar.

"Eric!" he said, holding the letter out. "Why didn't you come and get me when he dropped this off?"

Eric stood frozen, his hands holding a towel out in front of him, and his skin drained of all color. He had to be the one who blabbed. His silence confirmed his betrayal, but Big Al had to hear him say so himself.

"There wasn't anything in the mailbox a half-hour ago," Big Al said.

"I swear I didn't see him out there," Eric mumbled.

"Who's him?"

"OK, Al," he said. "I saw Billy running off. But neither one of us could've caught up with him."

"Why did you tell him about the bar?" Big Al said. "Now he's saying he's going to quit the team. You'd better come clean, or I'll fire your ass!"

"Oh, go ahead," Eric said, throwing his towel down on the bar. "One minute you're talking about a promotion. The other you're acting like firing me wouldn't be good enough, you damn nut!" Eric took his apron off and threw it on the bar. "Christ, don't you think he'd find out sooner or later?"

"How could you turn against me after all I've done for you?"

"Turn against you?" Eric said, pausing at the door. "You used to be someone I looked up to, but you've turned into nothing but a bully. You want to know why I told them, huh? Billy called last week wanting me to help them."

"What?"

"Yeah, I wouldn't even hear him out because I was too afraid to," Eric said. "I even know where he's been all this time."

"Where does Al live?"

"Sorry, Al," Eric said, going out the door. "But I quit, so I don't have to answer to you anymore."

Then he was gone, and Big Al went to the window to see whether he was still standing there uncertainly as if he'd made a big mistake, maybe even realizing he'd left without his jacket. But the cold didn't appear to bother him as he took long strides out of the parking lot and turned the corner.

ooo

Billy wiped the sweat from his forehead, hoping to see his father coming out of the bar after Eric. But the minutes kept passing, and he feared Eric hadn't given him the letter. He even questioned his own timing. If he had just waited until after school, Rich could've driven him back to practice. Maybe his tardiness would've been the last straw for the coach and he could finally have been done with everything. But he hadn't waited; he hadn't been able to. Listening to Mr. Stringer rambling on and on about class systems had made him so antsy he had gone out and found Rich in the smoking area, offered him a couple of bucks and had him bring him here, where he could approach his father's bar without being noticed.

He'd almost lost his nerve. The tinted picture window was so dark he could barely see through it, but he could've sworn someone had been standing there. It had looked like the outline of a man, but that's about all he could tell before turning and placing the letter in the mailbox and then running back toward the alley. Then he'd waited; for what, he didn't know — maybe to see his father coming through the door, calling his name apologetically. But when the door had opened, Eric had come outside and grabbed the envelope instead. He had waved at where Billy was hiding.

"We've got to go," Rich had said, coming up behind him.

Billy had put up his hand. "Wait a minute."

And they had waited, at least five more minutes, before Eric had come back outside, storming down the steps, and walked past them, disappearing around the corner.

"Now we've really got to go," Rich said. "We're going to have to fly just to get back on time." He got in the car. Billy got in, too. Then he saw his father come outside. Big Al was holding a briefcase. He put it inside the car before going back in the bar and turning the "open" sign around to the "closed" side. Then he came back out and drove away. Billy's heart kept pounding. There had been only one other day he had felt worse — when the principal, Mr. Hunt, had come down to the gym to tell him his mother had been in an accident and he needed to go home right away.

His mother's death had ruined them all, and his best efforts weren't good enough to keep his father, brother and him from going their three separate ways.

Rich did a U-turn and gunned the engine. Billy adjusted the side mirror away from the bar and slumped in the seat.

ooo

Nearly every shot went in, and every pass went right where Billy wanted it to go. Maybe that was all it took to make everyone happy — just to play ball and act as if nothing had ever happened. His mother was gone, and everyone thought he should just get over it. Boy, how they all laughed it up, all of them thinking he was fired up to play Kokomo. But he could hardly wait for the next day's game to be over. Firth came down the lane for a fast break, and Billy put the ball right in front of him with so much force it nearly went through Firth's baboon-like fingers. Everyone laughed as Firth caught the ball and let out a yelp — everyone except Firth, Coach Randle and Billy.

"OK, guys," Coach Randle said, staring at Billy strangely. "I want you to all get to bed early tonight. Get a good night's rest."

Billy walked away ahead of everyone else and dressed quickly. He was on his way out, when Lonny came over to him wearing the same irritating awkward smile he always had whenever he thought he'd screwed up. "I'm sorry about yesterday," he said, patting Billy on the back.

"Forget it," Billy said. "I just want to go to the couch and sleep."

"Couch?"

"I might not make it upstairs," he said as calmly as he could, even though he was seething. Lonny was something else. He probably didn't even remember Billy's asking for help only two weeks ago. Of course, Lonny had always put things out of his mind more easily than anyone Billy had ever known. He was the one who'd probably distanced himself the most after Billy's mother died, avoiding him until after a couple of months had dulled everything.

They didn't hang around as they used to, and now he acted as if he wanted something. Billy tried to move past him out the door, but Lonny grabbed his arm.

"Let's go to Hop's," he said. "I'm buying."

The thought of smelling tenderloins, chicken and fries—which usually made him hungry just walking through the door there — made him queasy. And it wasn't just that. The kids listening to the jukebox were always so happy, as if life were nothing but a party. Billy didn't want to be around any of them. But it was so cold outside, and even if they stayed there awhile, catching a ride would still be faster than walking. And if he had Lonny drop him off at Al Jr.'s, then he might remember their conversation from a couple of weeks previously. Tagging along would be worth it just to see Lonny's expression. So he went with him.

In the parking lot, Lonny rambled on about how to stop Tyrone Strong. They would trap him. With all of them ganging up, they would surely keep him in check. Double-team him into making bad passes on the perimeter.

"Who's going to guard Ellis and Harvey?" Billy asked. Ellis Talley was 6'4" and ran like a deer. Billy couldn't ever remember him being winded. Harvey, a 6'9" center, always outproduced Lonny, taunting him with the nickname Little Red Lonny, until he would actually turn red. It wasn't as if Harvey was tough or athletic. Many times, Lonny's hard fouls had sent Harvey to the ground, where he would sit cross-legged, laughing as the referee called the foul on Lonny. Then he'd go to the line, shooting his ugly praying-mantis shots, which only went in half the time. Either way, Lonny would still end up on the bench halfway through the third quarter with no fouls to spare or fouled out.

And Lonny knew it. That's why he kept his mouth shut the rest of the way to Hop's, where a couple of weirdo hippies gyrated near the jukebox in an odd style that didn't even look like dancing. Lonny went to the counter, while a steady flow of cars filled with teenagers drove aimlessly through the plaza parking lot or parked where they could congregate with the other lot rats. Karen's blue DeSoto pulled up, and Billy felt so queasy he had to go to the restroom to splash water on his face. When he came out, Lonny was sitting at the table, a tray full of sandwiches in front of him, eating a cheeseburger. The bells jingling on the door preceded a line of identically dressed cheerleaders — Karen, Tonya and Michelle— but Carla wasn't with them, and Billy chuckled, thinking about how vindictive Karen was. But then he stopped, feeling guilty because Carla would probably never be with them again, or at least for a long time. That's how Karen was, always acting as if a person only deserved one chance. When someone blew it, that person was done. She smiled and laughed, and Billy wanted to go up to her, maybe stand a little closer to her. But he sat at Lonny's table instead. Lonny finished his sandwich and smiled.

"Thinking about Kokomo, too, huh?" Lonny said before slurping half his drink. "You've got to keep your head clear. Tyrone's going—"

"I know all about Tyrone," Billy said. "He's the best point guard in the state. You need to mellow out, or you'll foul out by halftime."

"I can't," Lonny said. "It wouldn't matter to me if they win the state title as long as we win tomorrow."

"Sure, Lonny." He wanted to say more, but Karen and her friends had sat down across the dining room, and she acted as if she hadn't seen him. She used to ignore him all the time when she was angry with him. He never knew whether she was playing a game or whether she'd blocked him out so well she actually couldn't see him. But he could play games, too, and he stared at her until she glimpsed him. She frowned and then turned away. Billy convinced himself there was something more in her frown than coldness, maybe even a sadness that made her wish things between them had never changed. But he could never tell whether what he saw was the truth — for example, when he'd come downstairs to Karen and his mother laughing and wonder whether they were laughing at him. He'd be too irritated to even acknowledge them. God, he missed those days.

Without taking his eyes off her, Billy stood up. Lonny reached up, his long fingers wrapping around Billy's wrist as tight as handcuffs.

"Where're you going?"

"I've got to talk to Karen."

"Oh, c'mon."

Billy pulled away from him. "I'll be back."

Lonny mumbled something, but Billy was too far away to understand him. Karen got up to walk away, but he was able to move around the table and block her path.

"Get out of my way!"

"I've got to talk to you," he said. "Please."

She looked at her friends, both smiling uncomfortably, before she folded her arms and nodded. They sat down at a table underneath a window.

"What do you want?" Karen asked him.

"Things to be OK," he said, reaching out and touching her hand. "Don't worry. I know I blew it, and I know we're done."

"I know you did, too," she said. "This is a mistake."

"I don't want you to hate me anymore."

"Excuse me?"

"I don't want you to hate me anymore," he said, and he cleared his throat. "I wish you'd forgive me."

She leaned forward. "What's wrong with you?"

"I don't know," Billy said. He paused. "I'm through with basketball. I'm going to try and go to college without it."

"Why would you do something so crazy?" Karen said. "You won't be able to go to college without your scholarship. You'll end up over there." She paused and caught her breath. "I don't want you to die."

She began to say something else but then lowered her head down onto her folded arms. She hadn't said what he wanted to hear — and probably wouldn't, either. So he stood up and went back to Lonny's table. But Lonny had already left, leaving Billy's sandwich and Coke behind. Billy wanted neither and went to the door. Karen's friends were standing over her awkwardly as she wept. At least she didn't want him to die.

He remembered the first time he'd seen her, in the ninth grade. When they'd first noticed each other and she had smiled at him, he'd known she'd be his. Now there was a glint in her eye, just like she had when they first met, and a lump caught in his throat as he forced a smile back at her. He went out the door and into the cold, blustery night.

•••

Chapter 18

"Rich and Ralph are upstairs," Mrs. Blynner said. She was probably wondering what Billy was doing there at the door. His father had made him cut his ties with the brothers — even though his mother had insisted they weren't bad kids just because they'd been caught shoplifting from a dime store. They'd served their punishment, a weekend of detention. But one day, while all three of them played a game of 21, Big Al came outside and asked the Blynners to leave. Both wore confused frowns as they got on their bikes and left. Now, their mother, wearing an old, tattered blue bathrobe and her hair in curlers, clearly wanted to say something to Billy, something that'd hurt him as much as his father had hurt them. But she didn't. She just stood out of the way and pointed upstairs.

"Thank you," he said. Billy didn't want to be there any more than she wanted him there. His feet ached with every step, and he wanted nothing more than to go lie down on the couch and drift off thinking about Karen. The only problem was Sara had been at the apartment, giggling with Al Jr. behind his closed door. He could finally let Al Jr. go without worrying about him again; at least, for now, he wasn't alone. So he had tiptoed away from the apartment and walked aimlessly until coming here.

Halfway up the stairs, he heard muffled voices. Rich and Ralph sounded normal, maybe a little flat, but the third voice spoke fast and sounded argumentative. Billy stopped on the landing, trying to hear them better, but everything became silent. He knocked on the door.

"Who's there?" Rich asked.

"Billy."

The door opened slowly, and Rich peeked around the corner before motioning him to come in. Sitting on a chair was Brett Rand, a kid way too seedy to be hanging around with the Blynners. He barely looked at Billy as he nodded, and then he stared down at the ground. Beside him, sitting on the bed, Ralph forced a smile.

"What's up?" he said. "You need a ride?"

"No," Billy said. "I was just walking around and decided to stop."

Ralph shuddered. "Man, it's a little cold out to be walking."

"Yeah, well, Al's got a girl over, and you saw how small his place is."

"I can't believe you're still there," Rich said, smiling at Brett. "You should see the place. It's not much bigger than this room."

Brett didn't return his smile or even acknowledge him. He stood up and left without saying a word, stomping down the stairs and out the front door. Billy sat down on the chair and asked Ralph, "What's wrong with him?"

Ralph shrugged. "He's just moody. That's all."

"Yeah," Rich said. "I'm glad he left."

They were giving Billy the runaround. Last he'd heard, Brett had been sent to reform school for stealing parts off junked-out cars after the owner of Stanley's Junkyard had caught him pitching parts over the fence. That was a few years ago, but watching him sitting there pouting made clear that he hadn't changed much.

"What's wrong?" Billy asked, laughing. "Didn't he offer you guys enough money?"

The brothers exchanged quick glances before laughing. Then they took turns talking about the upcoming game against Kokomo. But Billy knew Brett had a one-track mind. Once, before his father had banned him from hanging out with the Blynners, he had gone to Brett's house with Rich. In the garage, Brett had close to 10 bikes up in the loft, along with several baseball bats and a couple of Red Ryder BB guns. Hell, there was even a stack of Hula-Hoops.

Nothing was too small to steal, and a lot of the junk probably hadn't even been reported to the cops.

Billy hung out with Rich and Ralph until 10 o'clock. They nodded at him as he went out the door, waiting, he supposed, to talk about Brett's plan. Outside, the wind blew at his back, and he hurried toward the apartment. Sara's car was no longer there.

"Man, it's nasty..." he stopped, laughing. Al Jr. stood just inside the wide-open bedroom door wearing nothing but a mangy old robe, and several lit candles sat on the dresser behind him. He started to close his door.

"Just because you got laid doesn't mean I should have to watch you running around here half-naked," Billy said.

"I'm going to bed now."

"How was she?"

"Good night, heathen."

ooo

Brett opened the front door of his house and stood back, surprised. "What do you want?"

"What've you got going?" Billy said, shifting his foot inside.

"Man, let me shut the damn door."

"You didn't count on them saying no, did you?"

Brett gasped and opened the door. "I'll kill them for—"

"They didn't say anything. They didn't have to." Billy said. "C'mon, Brett, I'm broke."

Brett came out on the porch. He watched a school bus drive by and then faced Billy. "Do yourself a favor, college boy, and go home."

"C'mon, Brett. What've you got to lose?"

"Plenty."

There was an uncertainty about him, as if he could go either way, but it didn't matter which way he went; Billy didn't even know why he'd gone there in the first place. He was running low on money, but he didn't really need much. Besides, Al Jr. had not so much as asked for a penny and, at times, even acted as if he wanted Billy there, which kind of freaked Billy out. But Billy wanted to know whether he was capable of doing something nobody would ever suspect him of, even if it just meant carrying a couple of rims to Brett's car. What harm could come from taking something from a junked-out car?

The absurdity of it all struck him, and he started to walk away, when Brett reached out and took hold of his arm. "I'll pay you a hundred bucks."

ooo

Al Jr. paced the apartment, fearing Sara wouldn't return, that the only reason she'd allowed things to go so far was that she felt sorry for him. But it didn't really occur to him until after 3 that he'd probably never see her again. Then the pit of his stomach hurt. A car pulled up outside, and he ran to the window. But he didn't see Sara's red Plymouth or the Blynners' jalopy. Instead, he saw an old Galaxie, Billy riding shotgun. The driver made wild gestures with his hands as he spoke, which he did for nearly 10 minutes. Then Billy got out and came up the sidewalk. Al Jr. opened the door and waited for him, noting the intensity on his face. There wasn't anything surprising about that; Kokomo was coming to town. Their father always ended up sulking for days after the games, unable to understand why Billy couldn't beat them single-handedly and blaming everything on Coach Randle. Then he'd pick Billy's game apart until he'd sulk and go up to his room.

Billy jumped back when he saw Al Jr. standing there. "Who's that?" Al Jr. asked.

"Just some kid from school."

"He must've…" Al Jr. said as another car pulled up, cutting himself off when he saw the red hood. He ran outside, where Sara sat in the car, brushing her hair. He waited until she got out before kissing her; she laughed and pushed herself away from him.

"Is Billy here?"

"Yeah, but he's got a game tonight."

"Why don't we go?"

"Oh, I don't know," he said. "I thought we'd just hang out here."

"You're too much of a hermit," she said, standing back and looking at him crossly.

"OK, OK, I'll go."

Billy cleared his throat from behind.

"How long have you been standing there?" Al Jr. said. "Were you listening?"

"Yeah, you can give me a ride," Billy said. "I'm sick of walking."

ooo

Big Al sat at the bar by himself. The closed sign had been up all day. Very few customers had been by, and a couple of them had rattled the door. He'd had to ignore them — keeping his mind clear — because there hadn't been any time left. Not with all the packing left to do. And after a couple of hours, everything — the shrine, pictures and anything else that mattered — had been packed up in a box, ready to go. Tonight's game against Kokomo, his boy's Achilles' heel, would probably be tough to sit through. He hoped Billy remembered what they'd talked about after the previous game against them. He couldn't race them, especially the Strong kid, and would have to play with the ball in his hands. And keep it as far away from Lonny as possible. It wouldn't do to give him the ball, as the kid as tall as a tree would take it away. But it was too late to worry about any of those things now. He took another sip of his most aged cognac and waited, watching the clock. Billy was coming home tonight, whether he liked it or not.

ooo

Billy always looked up to his father's seat several times during a game. The coach had noticed it when he was a freshman and told him not to because it was causing him to make mistakes. But no matter how many times Billy had lost his man or the ball, he wasn't able to stop. Tonight the coach didn't seem to notice him watching the stands when Chad's pass went right through his fingers during the pregame workout. He was too busy staring across the floor at the long, lanky Kokomo players going through their own drills, making fluid passes and draining their jumpers.

Then the buzzer sounded, and Tyrone jumped up and down before going to the rest of the Kokomo starters and pumping them up. Billy's father sat leaning forward, his head resting on his hands as he waited for the game to start. The coach was motioning for Billy to get over to the team huddle.

"OK, guys," Coach Randle said. "Listen up. They're way too fast and quick to get in a track meet with. Slow it down, just like last year, but keep the pressure up. Protect the ball, but don't hold on to it too long. And don't make any cross-court passes unless there's nobody near you. I want at least three passes, preferably five, before anybody shoots. Let's wipe those cocky smirks off their faces and send them home with a loss. Let's go!"

As they put their hands together and let out the team cry, the Kokomo players were already at the center of the court waiting for them. Harvey smiled his cocky smile at Lonny and waited for him to come over for the jump ball. When Harvey mouthed his taunt at him, Lonny turned red instantly and tensed up. The referee tossed the ball in the air, and Harvey tapped the ball toward the Kokomo side of the court. Tyrone ran to the ball and dribbled it, without breaking stride, all the way to the basket for an easy layup.

Billy hurried out of bounds to make the inbounds pass, but all of Kokomo's players had set up and were pressing, with their long arms out in front of everyone else. He was about to get called for a five-second violation and had to try to heave the ball over everyone's head, where Chad had the best chance of getting it. But Harvey came from several feet away and got his fingertips on the ball, and it fell short of where Billy intended to throw it. Ellis Talley was able to block Chad out and get the ball back. He lobbed it up toward Harvey, who tipped it in the basket.

On the next possession, Lonny took the ball out, and Tyrone tried to body Billy out of the way. Billy pushed back and took the pass as Tyrone flopped to the floor. The referee blew his whistle, and Billy pumped his fist until the referee called the foul on him.

"What?!" Billy said. "He's pushing me all over the place!"

The referee threw the ball to Harvey, who stretched his arms up and tossed the ball inbounds to Tyrone. Billy planted his feet, waiting as Tyrone drove forward and jumped in the air, his arm catching Billy and sending him to the floor, where he slid backward a couple of feet and closed his eyes as the referee blew his whistle again. But instead of cheering, the crowd started booing. He opened his eyes as the referee stood over him pointing down.

Billy hopped up. "I had my feet planted!"

The referee threw the ball to Harvey. "You keep it up and I'll give you a technical."

Billy started to say something and then closed his mouth. Tyrone walked up behind him. "You guys stink. We're going to run all over you."

Billy acted as if he hadn't heard him; he wanted to stew over his words. Maybe they could overcome Kokomo if Tyrone and the rest of them stayed cocky, Billy thought to himself. Last year, Richland had almost come back and won after the Kokomo coach benched his starters. Chad had gotten hot, hitting all five of his last shots, but Richland had then lost steam and the game by 8 points. But the Kokomo players weren't easing up, and their full-court press, the toughest in the state, forced Richland into 10 turnovers, five of them by Billy.

At the half, Richland was already down by 12, and Coach Randle had loosened his tie and taken his yellow blazer off. There were sweat rings underneath his arms. In the locker room, he spoke in a strained voice.

"You guys are doing exactly what I told you not to do," he said. "You've got to spread the floor and break free so you can get in your half-court sets."

And they tried to, but it didn't matter. Without any cross-court passes to cherry-pick, Kokomo dropped the press and alternated between a zone defense and man-to-man coverage. But even without the press, Kokomo dominated. By the fourth quarter, Kokomo had a 20-point lead, and Coach Randle benched everyone but Billy and Garner. With Garner in the backcourt, Billy let him handle the ball. If the kid wanted the ball that badly, he could have it. But all he could manage were a few forced bricks that clanged off the rim.

The crowd was getting ugly, yelling insults and booing. When the fourth quarter ran down and the final buzzer sounded, Billy put his hands over his ears. Harvey and Ellis danced off the court, pointing at the crowd. Billy lowered his head and went toward the locker room. Nobody would speak to him, but it wasn't any different than it had been any of the other three times they'd been beaten by Kokomo. He was the best player and always the goat when they lost. It didn't matter if Chad only had 5 points and Lonny had more fouls than rebounds. And the coach wouldn't look at any of them, either, when he stood by his lectern and gave them a speech about not giving up and finding inspiration in defeat. It was all a bunch of crap, just like the game. Billy dressed and went toward the door, where Lonny sat slumped in a folding chair, aping a damned soul to perfection.

"Jesus, Billy. You should've passed to me more."

Same old Little Red Lonny. Billy laughed. Lonny had the ball taken away from him so many times Billy wasn't sure whether he'd even taken a shot. He ignored him and went out to the thinning corridor, where he caught a glimpse of his father hiding in the small dark space of the janitor's cubbyhole.

ooo

As Billy backed up underneath a fluorescent light, Big Al took a step forward. What he saw was alarming. Billy looked as if he hadn't slept for days and was even thinner than he had been the previous week. "You look awful."

Billy grimaced. "So what?"

"I'm not talking about the game," Big Al said. "Doesn't Al feed you?"

"Go to hell!" Billy shouted. "You've screwed up everything! Mom would've—"

It was surreal, almost a detached motion. Big Al didn't realize what he was doing as his hand came up and hit Billy against the wall. The boy slid down, too shocked to speak or cry out in pain. The locker room door swung open, and Coach Randle came out in the hallway toward him.

"What'd you do to him?"

"What I should've done last week," Big Al said, leaning forward and helping Billy to his feet. "I'm taking my boy home."

Keeping their arms intertwined, Big Al led Billy down the hallway to the staircase. Shuffling footsteps came from the darkened hallway behind him and stopped so abruptly he let go of Billy and turned toward the sound. The only light came from a fire exit sign on the opposite end of the hallway, so all he could see was the outline of a man in the shadows. Big Al took a step toward him and could have sworn the man started shaking. But before he could close the distance any further, Billy took off running up the stairs. Big Al chased after him, almost tripping at the top, where he scanned the crowd and every exit. Whatever door Billy had used to exit, he was already long gone.

ooo

It wasn't until Billy had run upstairs and their father had gone after him that Al Jr. was able to take a breath. And when he did, he felt as if he'd been underwater too long. He felt painful stabs in his lungs. When the pain went away and he was able to walk back down the hallway, Sara stood at the top of the steps.

"What's wrong?"

He told her what he had seen, and she looked across the gym before grabbing his arm. "Is your dad over there?"

Al Jr. glanced over at the exits. He wondered how he could've thought his father was so frail the previous week. It didn't take him any time at all to shoot up the steps, running like a man possessed, but he couldn't have caught up with Billy. And there was no way he was still in the building. Al Jr. shook his head, and she pulled him around toward her. "What're you going to do now?"

"I've got to go home in case Billy's headed that way."

•••

Chapter 19

Where could Billy have gone? Al Jr. looked up at the clock again; it was after 2 in the morning. Maybe their father had caught him — spotted him somewhere near the parking lot — but he doubted it. So whom could Billy be with? One of his teammates? Maybe someone had taken him in. After all, Lonny and Chad had eaten supper and spent the night at their house many times in the past, all of them laughing it up in the room across the hall. But now they acted as if they could hardly stand him. Billy could've slipped over the guardrail on the Third Street Bridge and fallen in the river.

Al Jr. had to go find him. But then Billy slunk through the doorway, taking slow, dragging footsteps through the shadows and into the light.

"Where've you been?" Al Jr. said, but Billy ignored him on his way to the couch, where he collapsed. Al Jr. went to the chair and sat down. "I thought maybe Dad caught you."

Billy sat upright. "What're you talking about?"

"At the stairway after the game."

"That was you?" Billy said, laughing. "Good timing."

"Have you been outside all night?"

Billy nodded as he lay down. Al Jr. asked him where he'd been, but Billy was already snoring. So he took off his coat, went to his room and stretched out on the bed. He should've felt better knowing Billy was safe and nothing bad had happened. But he was more worried about him now than the time Billy had to go to the emergency room after a kid on a bike had run him over on the sidewalk in front of the house. Everyone had told Al Jr. everything would be OK, that it had only been an accident, but in a way it hadn't. He was nearly 6, and Billy had just turned 4. Al Jr. saw the big kid coming on his blue Schwinn and thought it'd be funny to see Billy pee his pants before jumping out of the way. But Billy did neither. He just stood there frozen, with his eyes wide-open, and before Al Jr. was able to pull him back, the bike had already gone over the top of him. The big kid stopped — looking kind of sick himself — and helped pick Billy up off the ground. Billy had a cut on his forehead, and they walked him inside, where their mother began crying as she picked Billy up. She demanded to know what had happened. Al Jr. told her they were just playing too close to the sidewalk. But Al Jr. knew the accident was his fault, even though Billy had a mild concussion and never remembered anything about it.

On the couch, Billy didn't wake up until 1 the next day. He sat up, stretched his arms in the air and yawned. "I feel like I've slept for days."

"I thought you would."

Billy frowned at Al Jr. "Man, we got slaughtered."

"Yeah, that was awful," Al Jr. said. "I kind of felt sorry for you guys."

"I don't know," Billy said, his face solemn as he stretched his arms. "At least I know where I stand."

"Where's that?"

"By myself."

"What do you mean?"

"I'm finished."

"With basketball?"

"With everything."

"I don't understand why you'd drop out," Al Jr. said. "Makes no sense running when you've got a way out."

"Who said I'm running?" Billy said. "I'm ready to fight."

"Are you ready to die?"

"Were you?"

The despair Al Jr. felt after their mother's death had made running the easiest thing to do. But he had run in the wrong direction. Maybe if he'd waited or thought about it, he would've hit the road south to Florida or north to Canada. But in his mind, he was already dead. Even the drill sergeants hadn't fazed him when they slapped him for being a ragbag. He thought he was tougher than everyone else until an incident his first week in Vietnam. A fellow FNG, a kid with a face full of peach fuzz and a name Al Jr. couldn't remember, was walking alongside him. The kid was bragging, talking smack about how much better the Cardinals were than the Cubs — especially how Fergie Jenkins couldn't carry Bob Gibson's jockstrap — when bullets went whizzing by them. Everyone jumped to the ground. The shooting went on for close to an hour. When the rounds stopped coming, Al Jr. stood. The kid's face had been blown off, and Al Jr. vomited. He wasn't so tough as he thought he was.

"I thought I was ready to die."

"Did you ever kill anyone?"

Though the room was cold, Al Jr.'s forehead started to sweat, and his stomach growled, forcing a coughing fit that lasted several seconds. When he caught his breath, he said, "I don't want to talk about it."

"C'mon, Al," Billy said. "You can tell me."

The bottle of whiskey on the table tempted him. Maybe Sara wouldn't notice the booze on his breath if he brushed his teeth and swigged some Listerine. But he knew a swig of whiskey wouldn't do anything except lead to another early drunk. Billy frowned impatiently.

"Well?" he said.

"It's scary over there," Al Jr. whispered. "I've seen guys get blown apart and still live—"

"That's not what I mean."

"I never wanted to."

"But you did?"

They'd ambushed three members of the NVA down a narrow trail. All three had died on their feet without knowing what'd hit them. But the whole squad had fired, and Al Jr. told himself his rounds may not have even hit any of them. There were a lot of fights like that — times when no one really had any idea who'd hit what because they had all been shooting at the same thing. You had to. Freezing up meant death or, at the very least, you weren't someone who could be counted on. But one time, they made a terrible mistake. A man with a bag over his shoulder was running away from them, toward a valley, where he was about to disappear. They took cover and shot him and then braced themselves for an explosion that never came.

They heard small children crying around the fallen man. Three boys hovered over him, trying to get him to move. The soldiers approached, and the boys disappeared in the tree line. Sgt. Tucker rolled the man over onto his back.

"Oh, no," he said, his voice sick. The man was an old farmer, not an enemy soldier, his bag full of rice instead of explosives. Who the small boys had been was something they never found out. They buried the old man and left the bag of rice near his grave.

ooo

The trunk was as full as it could get. Almost everything in there was irreplaceable and fragile, and Big Al made sure none of it was in danger of breaking before he gently closed the lid. Some of the stuff — including a picture of Jack and him behind the bar while several patrons, Stan in the middle, toasted them — had been in the office since Jack's time. Removing the treasures made him feel guilty, as if he were robbing the building of its personality, its soul. He also packed the two boxes that once held the Cuban cigars he and Jack had handed out after his boys were born. Half the men from back then were gone already, and some of them had turned out to be pretty good friends. Big Al stared at the bar. Everything had been so fleeting — Jack's life, Janet's life. Even he'd be forgotten soon. When Al Jr. was a little boy, he'd run up to Jack holding his arms up, wanting to be picked up right away. After Jack died, Al Jr. asked about him constantly. But after a month, he stopped asking, and as he'd grown older, he never mentioned Jack. Thinking about Jack saddened Big Al; the past was all he had left. Billy was gone and wasn't coming back. That much he finally knew.

A car pulled in to the parking lot, and Big Al turned around to wave the driver off, when he saw Coach Randle through the windshield. The coach rolled down his window.

"Bang-up job last night," Big Al told him.

"Last night doesn't matter right now."

"That's exactly what I'd expect from you," Big Al said. "You've never minded losing."

The coach's face reddened. Then he reached into the glove compartment, finding a folded piece of paper he held out the window for Big Al to take.

"I don't like being around you any more than you like being around me," he said as Big Al took it from his hand. "But if you care about your son, you'll want to read this."

"Care about my son?" Big Al said, leaning closer until he noticed Billy's handwriting. The penmanship was neater than in the letter he'd written him, but the words were more alarming. The note was apologetic and short. Billy wanted Coach Randle to call Evansville to tell the coach there that he was done. Billy would only be coming to school Monday to drop out.

"Christ," Big Al said. "Do you know where my son Al lives?"

"No, but you'd better find out." Coach Randle said, rolling up the window.

Big Al watched as he drove off the lot, and then Big Al got in his car and weaved aimlessly around town, trying to imagine where Al Jr. might live. For some reason, he thought it should've been clear where to go, but he couldn't think of why. Then he remembered Eric saying he'd already told Billy and Al Jr. about the bar's being sold. So he veered back toward the bar.

Inside, he picked up the phone and dialed Nick's number. When Nick answered the phone, Big Al strained to say hello.

"What's wrong, Al?"

"I'm hoping you'll let me off the hook."

"You're not feeling your oats so much now," Nick said, laughing. "That's all right. I really don't need any more bouncers anyway."

"I mean I want to call off the whole deal."

ooo

Brett opened the front door of his house and frowned at Billy. "You're not changing your mind, are you?"

Billy shook his head, though he had indeed been having second thoughts. It irritated him everyone read him so easily, but Brett relaxed a bit and slouched against the doorframe. "Good, because my fence isn't someone you'd want to mess with."

"Can we just get on with it?"

Brett laughed — an unsettling sound — and stood to the side, waiting for Billy to enter. "Sure, jocko."

Billy fumed. The little runt had some nerve. But something about Brett made him nervous. Crossing Brett would mean looking over his shoulder for a long time. But Billy didn't want to be around Brett in his parentless house. And Billy wasn't sure about the plan. They wouldn't be stealing rims from a junkyard, but that's all he knew. Brett led him down a dark hallway and opened the door to a room with fluorescent lighting. Going in, Brett turned around and smiled, the light making his buckteeth glow and his skin purple. The walls were painted the darkest shade of black Billy had ever seen, and the ceiling had a pentagram painted on it from one side to the other. A table in the center of the room had radios, televisions and knickknacks that looked like junk. Against the wall sat a desk, its open drawers filled with rolled-up bags of marijuana, all lined up perfectly.

Brett picked up a long water bong off the floor, pinched some weed from a bag, put it in the bowl and lit it, taking a hit that filled the chamber with thick white smoke. His exhaled smoke filled the room, and he coughed before trying to hand the bong to Billy. Billy shook his head, and Brett put the bong down and took a set of keys out of the top drawer.

"Let's go for a ride," he said, smoke still rolling out of his mouth.

ooo

Big Al headed up the steps to Eric's duplex. He'd been there many times in the past but only once since Janet died. Eric's wife, Darla, had been cold and rude, and Big Al had been so stunned by her hostility he'd never gone back. Big Al asked Stan why Darla was angry with him, and Stan, with a nervous smile, said he didn't have a clue. He might have gotten it out of Stan, if not for the fallout over the tab, but over time he'd forgotten about it. Until now. The thin curtain over the window moved, and Big Al cringed as the door came open before he even had a chance to knock. Darla came outside, her hair done up in rollers, a rolling pin in her hands, glaring at him. "You've got a lot of nerve coming here."

"Please," Big Al said, taking a step back. "I've got to talk to Eric."

Their baby cried from inside the house, the sound coming closer until Eric stood just inside holding him. Darla's cold stare softened when the baby reached out for her, and she took him and went back inside. Eric came outside and closed the door.

"I'd like you to come back and work for me," Big Al said.

"You mean Nick?"

"No, I mean me."

"But you signed everything over to Nick."

"He tore up the contract."

"Why?"

"Because I asked him to," Big Al said. "Everything's going to be better now. I promise."

Eric shifted around, as if he thought it was a trick, and Big Al asked him why his wife despised him so much. What Eric said shocked him. At the funeral home, when Al Jr. came inside the parlor, Big Al had gone after Al Jr. and then punched Eric when Eric had tried to hold him back. Big Al couldn't remember anything like that. But everything had been a blur after he made the funeral arrangements with the big guy, Swisher, whose solemn voice made everything feel so final. By the time of the funeral, he'd been so drunk everything had blacked out of his mind. It shamed him now that one of the grudges he held against Al Jr. was that he hadn't come to the funeral. Big Al had only assumed he hadn't because his name wasn't on the register. Now it choked him up knowing his son wanted to be there but wasn't because of him.

"I'm sorry," Big Al said, reaching out as Eric began to go back inside. "Wait."

Eric turned back around, and Big Al cleared his throat. "I need to know where Al lives."

ooo

Billy had expected Brett to drive downtown or to Erie Avenue, maybe even somewhere on the south side near Al's place. Anywhere but here, the upper east end, where all the houses were nice and well-kept. His family had considered buying a house in a tree-lined neighborhood off the boulevard several years ago, but the owners had wanted too much money for it, and Big Al had balked, saying there wasn't any way he could have afforded the mortgage on what he made from the bar. Their mother had been disappointed because the neighborhood was peaceful, and no one ever sped down Roselawn the way people did on North Street. This street was just a block away from his mother's dream house, and nothing was out of place except Brett's beat-up Galaxie parked along the street while he studied a map in his lap.

Billy was thankful it was too cold for anyone to be outside. Brett nodded toward one of the nearly identical colonials on the corner.

"There it is," Brett whispered. "We'll come back later when everyone's asleep."

"You want to go in there while those people are sleeping?"

"Christ, Billy," Brett said. "I'm not stupid. These people are out of town on vacation. I'll have everything fenced by the time they get back."

"Sounds like a crummy way to end a vacation."

"They're insured," Brett said. "You're not going to weasel out on me, are you?"

Billy gazed down at his lap. "No."

ooo

Big Al sat in the car in front of Al Jr.'s apartment for at least 10 minutes. The place was a rat trap. Roof tiles and siding littered the lawn. The porch bowed downward. And the screen door hung halfway off its hinges at an angle. Finally, he shut the engine off and walked up the sidewalk. The porch creaked when he stepped onto it, and he jumped back when he saw two men sitting in chairs off to the side. He grabbed his chest, nodding his head toward them, but their eyes were blank with drunkenness. He hurried past them through the screen door, and jumped again when it thwacked shut behind him.

Several mailboxes hung off the wall. He knelt over and found his son's name. He went down there, rested his ear against the door and listened. A barely audible voice of a man droned on, and the bubbly voice of a girl cut in every few seconds or so. Then they stopped talking, and the silence went on so long Big Al froze up. A light footstep came toward the door.

"Who's out there?" the girl said.

"Al's father," he said quietly.

The door flung open, and the girl — who was so short she barely came up to his chest — pointed up at him. "If you're here to hurt Al—"

"I'm not here to hurt him," he said, moving past her until he was in the middle of the living room. Al Jr. was standing behind a table holding his right hand out in front of him, while his left hand, for some reason, remained tucked inside the sleeve of his parka. His once chubby face had done more than lost its baby fat; it was so thin his eyes were as big as an owl's, and the fear in them was so intense he had to look away. When he looked back, he realized Al Jr. wasn't hiding his hand. His hand was gone.

Big Al was suddenly lightheaded. He collapsed on the broken-down couch and buried his face in his hands. "God help me."

● ● ●

Chapter 20

Seeing his father crying wiped away all the fear Al Jr. had of him. His father asked him, "What happened?"

"I was running. Everything went black. What're you doing here, Dad?"

Shame came across his face as he looked away. "I've got to find Billy," he said. "He left a note in Coach Randle's mailbox last night saying he was through with basketball. Do you know anything about it?"

"Yeah, he told me this morning."

"And that doesn't bother you?"

"I've been telling him he should go home ever since he got here."

"Are you sure?" Big Al said. "Why would he stay in a dump like this?"

"Because he's afraid of you."

Sara, whose expression never softened even as his father wept, hovered over him with her hands on her hips. "You're an asshole, Mr. Hennessy."

Al Jr. tried to move her away, but she wouldn't budge. She put her hands on his chest and pushed him back. "I don't care," she said, turning toward his father. "Why don't you go find your son?"

Al Jr. tried to remember whether he'd ever heard anyone speak to his father that way.

"She's right," Big Al said. "I should be out trying to find Billy."

Al Jr. followed his father as he went to the door. "Wait," he said. "If you stick around, I'm sure he'll be back."

ooo

Mrs. Blynner folded her arms and stood back from the door. She said Rich and Ralph were around back in the garage. Billy jumped off the porch and followed the sidewalk through their backyard to where their two-story garage sat on the edge of an alley. The smell of marijuana wafted out as Billy opened the side door and went inside. Faint voices came from the loft and stopped abruptly when he began climbing a ladder to the closed porthole.

"Who's down there?" Rich said, his voice so paranoid Billy laughed. Al Jr. used to be the same way when he smoked the junk, and Billy always wondered why anyone would want to smoke something that made him scared of everything. When Rich asked again, his voice was a little more urgent.

"Richland Police Department," Billy said, making his voice deeper. "Just kidding. It's me, Billy."

"Very funny," Rich said, opening the hatch. "Come on up."

Billy pulled himself through the opening. Rich sat beside Ralph on an old wooden bench, while two girls — including the one Rich had been with at the party — sat on a tattered love seat giggling to each other, both of them wearing sunglasses and smiling at him. Ralph looked at the girls and then frowned at him. "What's up, Billy?"

"I've got some time to kill before I go to Brett's."

The second he said Brett's name, he wanted to pull it back. Rich and Ralph both exchanged glances.

"I heard you guys got smoked last night," Ralph said.

"Yeah, we stunk."

"You're Billy Hennessy," one of the girls said, smiling. "You should hang out with us and get high."

Ralph's face got as red as a tomato, and he sat back on the bench and sulked. "I'm sure he's got other things to do."

Billy backed up and almost fell through the porthole, and the girls laughed as he regained his balance. "I'd better get going," he said, turning toward the opening and climbing back down. "I'll see you later."

One of the brothers stood up and walked across the room, the wood floor making cracking sounds with the forceful footfall. Then Rich came down and motioned for Billy to follow him out to the alley, where they stood underneath a bright light.

"What're you up to?"

Billy frowned. "What do you mean?"

"Brett doesn't have any friends," he said. "Never has. You hang out with him and he'll get you busted."

"I'm just the…" Billy said, slapping his sides. "I caught up with him the other night. We're just hanging out."

"Bullshit, Billy," Rich said, stepping closer. "Brett doesn't hang out. He steals. Go back to Al's and forget it."

"I'll see you later," Billy said. He went down the alley, turned around at the sidewalk and saw Rich still standing underneath the light. Without breaking stride, Billy waved at him and kept on going.

ooo

"He should be here by now," Big Al said, standing up and going to the picture window. Outside, the houses were dark and gloomy, and the glare of the streetlight shone on an empty sidewalk. "Didn't he say where he was going?"

"No."

Big Al felt sick when he saw it was already past 8 o'clock. He wondered whether Billy hadn't come back because he'd seen his car parked out front. Maybe he was afraid to come inside and was walking around in the cold waiting for him to leave. Regardless, he'd wasted too much time sitting around, so Big Al took his keys from his coat. "We need to go find him."

Big Al went out to his car, started up the engine and waited for Al Jr. He finally came outside, with his lazy, shuffling walk, picking up his pace only when he noticed Big Al waiting impatiently.

"Why would Karen know anything?" Al Jr. said after Big Al asked whether they should try her house. "They haven't been together since last year."

Last year? How could that be? Billy had never told him they broke up. But he and Billy hadn't really spoken much in the past year, sometimes letting weeks go by without much more than a passing greeting. They hadn't even put up a Christmas tree or exchanged gifts. On Christmas, they ate bologna sandwiches. None of it seemed screwed up at the time. After all, they'd always put the tree up on the eighth day in December, Janet's birthday, and neither one of them could cook a lick. But they'd become strangers by then, and now it had gone on so long he couldn't even find his boy in a town with barely 20,000 people. Big Al had to keep himself from crying, if for no other reason than he didn't want to cry in front of Al Jr., who, in many ways, was more like him than Billy ever would be. Seeing him with the girl, whose toughness was a lot like Janet's, made it clearer. Maybe their similarities were the reason they'd never gotten along, and he wanted to say so now. But the urge went away the second he noticed Al Jr. out of the corner of his eye twitching his fingers the way he always did when he was holding out on something. The damn boy, insolent as ever, was...

"Go to Erie Avenue, around 15th Street," Al Jr. said. "I'm pretty sure the Blynners live somewhere around there. I'll know the house when I see it."

Big Al thought Al Jr. was telling him some kind of joke. "I told him a long time ago I didn't want him hanging out with those bums."

"Those bums have been giving him rides."

"I wish you'd have..." he said. Al Jr. sat slumped down, waiting for a bawling. But this time, Big Al held back, and they drove over the Third Street Bridge and veered onto Erie Avenue.

ooo

"Be cool," Brett said, his voice harsh. The scolding irritated Billy so much he nearly got out of the car. Brett had been on him ever since they got in the car, after hours of sitting in his creepy room, listening to his creepy music and watching smoke coming out of his glowing head as he lit one bowl after another. But leaving would have made him look weak. Brett seemed as if he was on the verge of telling him to get out of the car anyway, especially after Billy asked him why he needed the hunting knife in his boot. Brett had said to pry open any locks he might find, but he was also planning on taking a screwdriver and a crowbar in with him, too, and wouldn't say why he needed all three. Instead, he went over the instructions again. He put on black leather gloves, removed a flashlight from underneath his seat and placed it in between them.

"Once we're there, drive around for a half-hour and come back," he said. "You got it?"

Billy nodded even though he had no intention of obeying him. He'd drive around all right. Around the block. Then he'd come back to see whether the house really was empty.

A car came around the corner, its blinding lights shining through the windshield as it came to a halt a few feet away from them. Brett mumbled something about the police and turned toward him.

"Remember," he said. "We're just out for a ride."

The headlights shut off, and Billy's eyes splotched up with bright dots. As they faded away, the driver got out of the car and stood next to it. Billy gasped. "It's my dad."

"What?" Brett said. "I knew I couldn't trust you."

"How'd he know?"

"Get rid of him!"

"Billy, it's time to come home," his father said, pointing at his car, where a man sat in the passenger-side seat, hidden in the shadows until his father motioned for him to get out. There was something familiar about the man's shuffling walk and the way he stood slouching next to his father, and Billy recognized his brother. He reached over to open the door, but Brett grabbed hold of his wrist with his long bony fingers.

"We've got work to do," he said, his voice an angry whisper.

"Too bad," Billy said, pulling away from his grip. Once he was outside, he leaned over the open door. "I wouldn't go to the house if I were you."

The streetlight illuminated Brett's face. His nostrils flared, and his mouth drew into a sickened grimace. When he spoke, his voice cracked. "You'd better keep your mouth shut," he said. "You're nothing but a lying scumbag."

Though Billy hadn't heard him approaching, Billy's father stood behind him, pulling him away from the car. "You'd better watch your mouth, boy," he said to Brett.

Brett put the car in drive and sped away, the door slamming shut halfway down the block as he yelled out the open window.

"Screw you, old man!"

ooo

Inside the car, Big Al sat next to Billy, who was so tired he kept nodding his head up and down. They drove back to Al Jr.'s apartment. When they got there, Al Jr. went inside, and Big Al and Billy waited for him to come back out, and when he finally did, he stopped on the sidewalk and stared down the street for several seconds. Big Al wondered whether he was in one of those stupors the news always reported, in which young men coming home from war couldn't tell where they were. Big Al had offered to show the boys the bar when he couldn't remember whether he had locked all the doors. Now he questioned whether they should all go or he should leave Al Jr. at his apartment. Big Al began to get out, but Al Jr. started walking toward the car again. But once he was inside, he asked, "Did you bring a friend, Dad?"

"No," Big Al said. "Why?"

"Because that car pulled up when we did."

Big Al turned to see the dark sedan behind them. But it didn't seem too suspicious to him. The driver bent over, his head occasionally moving as if he was trying to find something that had slid off the seat. Al Jr.'s hand trembled.

"It's just some hippie trying to find his dope," Big Al said. He hoped his lame joke would put Al Jr. at ease, maybe even make him laugh.

"I don't know," Al Jr. whispered. "This isn't the kind of neighborhood someone pulls over in to look for something."

"Christ, Al," Big Al said, laughing. "You're as territorial as a cat."

ooo

Something about the driver wasn't sitting well with Al Jr. As soon as he'd pulled up behind them, the driver had ducked down in his seat. Al Jr. could have sworn the longhair hippie was up to something bad. But his father acted as if he were nuts. So he waited for the man to sit up again and show himself. Then he'd know for sure whether he was up to something or he was just some hippie looking for his dope. But the car remained parked as they drove off, and the driver never raised his head. His father kept giving him sad, guilt-ridden glances through the rearview mirror, and Al Jr. smiled, hoping to make him feel better.

"I guess I'm a little skittish."

"I can see why," his father said softly. "It looks like you've been through—"

"A war?"

"Hell."

"I've never been there," Al Jr. said. "But there's probably not much of a difference."

Then the car fell silent, the only sound an occasional snore from Billy, and they veered off in the direction of the bar. Al Jr.'s chest ached, and he could hardly breathe. He hadn't been to the bar in over 10 years, since back when they all planned on working together someday and his mother kept saying she'd teach him to bake and cook. At the time, he moaned and groaned, saying he wasn't a girl, and she laughed and rubbed his head. God, it seemed so long ago.

When they went inside, Al Jr. gasped. Back then, the bar had only been one big skeletal room. Now there were walls where the empty space had been. One room off to the side had a pinball machine, its lights flickering on the sports memorabilia on the walls.

"I didn't think it'd look so sharp in here."

"It should," Big Al said. "I'm still paying off the loan. Maybe if I'd have had the kitchen going, it would've paid off a lot quicker."

Al Jr. went past him to the swinging doors behind the bar. The small kitchen had a grill and oven covered by a tarp. Under the tarp, a layer of dust covered the top of the grill. Otherwise, the stove looked as if it had just rolled off the assembly line.

"Doesn't look like there's anything wrong."

"There isn't," Big Al said, relaxing against the doorframe. "But nobody around here knows how to cook."

"Christ," Al Jr. said. "You'd probably make a fortune if your customers didn't have to go somewhere else to eat."

"I doubt it."

"Well, let's find out. I can bake pizzas and fry burgers."

Big Al laughed. "We could give it a shot."

"I could come in on Monday, and we can see what we'd need."

"Why not?"

Al Jr. examined a wall covered with miniature baseball bats, mugs adorned with monikers from almost every pro team from almost every sport and a poster of Cassius Clay standing over Sonny Liston, along with the schedules from all the local schools. But what stood out was a red, white and blue basketball.

"What's this?" Al Jr. said, picking it up off the shelf.

"An ABA ball," Big Al said, smiling. "We've finally got a pro team to root for around here."

"The Pacers?" Al Jr. said, putting the ball back on the shelf. "They kind of stink, don't they?"

"They'll probably fold," Big Al said. "Hell, the whole league will probably fold, but they're ours for now."

Billy sat at a table, his head buried in his arms, and Al Jr. sat beside him. Their father filled two mugs with soda, brought them to the table and sat them down. Al Jr. picked his up and frowned. "You didn't pack up all your booze, did you?"

"No," he said, "but I don't serve minors."

Billy lifted his head up and yawned. "Can we go home now?"

ooo

The short drive went on endlessly; his father and brother babbled on, their mingled words making no sense. Billy drifted in and out of sleep. A couple of times, he sat up, rubbing his eyes, and tried to stay awake, only to slump back down. Then the car jerked to a halt when they pulled up in front of Al Jr.'s apartment.

"We should just serve cold cuts," Big Al said.

"Are you kidding?" Al Jr. said, getting out of the car. "We could have burgers, pizzas and chili, anything they want."

Big Al grunted. "What they want is free booze."

Al Jr. laughed as he got out and shut the door. They drove away, and Billy could see Al Jr. staring at them through the side mirror, becoming smaller as the car went down the street.

ooo

His father's car turned the corner and disappeared, but Al Jr. couldn't move until the cold wind forced him to head into the apartment building. He wished Billy's sleepiness hadn't cut the night short, though he could barely keep awake himself. He could've gone with them and slept in his old bed, but doing so would've been a strange way of pretending nothing had changed. Besides, his apartment might not have been much, but it was his, and even though his sheets didn't get changed often or smell as fresh as the ones his mother used to put on his bed, he couldn't wait to get underneath them.

Then a car drove slowly down his street. It was the same black sedan that'd been behind them earlier, and now the driver was sitting upright, his long hair pulled back in a ponytail and his gloved hands clutching the steering wheel. He sped to the end of the block and turned toward the Third Street Bridge, just as Big Al had done.

Something seemed suspicious, something Al Jr. couldn't grasp until he remembered how Eric had told him about the fight his father had been in. Eric had said that the guy looked like a hippie but didn't act like one and that in fact, many thought him guilty of murder. Al Jr. started running to the end of the block, went around the corner and got to the phone booth, where he dialed the operator.

"Insert one dime, please."

"I need the police, ma'am," he said. "There's a man chasing after my dad and brother."

The operator said nothing, and the line sounded as if it had gone dead. Fearing she thought him a nut case, Al Jr. almost hung up and dialed again, but then a man with a deep voice spoke.

"Richland Police Department, Sgt. Brown."

"Ronch Laroy's going to kill my dad and brother!"

"Back it up here," he said. "What's your name?"

"Al Hennessy."

"Where're they, Al?"

"They're driving home, and he's right behind them," he said. "They live at 2000 North St."

"I'll send someone over," Sgt. Brown said, and then he hung up.

Al Jr. dropped the receiver and began running toward his father's house, crossing the bridge, where a cold fog rose from the river, making it impossible to see more than a couple of inches in front of him. A few times, he bumped up against the concrete wall and fell. And when he finally made it across, his shirt was drenched with sweat, and his legs felt as if they weighed a ton apiece. But sirens began to sound off in the distance. As he made it to 17th and North, blue and red lights lit up the sky over the hill leading to their house. Several shots rang out. And then he heard his father yelling his brother's name.

ooo

Billy woke up when his father touched his arm. He sat straight up in the seat. For a moment, he wondered whether he hadn't been dreaming about his father and brother getting along, working together. He'd love to see their first day, see how many times they would clash. But Al Jr. had been excited; this wasn't just taking out the trash or doing everyone's dishes. He'd be running the kitchen. Ha! At least the guys he'd be cooking for would be too skunked to worry about whether the food was any good or not. Maybe he could work there during the summer before going to Evansville in the fall. Then both of them could screw up everyone's order. He looked over at his father to say something and saw him staring at the rearview mirror. Sirens rang out in the distance. In the side mirror, he saw three squad cars approaching and — if it wasn't the damnedest thing — the black sedan Al Jr. had obsessed over. His father pulled over. He opened his door, and Billy grabbed his arm. "What're you doing, Dad?"

The black sedan parked behind them. "I want to see what this guy wants," he said. The other driver got out, the hood of his parka pulled over his face, and reached inside his coat. His hand came out with a revolver, and he fired a shot that went past his father and hit the rear window of the car, sending glass all over the place. Before Billy crouched down in the seat, he saw his father running toward the man in a zigzag pattern. The man fired three more shots. Billy slunk as far as he could and heard his father call out his name.

The sirens came to a halt, and he heard mingled, excited voices yelling. An older officer opened his door, craned over and then laughed.

"How'd that bullet not find your head?" he said. He called out to his father. "Good thing your boy's got good reflexes."

Billy got out of the car. The man was on the ground, handcuffed, cussing and calling the officers pigs. They pulled him to his feet and threw him in the back of one of the squad cars. His father stood to the side trembling.

"Jesus Christ," Big Al said. "I didn't think he'd come after me again."

The older officer asked, "Why'd you think we wanted you to press charges?"

Big Al took a deep breath. "I'm glad you guys were watching him. I just wish you'd have gotten here a little sooner."

"Sooner?" the policeman said. "Why'd we be watching him?"

"Your son called us," a younger officer said. "Or we wouldn't have known anything."

Pounding footsteps ran down the sidewalk toward them. Once Al Jr. came out of the shadows, he looked at Billy first before facing their father. Both of them seemed to have something to say, but as was the case many times in the past, neither was able to find the words.

• The End •

About the Author

Jeff Regan has worked in the mental health field for over 20 years in various capacities. He was inspired to write this novel by many of the conflicts he has seen that have led to many unresolved rifts and fractured relationships. This story is a dedication to those he hopes have found peace with one another in the great beyond. He currently works as a community mental health worker in Logansport, Indiana.

UNOPENED LETTERS FROM DEAD MEN
is also available as an e-book
for Kindle, Amazon Fire, iPad, Nook and
Android e-readers. Visit
creatorspublishing.com to learn more.

○ ○ ○

CREATORS PUBLISHING

We find compelling storytellers and
help them craft their narrative,
distributing their novels and collections
worldwide.

○ ○ ○

15013515R00143

Made in the USA
Lexington, KY
11 November 2018